JOHN MOZIE

THE
ENCHANTED
GIFT

Michael Terence
Publishing

First published in paperback by
Michael Terence Publishing in 2020
www.mtp.agency

John Mozie has asserted the right to be identified as
the author of this work in accordance with the
Copyright, Designs and Patents Act 1988

ISBN 9781913653699

Cover image by Uche Mere

To the memory of my mother, Agnes Azuka, my abiding angel.

Contents

1

The Necklace

Siyonna stood on the balcony of her family home in Umuabado and looked out at the narrow road that led to the stream. Umuabado did not have any rivers. The reason for this lay steeped in ancient Igbo mythology. Legend had it that the goddess Okwuno had angered her mother Idemmili by running away with a human, Oja'dili and having a child with him. Idemmili found Okwuno and took her back home but cursed Okwuno in the process, promising her that the child would never see water. That child, Abado, grew up and settled in a land just by the cusp of the great Idemmili River, a good place to raise a family and plant yam seedlings. Idemmili kept her promise and the river mysteriously moved, cutting off his dwelling. Abado, crying out to his mother for help, eventually touched Idemmili's heart and she gifted his land with the Uruku stream.

As Abado's descendants grew and the area became Umuabado, the stream flowed through the village, providing drinking water and the bare essentials the village needed. However, there would be no big fish coming from Umuabado, unlike the other villages served by the great River Idemmili and the River Niger in Onitsha.

Uruku stream lay about two miles from Siyonna's home in the village and people skirted around her compound to reach it. Siyonna loved these days of sitting on the rear

1

balcony. It was one of the few occasions she had time alone with her thoughts here in Umuabado. She was the youngest of five children and at a full nine years younger than her nearest sister, the baby of the family. On more than one occasion she had heard her mum describe her as their 'pleasant mistake.'

Siyonna did not doubt that her family loved her. Her full name was 'Kamsiyonna' which translated to 'God gave me all I asked for', but everyone at home called her Siyonna, or Onna-mma (Onna the beautiful) and her dad would sometimes call her 'Siyonna'm', adding the extra personal touch, claiming both daughter and God as his!

She found it hard to believe that a whole year had passed since 'the incident', the one which changed her life forever. She was 15 and the family had come back to Umuabado for her older sister Chieme's traditional wedding and she had sat in this same spot on the rear balcony, escaping. Siyonna found the visits to the village relaxing with little to do. However, this particular visit threatened to be tricky as a lot of fuss and disquiet surrounded the planning of the traditional wedding. She felt like all she did was run errands for the myriad of relatives older than her and that pretty much included everybody. To make matters worse, her older brother Ikechukwu had a toddler, her nephew Afam whom she adored, but would love to put down sometime! Ikechukwu's wife, Nnedi, on the other hand, saw her as a convenient nanny for her infant on these visits, so in-between the "Siyonna get me this" and "Siyonna fetch me that" of her older relatives, she also had to mind Afam. Some holiday, she thought. At every opportunity, usually when Afam was asleep, she'd hand him over to his grateful mum and escape to the balcony at the back of the house.

Siyonna was sitting there when an old woman walked by with a big water pot on her head. Initially, Siyonna ignored her but as the old woman got closer, she could tell that she was really struggling with the weight of the pot. She watched as the poor woman steadied herself on the walls of the compound and her thin, spindly legs threatened to give way under her. Each time she staggered Siyonna's heart skipped a beat. After what felt like the umpteenth attempt at walking straight and balancing the pot, came yet another stumble, this time with some of the water escaping from the top of the big clay pot. Siyonna could no longer simply watch and do nothing. She called out to the old woman and asked her to wait, she would lend a hand.

Siyonna flew down the stairs to calls of "where are you going? What's the mad rush?" from her mum and sisters, sitting in the big family room just at the bottom of the stairs. Like any self-respecting Nigerian, she responded with the familiar "I'm coming!" as she firmly headed for the side entrance, dodging chairs and canopy stumps set up for the traditional wedding ceremony the next day.

To reach the side entrance, she faced another obstacle. She had to run behind the house belonging to her father's younger brother, Udozor. Fortunately, Uncle Udo and Auntie Aku had gone to her father's as well, otherwise she would have had to explain her hurry to yet another party.

She yanked open the rusty iron gate and ran around the side of the compound to find the old woman leaning against the wall, panting heavily.

"Ahh, my daughter," crowed the old woman with delight. "These trips are getting harder and harder as the years go by."

back home just before the civil war. I taught in Enugu whilst my husband took a job in the civil service. When my family died, I left Enugu to teach in Awka. Then, after I retired, I came back to live here. As my pension buys fewer things these days, I try to do what I can for myself."

Siyonna thought for a while about what it must be like to be on your own at that age.

"But you must have other family who can help?" she said.

"Yes, but it's difficult. One set believes I am a witch because my husband and children died and I survived and the other believe I am greedy because I did not share the little money I received as my husband's pension with them. So here I am!"

Siyonna thought that this must be quite cruel but said nothing. How fate could visit such misery on someone so nice was beyond her.

"Enough about me," said the old woman. "What about you, my daughter? Where will life be taking you? What are your dreams?"

"I'd love to go to university in the U.S," said Siyonna, smiling. "I'd love to study English and work in the media. But I doubt my parents will let me go or can afford it for that matter. So right now, I don't know, but I just know it would be lovely to study in the States."

"If that is what you want," smiled the woman. "Then pursue it. Follow your dream and work at it. Look for scholarships and apply yourself, my daughter. The world today is a far cry from the one I lived in. There is so much you young ones can do, that people in my generation couldn't. Go follow your dream. Everything is possible in this life, so long as you believe."

"Funny," said Siyonna, after thinking about it. "That's exactly what my brother's wife tells me whenever we talk when she isn't using me as a nanny for my nephew, that is," she added, pulling a face.

The old lady cackled with laughter.

"Listen to your sister-in-law; she seems like a very wise woman!"

She got up and came back with a cool bottle of Fanta for Siyonna.

"You shouldn't have bothered," said Siyonna but the old woman would have none of it.

Siyonna drank the Fanta and got up.

"I really must go now, Ma. I will come back and see you before we leave for Lagos."

She smiled and Siyonna saw a shadow of the once-beautiful, fulfilled woman in the picture with her family.

"I have something to give you. Please wait?"

She scuttled off to one of the rooms before Siyonna could complain and came back moments later clutching a string of the most amazing beads Siyonna had ever seen.

"I want you to have this," she said. "I have lost most of my jewellery and I really have no one else to give this to. This necklace will bring you luck. Keep it close to you."

"Oh my!" Siyonna exclaimed. "I really couldn't."

"Yes, you can and you will," said the old woman sternly. "In your act of charity to an old woman today, you have given me hope and renewed my faith in humanity. Please take the necklace, it is no longer of any use to me. If you

Obiageli's face began to soften even though the frown remained.

"You should have told somebody where you were going," Obiageli said. "Whatever the reason, somebody should have known where you were going. Now run along and go help Nnedi with Afam so we can get on with supervising the caterers. And don't you dare leave the house again today, do you hear?"

"Yes mum," Siyonna answered timidly and trotted back to the house.

She ran up the stairs to her brother's room where she saw Nnedi frantically trying to get Afam to settle.

"Oh, there you are! Please could you take him? He's fed and all that but just won't go back to sleep. I desperately need to go help mum and Afam will be in the way if I take him with me."

"It's ok," smiled Siyonna. "I'll take him."

She took the baby and strapped him to her back as Nnedi left the room. It was now dusk and the balcony no longer presented an option because the mosquitos all seemed to wake up at night. When they were not biting you, they were buzzing your ears. Besides, the last thing she wanted was for Afam to get the dreaded malaria, passed on by mosquitos biting their victims. The only options remained her bedroom, the family living room on the 1st floor or her parent's little alcove adjoining their bedroom.

The family living room did not really offer peace and quiet. With all the excitement of preparing for her sister's traditional wedding, this room was very busy with people coming and going. She shared her own bedroom with Ebele, who was unlikely to want the intrusion of babysitting Afam.

Siyonna settled for her parent's room, crossed her fingers and prayed her dad was not already asleep in there.

Luckily, her dad had stayed downstairs with his brothers and cousins so the room was free. Afam stirred and started kicking as she walked in. She held him with one hand whilst dexterously undoing the wrapper with the other and rocked him as she settled down in her father's easy chair and flicked on the television. African Magic! Yes! Just what the doctor ordered. As the screen came to life, Afam appeared to relax, gurgling happily at the bright lights and sound. Result! Thought Siyonna. She wouldn't now have to do that endless walk up and down the room to lull him back to sleep. What a relief.

A Nollywood movie was playing on African Magic and Siyonna settled back to watch it. She had seen it before but felt happy to see it again. Besides, she knew it was easier to watch something that required limited concentration whilst with Afam. Who knew how long the quiet truce would last? Knowing him, he'd soon remember that his 'chariot' had been stagnant a while and complain. But for the moment, peace reigned.

"How are you guys?" said Ebele, shattering the moment in her low throaty voice.

Although of average height, Ebele stood shorter than the rest of the family where everybody else bordered on six feet or more. This made her appear short, much to her chagrin. Ebele was also pretty. And smart. She had graduated from medical school last year and now in her training program as a junior Doctor. Very insightful, she had an uncanny ability to pick holes in Siyonna's stories.

"We're fine," replied Siyonna, knowing that Ebele hadn't come all the way here to just to find out how she was doing.

Siyonna came in and put Afam in the bassinet at the corner of the family room, then sat on the settee opposite Odera. Odera continued to listen to Ebele, and Siyonna looked at him, waiting for Ebele to finish talking. Odera appeared almost long; the only way Siyonna found to describe him. Gangly and long, features he must have inherited from his mum as Uncle Obi was not that tall. Siyonna hardly remembered her aunt, Odera's mum. She had died very early, long before he turned 5. Since going to university, Odera had adopted the style of wearing an unkempt Afro, with a life of its own, and the wild beginnings of a moustache seemingly stuck in pre-pubescent scantiness. Siyonna smiled to herself. Goofy Odi feeling cool.

"So this woman, you say her name's Mabel?" Odera asked Siyonna, breaking her reverie.

"Hmmm," she said, nodding.

"There definitely was the story of a widow who had lost her entire family, living in the village," said Odera, looking knowledgeable. "But rumour has it that she died a long time ago and that her house was haunted. That was so long ago I grew up believing it was a mere urban legend. Do you think you could find her house again?"

"Sure, I think so," she said.

"You really don't sound convincing, Onna-mbe," said Odera, reverting immediately to his childhood pet name for his cousin, loosely translated to mean Siyonna the tortoise.

Siyonna could not quite understand what about her reminded Odera of the tortoise, but her mother told her that as a baby when she started crawling, Odera had concluded she took the shape of a tortoise, and tortoise she remained from then till now.

"Don't call me that," said Siyonna, anger flashing in her eyes just as Odera smiled mischievously.

"Stop it you two, this is serious," said Ebele.

"Ok, if Siyonna can remember the way to the house, I'll come out at 7.30 tomorrow morning so we can go find it. We'll probably have an hour and a half tops before your mum starts looking for us, what with all the things we need to do tomorrow. I will be waiting for you at the side gate by our house," said Odera, looking from one to the other.

"Good," said Ebele. "That's a plan. Thanks, Odi, we'll see you in the morning. Want something to eat?"

"No thanks," smiled Odera. "I just had some delicious Onugbu soup with pounded yam and trimmings! Meant for my father but he had already eaten here with your dad."

"Odi! You and food!" laughed Ebele.

Odera smiled and waved as he left, with a parting:

"Bye, Onna-mbe! See you in the morning."

Siyonna groaned and hurled a cushion that landed harmlessly at the doorway Odera had just exited from.

The next morning, the two sisters arrived at the gate early. The large communal compound was decked out in bright colours, with over twenty large marquees ready to accommodate the traditional wedding guests. Siyonna loved traditional weddings. Scratch that. Siyonna loved all weddings! The opportunity to dress up and the fiesta atmosphere of a Nigerian wedding of any sort delighted her in every way, something beautiful to behold. Her family were hosting their third traditional wedding. One day it would be Ebele's turn and eventually hers.

They walked 200 yards to the end of the last marquee and turned the corner which led them directly to the back of Uncle Udozor's compound. They walked on and reached the gate, slightly shielded from Uncle Udozor's back garden by a rough gazebo. A few minutes later, Odera walked through the back and said an airy good morning to the girls.

They all set off down the road that Siyonna had walked the previous evening. She led them easily through the village towards the unkempt path she had walked with Ma Mabel. When she came to the path that led to Ma Mabel's, she turned towards it then looked back at them over her shoulder.

"This is it," she said, excited.

They waded through the grass and came to an opening where Mabel's pristine bungalow should have stood. Only there was no pristine bungalow. What confronted them was a ramshackle hut that looked deserted.

"I don't understand. I am certain this is where we came. This really does not look like the house," said Siyonna, utterly perplexed.

"Are you sure this is where you came?" Echoed both Ebele and Odera at the same time.

"Yes. I am pretty sure it is. I recognize the Udala tree over there. This is where we came."

For the first time ever, Odera did not needle his cousin. He looked at her then turned to Ebele.

"I think I believe Siyonna. There is a possibility she did go to somewhere that looks similar to this one. But we probably cannot solve this one today. We could ask Mama Obele. She should know Ma Mabel and where to find her. But I think

Siyonna should keep and use the necklace the lady gave her. It is her gift and it isn't ours or anyone else's business why the old lady gave it to Siyonna. That's what I think."

"I guess you're right," said Ebele after considering the situation. "We'll pick this up again after the traditional wedding. The trouble is, I have to leave tomorrow because I'm at work on Monday. You two could follow up with Mama Obele and maybe Uncle Udozor too? Right now, we'd better head back home before mum notices Siyonna is gone."

Siyonna's eyes opened wide and her mouth performed a silent shriek.

"I thought you were going to tell mum we were going to Mama Obele's?"

"I forgot," shrugged Ebele.

"Yee, I'm dead!" shrieked Siyonna, bolting back along the path and running as fast as possible towards the compound.

All that had happened a year ago. Siyonna could not believe how quickly time had flown. There was the added sadness in the knowledge that she never saw Mabel again even after all that. One year on and save for her striking blue necklace, it almost felt like they had never met. Odera still looked at her funny and thought she had communed with a ghost. Whenever she mentioned it, Ebele would smile:

"Don't be silly, ghosts don't exist. Odi is simply trying to scare you."

2

The Traditional Wedding

That day, Siyonna had run full speed all the way from the ramshackle hut in the village she had thought was Mabel's home to her family compound. As she approached the compound, she worked feverishly to formulate a plan that would ensure she averted her mother's wrath should she run into her. Obiageli Nduka was an early riser, a habit honed by a lifetime of living and working in Lagos, where life started at 5.00 a.m. for most families. On a day like today, with all the activity and buzz of the traditional marriage, Siyonna fully expected her mother to be up and about, supervising all the last-minute preparations and confirming, for the umpteenth time, that the caterers would be on time.

Obiageli did not believe in leaving things to chance and had very little faith in suppliers meeting her exacting standards without her supervision. Fortunately for Siyonna, Obiageli was so exhausted from the preparations she had supervised for the past week, not to mention the endless meetings with suppliers that not even her 6.00 a.m. alarm call could wake her up today. By the time she finally jumped out of bed and into the shower at 8.30, Siyonna was back.

Siyonna quietly went to the kitchen already abuzz with activity, grabbed some bean cakes from the breakfast tray at the corner of the room, poured herself some tea and disappeared to the family living room upstairs. By the time her mother came out, she was just finishing breakfast.

"There you are," said Obiageli, the surprise evident in her voice. "Up already without prompting? What happened, was your bed on fire?" she teased.

"Oby, let the child be," said her dad with a smile on his face. "Siyonna does have a busy life you know?"

"Thank you!" said Siyonna. "Thank God someone here appreciates the fact that I am no longer a child."

As if on cue, both parents burst out laughing, shook their heads and headed for the stairs.

"Please adult," said Obiageli over her shoulder. "Don't forget to be ready to help serve the guests coming for the *ime'ego*. Dele and his people should be here about mid-day. Be ready oh!"

"Yes mum," Siyonna said, as she grabbed the remote and tuned into African Magic. Two and a half hours just about gave her enough time to watch a quick program before the ceremonies began.

Siyonna lamented the fact that whenever the house was full, her time was not her own. Just as she settled to watch a nice movie about two competing suitors after the same bride, a loud shout of: "Siyonna!" rang out from Chieme's room.

Chieme was the second daughter and the third child, and the bride. She stood tall like all the other Ndukas, and very pretty. After graduating in Languages, Chieme had gone on to a University in France for a postgraduate degree and progressed to work for the United Nations as an Interpreter, travelling the world. On the few weeks a year when she was home between assignments, she regaled the family with tales of faraway places and strange customs. Siyonna loved her world-travelled sister a lot and showed off with pride the gifts and hand-me-downs she got from her. Ebele was too short to fit into most of the clothes so Siyonna would naturally get them as soon as Chieme was done with them.

Their parents had been concerned about Chieme for a while, wondering if she would ever settle down and get married, when she suddenly showed up with Dele and announced their engagement. Dele Bankole worked as an Engineer with one of the power companies in Lagos. They met when he was in Washington on vacation and Chieme worked at the United Nations offices there. Friends introduced them at dinner, they hit it off immediately and had been seeing each other for over three years now. In all that time Siyonna's parents were not told she was dating and had sent at least four prospective suitors to Chieme who had flatly refused to entertain any of them. So, when she showed up with Dele, her parents were relieved that she had actually found someone to spend her life with.

He was also very easy to like. He was funny and very handsome. His father came from Lagos but his mother was Scottish. Surprisingly Dele knew as much about Scotland as anyone else. So continuous prods from Siyonna and her friends to tell them about the Kilts and Haggis came back with blank looks of 'dunno'. Dele's mum had immersed herself in Africa and the African way of life as soon as she arrived in Lagos, with the result that her children knew very little of the Scotland she had left behind. Once it became obvious Dele could not feed their curiosity, they found another use for him. On the days he visited Siyonna's parents back in Lagos, Siyonna and her friends made sure they got him to take them out and buy Iced Cream from one of the malls in Victoria Island.

Obiageli felt particularly fond of Dele. As she said repeatedly to her friends:

"The boy is fine and so respectful. What's not to like? My daughter's wait was well worth it!"

His visits always cheered Siyonna's parents up.

Dele came from a different tribe from the Ndukas. The Nigerian fixation with tribes could be very intriguing. There were more tribes in Nigeria than anyone could imagine, each with their own customs, languages, food and dress. Siyonna had been born and bred in Lagos and apart from vacations in Umuabado and occasional trips to Uncle Obi's at Enugu, considered herself a Lagosian. Lagos was such a melting-pot of Nigerian cultures you could not possibly reduce it to a tribe. But Siyonna was also aware that Lagos was home to the Yorubas, the tribe Dele belonged to.

As different as they were, all the tribes had some strong shared values, especially around the concepts of respect for elders and authority figures. They also all had their own forms of traditional marriages. Siyonna understood most of the major Yoruba traditions because a good number of her friends were Yoruba, but she couldn't call herself an expert at Yoruba nor Igbo traditions.

The Igbos, as Siyonna began to discover, had a very specific approach to marriage. In Igbo culture, the marriage was not just between a man and a woman, it was between the two families. So first, the suitor would find a close friend of the girl's family to undertake the task of introducing him to the girl's family so he could formally ask the woman's father for her hand in marriage. Then the suitor would come back to do the '*Iku'aka*' which was the official announcement of his intention to marry the young lady, accompanied by members of his family. At this event, senior members of the bride's family would also be present. Then a date would be agreed for the dowry payment and wine-carrying, or traditional marriage. Even with the advent of Christianity, the Igbos would still insist on completing the native rites before going on to have a church or registry office wedding. Because Dele was getting married to Chieme who was Igbo, they had to complete the marriage rites as defined by the Igbo tradition.

So after Dele and Chieme told Siyonna's dad they wanted to marry, Siyonna's dad told Dele to get his relatives together and perform the traditional 'Iku'aka' ceremony. Mr Nduka sent word back to his brothers, Uncle Obi and Uncle Udozor, his cousins and wider family (his Umunna), telling them that Chieme had a suitor who was now ready to perform the 'Iku'aka' ceremony. All the men, including Ikechukwu, had gone back to Umuabado for the ceremony, and Dele, accompanied by his father and uncles, came down from Lagos with gifts of Whiskey, Brandy and Brocade and Lace fabrics for the family. It was an opportunity for Dele to meet the wider family and also for the Ndukas and their relatives to get a feel for the family their daughter Chieme was going to be married into.

Siyonna had not attended the 'Iku'aka' ceremony but it must have gone well because today, Chieme and Dele would do both the dowry and traditional wedding. It had taken two months to get to this point and everybody was excited, no-one more than Chieme. She seemed to glow every day with the joy of love and her impending nuptials. When Dele was around, she exuded love and life, in a way that Siyonna could hardly put into words. She couldn't explain it, but she concluded simply that this must be what love looks like. Ikechukwu and Nnedi were definitely not that expressive, at least not in front of her. Her eldest sister Adaobi lived with her husband in Canada and Siyonna hardly ever saw her. She had hoped to make it back for the traditional wedding but Adaobi had sent word she would come for the church wedding instead. Because of both their work commitments, she and her husband Nnamdi, just couldn't get away.

Siyonna walked into Chieme's room to see her struggling with her traditional headscarf (*Ichafu*).

"You called, are you ok?" she asked.

"Not really," said Chieme. "I am having serious problems with this *ichafu*. Could you please help me? I need to finish with this and get on with my makeup."

Siyonna walked up to her sister and deftly sorted out the scarf, holding it in place with pins. She had become a bit of an expert at tying the intricate scarf from helping out at her mother's shop. One of her mother's businesses was a clothing and fabrics shop that sold the lace, Jorge and '*abada*' fabrics used for making Nigerian traditional attires. Her mum's shop was always a hub of activity and Siyonna would help every holiday, earning good money by helping shoppers with design advice for fabrics they bought and also helping with the scarves.

As soon as they were done, Chieme delicately moved the now firm scarf from her head to a mannequin's head to keep it in shape until she needed it. She then turned her attention to the abada and bead attire she would wear for the 'ime-ego' or dowry ceremony, before changing to the beautiful maxi dress her mother had made for her to wear for the wine carrying. Her mother insisted she wore three different outfits for the wine carrying, marking different stages of the ceremony.

"Thank you Onna-Mma," Chieme smiled, using her pet name for her little sister.

"It really is no bother," smiled Siyonna.

"You better go get ready. We can't have you late today. Mum will skin you alive. And me as well," said Chieme, kissing Siyonna on the cheek before starting on her makeup.

Siyonna had just finished getting dressed in her wrapper and '*jigida*' (bead) attire when she heard an excited cheer from the crowd gathered in the compound. She knew that meant Dele, his friends and his family had shown up for the ceremony. All the girls had to wait in the family room upstairs and would be called to accompany Chieme to Uncle Obi's house to confirm she would marry Dele. All the brothers had houses in the compound, and Uncle Obi's was the first one, right in front of the big front gate because he was the first son of the Ndukas. His brothers' houses flanked his but set just behind as you came into the compound, separated by the huge courtyard where the ceremony today would be held. As the first son, Uncle Obi stood in for grandfather as the head of the family and would be giving Chieme away today.

About an hour after Dele's arrival, the ceremony started with a prayer from Uncle Obi and the breaking of the kola nut by Ogbuefi Aro Oli, the oldest man from the Umunna. The Kola nut is a fruit and widely respected in Igbo tradition. A ceremony would not start until the Kola nut had been broken and shared amongst the guests and the Kola nut, of course, could not be broken until a prayer had been said over it, calling on God to bless the occasion and the food that would be served and consumed during the event. Before the advent of Christianity, the prayer had been to different gods the Igbos worshipped. These days, however, it was restricted to the Christian God, ensuring tradition lived in comfortable harmony with the new ways and remained relevant in the years to come.

Siyonna did not care very much for Kola nut. It tasted bitter and the only time she did eat it, she stayed awake for most of that night. At events like this, as Ikechukwu, her dad and Uncles munched away happily on the fruit, she always looked on in amazement, marvelling at the complexity of people and life in general. What one person found delicious, came as a complete and utter anathema to another.

Ikechukwu, Siyonna's older brother, called the girls and they danced across the compound to Uncle Obi's. All the girls wore Jigida beads just like the bride. Festive banners and balloons decorated the whole compound and the brightly coloured gazebos and canopies shone in the sunshine. Many of the guests had already taken their seats in the shade provided by the canopies. A festive feel surrounded the whole ceremony. Music blared from the speakers provided by DJ Pedro and the MC excitedly announced that the bride was on her way to the compound, to confirm her suitor as the man who had come to pay her dowry.

Guests stood and clapped as the girls danced by and went into Uncle Obi's house. As everyone else waited, Chieme and Ebele were called into the living room where Chieme identified Dele, to loud applause and the girls danced back to Siyonna's home.

As they came through the door and the group broke up, Siyonna couldn't help but be impressed at the number of women who'd come from all over Nigeria to support Chieme. She had friends from University who now lived and worked in various parts of the country and quite a few from the Federal Government College in Kaduna where she'd been a pupil. All of them had made versions of the women's uniform for the day, or what the Yorubas called the '*Asoebi*'. The very concept of Asoebi, though Yoruba in origin, seemed to have seeped into Igbo tradition as well, as friends and family wore matching fabrics to support the celebrant at special occasions like weddings.

Chieme's friends, in their Asoebi, would dance with her at various stages of the ceremony. Siyonna was young but also knew these outfits did not come cheap. She thought Chieme deserved to have so many friends who loved her, and wondered if she would have such a following on her own wedding day.

Her mother broke her reverie by coming in and asking the ladies to change and get ready for the next event. In between events, Siyonna's parents had arranged for a popular traditional dance troupe to entertain the guests. Drinks and light snacks were passed around whilst preparations were made for the '*Igbankwu*', the wine-carrying event which marked the completion of the wedding ceremony in accordance with Igbo tradition. A visit to the in-laws should follow at some stage but that could be scheduled later.

The dance troupe performed the acrobatic displays and intricate moves perfected by the famous Atilogwu Dance Troupe many years earlier, much to the delight of the crowds. Siyonna had slipped away from her sisters and the other ladies in the living room and stood in a discrete corner of the house where she had a good view and could see the dancers well. Just as she arrived, the troupe proceeded to build a pyramid, with the smallest member, a boy of no more than 8 or 9, at the very top. Siyonna couldn't guess at the height of the pyramid but it looked extremely tall. As the boy tumbled from the top of the pyramid and did two perfect pirouettes before landing firmly on his feet, the crowd cheered wildly and Siyonna couldn't help but cheer with them, she enjoyed it so much.

The pyramid disintegrated and the dancers gracefully fell into position as the beat changed and they all went into a fast tempo dance. Their feet moved quickly in tune and they shifted and shuffled in unison, in perfect beat to the music. As the drumming rose to a crescendo and died with a final beat, the dancers all stopped and ended up on one knee, in time and perfect unison. The crowd cheered wildly as the performers retired. Siyonna sighed audibly. She did love these dancers and had been so excited when her dad had invited them. What a treat! She could have spent the whole day rooted to this spot but the show must go on and she made her way back to the house to join the ladies for the Igba'nkwu ceremony.

All the ladies emerged resplendent in sky-blue blouses and wrappers and matching sky blue ichafus. With their makeup in place, they looked absolutely radiant. Chieme, of course, stood out in her own attire, trimmed with gold and worn with matching gold-covered sandals. Dele, waiting outside with his family, wore a gold kaftan and the red and gold embroidered cap of a Yoruba gentleman. Naturally, Chieme should be the only one wearing something gold in the ladies' procession.

The ladies started their dance when they were called by Nnedi, who danced right next to Chieme and fell in behind her. To music and the uproarious cheering of the guests, Chieme and her accompanying ladies danced to the canopy where Uncle Obi, Siyonna's dad, Uncle Udozor, Siyonna's mum and aunties were sitting with other senior members of the family. Chieme went up to her father and knelt before him. Mr Nduka put his hand on his daughter's head and blessed her, calling on God to bless her marriage, bring her joy and give her many children. He also asked God to help her be a good ambassador to her family and her tribe, bringing pride and joy to her new family. As the gathered crowd said 'Amen' at the end of the blessings, Mr Nduka handed his daughter a wine tusk filled with rich, fluffy palm wine.

Chieme took a sip of the wine, rose to her feet and then started dancing as she made the traditional show of trying to find her husband in the crowd. During the dance a few of the guests would call out 'I'm here!' in mock efforts to distract her but Chieme would shake her head as she led her troupe of accompanying ladies resolutely across the grounds directly to the tent where Dele and his family waited.

Dele sat between his father and his mother, a pretty, middle-aged woman with flaming red hair now beginning to show signs of grey, her skin tanned an even light brown from years of living in tropical Nigeria. His brother and sister sat on the other side of their father and cousins and friends filled this Canopy, as well as the next two canopies beside it. As Chieme's party approached the canopy, Dele's younger brother Femi jumped up to receive the wine, saying he was the groom and Chieme smilingly shook her head and went straight to Dele, knelt down, took a sip of the wine and handed the tusk to him to drink. Dele smiled, sipped the wine, and with his spare hand helped Chieme up, hugged and held her in his embrace, much to the joy of the guests who erupted in loud cheers.

Then holding her and dancing with her, they made their way back to her dad's canopy where they both knelt down for further blessings, went back to Dele's parents for even more blessings and then danced to their own canopy where a wedding dais had been festively decorated for them. They sat down next to each other as the MC announced they were now married.

As food and drink were passed around for the guests, Siyonna's mum grabbed Siyonna, Ebele and their cousins and friends to help. Siyonna was asked to make sure Dele's family and friends were looked after. Whilst this was going on, friends and guests would go to the canopy where the couple sat, to congratulate them and wish them well. Guests left them envelopes with money and other gifts, and some even brought household items.

Chieme had changed into a beautiful gold, long skirt and blouse her mum had made, topped off with a wine and gold scarf tied around the waist and an *ichafu* made from the same wine and gold material. As she led her friends and sisters around the compound for a final dance, Siyonna's dad beamed with pride. He could not have felt happier than at this moment, knowing that Chieme had at last found a life partner, a soulmate with whom she would share her life, hopes and dreams.

The bride danced up to her parents, hugged and kissed them, then led the ladies over to her new parents-in-law, hugged and kissed them too. She then danced around the compound one more time before retiring with her new husband to the house. The crowd clapped and cheered her all the way to the front door.

Soon after that, some of the guests started leaving, especially those who had far to travel. Dele and his parents had booked a hotel in Enugu for the night and would fly back to Lagos the following day. True to tradition, after the wine carrying, Chieme would go with her husband and his people to start her new life. However, both parties agreed that Chieme would come back to Umuabado after seeing them off in the morning.

As the party made their way to the car, Chieme started crying. Siyonna had seen this with brides at previous wine carrying events and could not understand why brides cried. Surely, they wanted to get married otherwise the ceremony would not happen? Nobody forced them into it, certainly not in Chieme's case. Siyonna suspected that had anyone tried to stop Chieme from marrying Dele, all hell would have broken loose. So why the tears? Were they tears of joy? Siyonna doubted it.

Just as Siyonna walked up to her sister to ask why she was crying, Dele appeared and gently put his arms around Chieme's shoulders soothingly, before walking her to the car. Amidst calls of goodbye and safe journey from the throngs of relatives and guests gathering to see them off, Chieme, Dele and his family left for Enugu.

Back in the compound, the party continued as the DJ did his best to entertain the crowd. There was still plenty to eat and drink as the guests chatted, ate and danced. As the evening wore on more people left, especially the ones who wouldn't be spending the night in Umuabado. Siyonna felt beat. A few of Chieme's friends remained who would be staying the night with the family. Siyonna's mum had settled them into the guest annexe, as well as some of the spare rooms in the house. Most people were tired and had by now headed off to bed. Siyonna came up to the family living room upstairs and saw Afam asleep on a hastily made-up pile of blankets on the carpet. Her parents and Ebele, Ikechukwu and Nnedi lounged back on the settees, talking. Siyonna came in and lay next to Afam.

"Won't you go to bed?" asked her dad.

"In a minute," Siyonna replied. Mr Nduka smiled. Siyonna's minute, he thought.

At some point during the night, her parents must have put a blanket over her. The next thing she knew, the sun had risen and she could hear the sound of workmen taking down the canopies and gazebos outside. Siyonna got up, looked around, stretched, gathered her blankets and headed for her room. As she walked through the short passage to her room she passed her mum.

"Morning mum," she muttered groggily.

"Morning my daughter. Did you sleep well?"

"Not sure mum, I'm going back to bed," sighed Siyonna before Obiageli had a chance to complain.

Siyonna woke up much later, feeling ravenous. She remembered she had been so busy during the ceremony yesterday that she hadn't had time for either lunch or dinner. She jumped out of bed, stripped off the dressing gown she'd slept in and jumped into the bathroom for a shower. She didn't see her sister Ebele who she shared the room with, so assumed she must be downstairs. After a quick shower and getting dressed, Siyonna quickly made her bed, folded the gown and put it in her laundry bag and went off to find something to eat.

The problem with big houses and ceremonies, thought Siyonna, is one could quickly get lost or be forgotten, as she flew down the stairs towards the kitchen.

"Good afternoon Mama Joe," she called out to the buxom lady working the stoves in the family kitchen.

Mama Joe was married to one of her father's cousins and always turned up to help with cooking whenever her parents had events in Umuabado. Obiageli paid her handsomely for the help and Mama Joe was quite fond of her. She had known all the children from birth and seen them grow up, but she was always Mama Joe. Siyonna did not know her real name and never asked because it did not matter. In Nigeria, parents quite regularly received the same name as their first child, so 'Mama Joe' as a moniker, also served as a badge of honour for the mother and identified the bearer perfectly.

"Onna-mma!" Mama Joe called back. "You are finally awake? Go sit at the table and I'll bring you something to eat."

"Ah, thanks, Ma! But I better take it in myself or my mum might just kill me for being spoilt," said Siyonna.

Mama Joe roared with laughter, grabbed a plate and filled it with spicy, hot jollof rice and beef, then handed it to Siyonna.

"Here you go my dear daughter, get that into you and you'll feel alive again!"

Siyonna thanked her and took her plate to the dining room, said hello to Ebele and settled down for lunch.

Just as she finished her food, she heard sounds of excitement coming from the living room.

"The bride must be back," said Ebele, smiling.

Sure enough, Chieme burst into the dining room.

"Hello girls," she said breezily, picking a piece of beef left on Siyonna's plate.

"Shall I get you a plate? Are you hungry?" asked Siyonna.

"No thanks," said Chieme, shaking her head.

After the pleasantries, Ebele made her excuses and left. She had to get back to Enugu and then a flight to Lagos, ready for work on Monday. The rest of the family would be leaving on Monday instead.

Siyonna found herself alone with Chieme.

"Chi," she said. "Do you mind if I ask you a question?"

"Of course not."

"Why were you crying yesterday when you were going to Enugu with Dele?"

Chieme thought for a while.

"I guess it was the realization that I was now leaving home for good. Don't get me wrong, I have lived on my own in many different countries and have been away from home since I was 11 and in boarding school at Kaduna. But that was different. I always knew I would come home, someday. This time it's different. I am really leaving to start my own home. I just think it will never be the same again. The next time I'm here, I'll be a visitor and people will be asking me, how's your husband?" Chieme smiled, and took her sister's hands in hers, rubbed them gently and repeated, "It's different."

All that occurred last year. This year, they had come back to Umuabado for her cousin Ada's *Igba'nkwu*. Ada was Uncle Udozor's daughter. She had met Joseph, a pilot in the Air Force when she worked in Makurdi during her compulsory National Service. Ada had worked in the hospital on the Air Force base and met Joseph who had come to her to fill out his prescription. Joseph had been smitten at first sight, so the story went, and kept coming back until Ada agreed to go on a date with him. As soon as Ada's National Service ended, Joseph had proposed. And here they were, the day after Ada's *Igbankwu*. The Church wedding would be in Makurdi where Joseph was still based and Siyonna was not sure she could go. She'd be back at school and it was unlikely her schedule would allow her to take a whole weekend off. But the *Igbankwu* had been a lovely ceremony with the Ndukas pulling out all the stops again.

Tomorrow the family would all disperse. Uncle Obi was now spending more time in the village and would not be leaving. But Uncle Udozor and his family and everyone else would head back to their homes in the city. She had to go home to start school on Tuesday. The holidays were over for her. She always enjoyed her days in Umuabado. Quiet and unobtrusive for the most part, they represented her only opportunity to reconnect both with her thoughts and with nature in a way that Lagos never could.

Speaking of nature, she saw the big lazy snake that often chased rodents around the back of the compound, crawl leisurely past again. She did not like snakes and was uncomfortable with the fact that this one lived in her compound and had the run of the place.

Odera must have been thinking the same thing because he surreptitiously crept up and hit the snake on the head with a large stick. The snake writhed in agony for a while, then lay still, dead, as people rushed out to look at it and snap their fingers at how big it had grown. One of the men picked it up and walked out of the compound, dragging the serpent behind him. Odera looked up at her and smiled. He had by his singular act of killing the snake and inviting a crowd to witness it, deliberately broken her peaceful reverie and knew it. Siyonna frowned, stuck her tongue at him and went back indoors.

3

Mr Bellamy

Back at school, Siyonna felt like the break had never happened. So much had occurred since they returned from Umuabado. Ada had since had a church wedding and her parents and her brother Ike had all gone on to Makurdi for the nuptials. Siyonna couldn't go because she was at school. However, the photographs from the wedding looked simply breathtaking, especially with Joseph in his Air Force dress uniforms and the couple walking out to an honour-guard by Joseph's brother officers. Siyonna had never been to a military wedding and really wished she could have been there. When she said as much to her parents, her mother remarked drily that it wasn't too late yet. She, Siyonna, could always go and marry a military man so she could experience the wedding first-hand for herself. Her father had thought this was funny and roared with laughter. Siyonna smiled as she remembered the conversation. Obiageli Nduka was just something else, she thought. Funny how she always thought about her mum as Obiageli whenever she felt not so charitable towards her. Obiageli Nduka. The name sat comfortably in her conscience. It would be a cold day in hell when she'd have the brazen effrontery to call her mum 'Obiageli' to her face!

School proceeded at breakneck speed. Everyone felt there were not enough hours in the day to get all the work done. It seemed less of a chore for Siyonna however because she actually loved school and enjoyed her lessons. Out of all of them, none caught her interest like Literature. Siyonna lived for literature. She loved the stories Literature brought to life. She loved how literature painted a thousand pictures with words. Her father always marvelled at how she could disappear in a daydream at the drop of a hat and often declared in utter bemusement: "Onna-mma, you're always either lost in a book or a daydream!"

By the time she was 12, her father had given up any notion that perhaps, maybe, Siyonna would follow in his footsteps and study engineering. As much as she liked maths, she had no patience for anything that took her away from her beloved stories. She would do just enough to pass her maths and no more, to the frustration of both her father and her teachers. Mr Nduka's gentle exhortations about the logic and intrinsic beauty of figures were mostly lost on her. For Siyonna, beauty lay in the unending humanity of the stories brought to life in the pages of a book. History, Literature, and the magnificence of the English words and phrases that brought them to life. Reading these stories and getting lost in them, felt so fulfilling for the young Siyonna.

One thing that Siyonna knew about her school, Our Lady of the Sacred Heart, they spared no expense at getting good staff. How else could the school justify the fees parents paid every year? Her father always complained that her fees 'could build a house in a township.' Siyonna did not quite know how much a house in a township cost, but had no doubt that the school charged a lot of money. That was part of the reason her father insisted she went to school from home rather than board at Our Lady's. In his opinion, it cost less to get her to school every morning from their home on Lagos Island than to pay the bloated boarding fees on top of the school fees. So, every morning, Siyonna had to be up and ready by 5.30 so that Mr Sunday, her dad's chauffeur, could drop her off at school. Mr Nduka ran an engineering firm in Apapa, about 6.5 miles from their home on the island, but on a bad day, it could take as much as 2 hours to get there. Lagos was notorious for its traffic jams and roads could literally shut down for hours on end because of a traffic incident. Lagos drivers were quite peculiar. As Mr Nduka had pointed out to his daughter on many occasions, it was as if people forgot all their manners when they climbed behind their wheels in Lagos.

This Monday turned out to be no different from any other Monday for Siyonna. Her dad was already in the back of the car when she flew out of the house, slamming the front door behind her, her breakfast sandwich in one hand, school satchel in the other. Mr Sunday reached out from his seat and opened the door for her.

"Thank you, Mr Sunday. Good morning," she gasped as she settled into her seat and clicked the seatbelt into place.

"Morning my dear," he replied. *"How your weekend take be?"*

"It was fine, thank you, Mr Sunday," Siyonna replied as Mr Sunday turned around, drove through the gates and joined the already busy traffic of cars heading through the thoroughfares of Lagos Island to work. Mr Sunday only spoke Pidgin English and it always made Siyonna smile. Siyonna turned to her dad behind and said good morning.

"Morning Onna-mma" her dad responded, using her pet name. "I see we have breakfast on the move again. Can't be healthy you know? It will be much easier to wake up slightly earlier. Do you want me to wake you up when I wake up?"

"Ah noo!" replied Siyonna in horror.

As far as she was concerned her dad never slept. No way did she want him rousing her at 4 a.m.

"I will work at getting ready sooner, daddy, and I will get there, you'll see."

Mr Nduka smiled and grunted a 'hmmm' as he buried his head in his morning papers again. He knew how tough it was for his daughter and knew she really would have preferred a few more hours in bed every day. However, he also felt that his occasional encouragements for a change in approach were in all their interests, otherwise they'd never leave the house on time.

Mr Nduka's other children had all gone to federal colleges outside Lagos, apart from Ikechukwu who attended Kings College in Lagos and went on to read Engineering at the University of Lagos. Ikechukwu had been different, informing his father in no uncertain terms that he did not intend to go out of state and would defer admission if the University of Lagos did not offer him a place. It had been a huge relief for everybody when he got the place. A good school, it was one of the best in the country so it had thankfully all worked out well for them.

With Siyonna, it was different. Her mother would not have her go to any school far from home and they both felt that the private school they chose was the best option for her.

"She is our youngest. She needs to be near us," Obiageli had declared defiantly 6 years ago when Siyonna was ready for secondary school.

Mr Nduka found himself powerless to stand up to his wife and had given in without much of a fight. Even though he'd never admit it, he also secretly loved having his youngest daughter around. And because he worked shorter hours now than when he was building the business and Ikechukwu had come in as the de facto Chief Executive, he had more time to spend with Siyonna and bond with her in a way he could not with her other siblings. He winced with regret at the thought. Thank God they'd all turned out all right. Thank God for Obiageli who had made the sacrifice and stayed at home to raise the kids, only starting a business after Ebele had gone into secondary school. Working 16 hour days when he was trying to build his engineering business, it would have been impossible to combine that with being fully involved in the children's lives. Well, he thought, he would more than make up for it with Siyonna.

He stole a glance at his daughter and marvelled again at how so very like her mum she looked. She had a slight frown, as she munched away at her sandwich and stared into Five Cowries creek, where the Lagos Lagoon formed a distributary. At this time of the morning, there was very little traffic and the car went through the tollgate as Mr Sunday expertly navigated them into Chrisander Road, Ikoyi, and turned off into Our Lady's. Mr Nduka could not fault the school its site. Beautiful and well presented, the school stood on a sizeable expanse of land that had once belonged to a British trading company. Rumour had it the company had run into tax problems and offloaded its assets in a hurry before the Nigerian government caught up with it. The property had been bought by an educational company who built a school and got Catholic Nuns to run it. The result was a beautiful, modern school in agreeable surroundings that also turned out good results every year. Highly sought-after, it had become one of the most desirable schools for girls in Nigeria.

Mr Sunday stopped at the gate and popped the boot for the usual security inspection. The guard completed his checks and waved them through. The car pulled up at the concourse and Siyonna thanked him, waved her father goodbye, and left to join her friends, also just coming in, as Mr Sunday swung the car around and headed back to the gate.

Siyonna walked to her best buddy Bunmi and hugged her. They were soon joined by Amaka and Dupe, and all headed off for their assembly. The other member of their little clique, Amina, was a boarder and would be coming to the assembly from the dormitory. The girls chatted happily along and fell quieter when they saw Mother Joseph, the Head Teacher. Mary Ajose Joseph had been a nun for over 30 years. She had started teaching just after her national youth service. However, the pull to dedicate her life to the service of God had been quite strong, so she joined the Catholic Convent. After taking her vows, she had been delighted when the church offered her the opportunity to go back to work as a teacher whilst still retaining her religious orders. In the years that followed, she had risen to become a Senior Principal, and Our Lady's was to be her last school before she retired. Unfortunately, she loved the school and the girls who passed through it too much, and she didn't know how she was going to be able to leave.

"Hurry along, girls, and no chatting. That's what we have breaks for!" she called out to Siyonna and her friends, who all giggled at hearing Mother's familiar morning chide.

"Morning Mother Joseph," they sang out in unison to the Principal.

"Good morning girls, and welcome back to school," she said as they filed past into the Assembly hall.

The girls met up with Amina who'd saved them seats around her. As the catch up started, Amina let out that there seemed to be a big announcement brewing this morning. Apparently, the Physics tutor, Miss Ojo, was to be replaced. As the others let out yelps of shock, Siyonna gave them a bemused look.

"Not one of my subjects, I'm afraid. Sorry girls!"

The other girls did not quite share her good humour. Miss Ojo was well- liked and quite helpful. A few of the girls who did not ordinarily shine at Physics were actually taking the course because of her encouragement and the extra help they got from her.

"Yee I'm dead," said Bunmi. "How on earth am I going to make my grades in Physics without Miss Ojo's help?"

"Ah come now," said Siyonna. "Let's wait for the announcement first. Who knows, it may not even be Physics. You know how these rumours go. Let's wait and hear what Mother says first, why don't we?" she said, putting an arm around her friend.

Mother Joseph walked up to the stage and stood behind the lectern in that manner that quietly commands silence even when one doesn't say a thing. Siyonna admired Mother Joseph. The very nature and composure of the woman just screamed respect. Not that she was tall, no, and she never quite did anything to accentuate her height. Nor was she big. In the typical manner of a nun, Mother Joseph seemed almost austere in appearance but elegant in her austerity. Dignified and elegant, how could this be? Siyonna wondered, watching Mother Joseph and marvelling at this woman. As she stood ramrod straight, arms tucked into the sleeves of her habit, the sounds of giggling schoolgirls subsided immediately. And Mother Joseph hadn't even said a word yet!

"Good morning," said Mother Joseph. "Mrs Olu who has been our Literature-in-English Tutor for the senior school certificate preparatory classes for the past 5 years, has sadly had to leave the school to join her husband abroad. Whilst we knew this day would come, I must say it did come as a surprise when she told me on Friday that she had to go. However, we have been fortunate to find a replacement willing to step in and pick up the reins, so to speak. Please join me in welcoming Mr Adrian Bellamy. Mr Bellamy?"

Mother Joseph turned her head in a slight incline and everyone followed her gaze to where a lanky, young-looking, Caucasian man sat near the podium. He stood up and walked over to stand at Mother Joseph's side. All the girls groaned and giggled at the man who looked like he had only just stepped out of secondary school himself.

Mother Joseph cleared her throat and the noise ceased.

"Mr Adrian Bellamy is an accomplished English Tutor who has taken time off from his work in England to visit and work in Africa. He has been in Tanzania for a year and will be in Nigeria for a further two years before returning to his post in England. Whilst he is here in Nigeria, we have the privilege of welcoming him to our school and hope he'll be happy here You girls must do your best to accommodate him and show him what well-rounded young ladies you are!" continued Mother Joseph enthusiastically. "So stand up and let's give Mr Bellamy a warm Our Lady's welcome!" She declared, throwing a jubilant half-punch in the air for good measure.

The girls all stood and applauded the new teacher, who beamed sheepishly in return. As the assembly broke up, the girls wandered off to class and the conversation turned to the new '*oyinbo*' tutor. All the girls declared he was young and quite good-looking. Siyonna said goodbye to her friends as she headed for lecture room C where she would have literature as her first lesson of the day. Siyonna quite liked Lecture room C. It felt cosy, with its wood panelling and polished, exposed beams. It also had large windows that looked out at the school's carefully manicured lawns. There'd been occasions when during mid-morning lessons, you could see Mr Okun, the school's grizzly, aged gardener, carefully working the lawns and pruning the flowers and ornamental plants that edged the garden. If one wasn't careful, one could lose oneself in the sheer tranquillity of the views. Mrs Olu's favourite expression had been: "Lose yourself in the prose, not the garden. Staring out of the window will not help you pass those exams!"

Siyonna came into class with a group of other girls and headed for her favourite desk, only to find Sally Eze already there. Sally looked up at her with a satisfied, smug expression, blatantly challenging Siyonna to say something. Siyonna pointedly ignored her.

"Siyonna here, this desk is free," sang out Lola Abiodun, a girl from 6B she got on quite well with. "You can come and sit next to me."

Siyonna smiled and went and sat next to Lola just as Mr Bellamy walked in.

"Morning again," he said in a confident voice. "Let's get cracking class, shall we?"

He perched on the end of the teacher's desk and surveyed the class.

"No, no, no this won't do. Please leave your desks, bring your chairs with you and form a half-moon right here," he said, pointing to a spot at the front of the class.

The girls moved their chairs and as they all sat down, Siyonna found herself sandwiched between Lola and Sally. She turned to Sally and smiled. Only sixteen girls had joined the literature class which surprised Siyonna because she couldn't believe how unpopular literature was. Whenever she broached the subject with her more science-inclined friends, they all bemoaned the amount of reading and writing that came with literature.

"The grammar is just too much!" Bunmi would often declare.

"I agree," Amaka would add. "All that long grammar and for what? Give me a good question on equations. When you know it, you just know it. There's no logic or trying to second-guess what the teacher is asking! Ah not for me, Literature, Siyonna, no thank you!"

Mr Bellamy ran his hand over the papers stacked on the desk beside him then stood up.

"I have been looking at the last essay you did for Mrs Olu, on the book 'Things Fall Apart.' So why in your opinion, did Okonkwo kill the messenger?"

He looked at the class and as there appeared to be no takers, he picked up the top paper in his pile.

"Sally?" he asked.

Sally sat up and stared back at him for a moment.

"I-I guess he did not like the messenger?" she stuttered.

Mr Bellamy waited as if willing her to say more.

"Well yes, Sally," he replied eventually. "We can assume he did not like the messenger. But there was a much broader driver for attacking this man and killing him. What was it?"

Sally was not making any effort to answer the question so Mr Bellamy turned to the rest of the class and settled on Siyonna.

"What's your name?" he asked.

"Siyonna, sir."

"Erm, about the sir thing," he said quickly. "Please call me Mr Bellamy or Mr Adrian but not quite the sir. I think we should approach learning as partners and work together in a friendly atmosphere?"

This seemed to please the girls who all nodded.

"So, Siyonna, what was up with Okonkwo?"

Siyonna cleared her throat.

"Well, he felt that his world was changing and his values were being eroded. After he'd been locked up with Obierika and the other men from the village, he had expected that, based on conversations they'd had, people would mount a firmer opposition to what he saw as the invasion of the white man. That did not happen and Okonkwo had already concluded that his clansmen lacked the will to engage and fight the invader to save their way of life. So, long before the messengers showed up, he had already decided to go to war which is why he wore his war-dress and took his machete to the meeting at the village square. Whatever the outcome of the meeting, Okonkwo was hell-bent on doing something about this scourge on his way of life. The messenger just happened to have been at the wrong place at the wrong time. He was killed, not because Okonkwo disliked him, he was killed because of what he represented, the messenger of the invader."

"Well done Siyonna," said Mr Bellamy. "Absolutely brilliant. I couldn't have put it any better myself."

He leafed through the pile of marked scripts on the desk and found Siyonna's.

"I might as well give you your paper, Siyonna. Mrs Olu was also impressed with your work on 'Things Fall Apart'. This is an A-star. Quite impressive."

He proceeded to hand out the papers to the rest of the class.

"In answering questions on literature, think," he continued. "You must engage your reader with the responses you give. Look at the substance of the text and provide a response that adequately analyses the text and provides a meaningful response to the question put to you. Literature is all about stretching your imagination and understanding what you have read. Think."

The rest of the lesson was spent going through the impact of the colonization of Nigeria on local life, far beyond the confines of 'Things Fall Apart'. Mr Bellamy sought to create some context about what Okonkwo's character must have perceived to be an immense upheaval of his society, a direct affront to his gods and sweeping change to everything he believed in and had worked for all his life. He had, as Mr Bellamy put it, been pushed to the very limits of his patience.

"Next lesson, I'd like you to write an essay on the possible links between Okonkwo's approach to the invasion of the white man and the effect of his father Unoka on him. Have the essays on this desk as you come in for your lessons. Good day, girls, and good session."

Mr Bellamy smiled as the girls picked up their bags and headed for the door.

"Miss Know-it-all," muttered Sally under her breath as Siyonna walked past her. "You think you're better than everybody with your analysis? You need to be brought down a peg or two," she snarled.

"Leave her alone Sally," said Lola, taking Siyonna's arm. "You leave her alone. How is it her fault that you spend all your time on that face of yours and boys, rather than working? Just back off or you'll have me to answer to."

Sally backed away, swiftly.

Lola was nobody's pushover and after she had given the ex-bully Tessy Lampon a bloody nose in their third year, most girls steered quite clear of her. Whilst fighting was frowned on at Our Lady's and would lead to instant expulsion, fights still broke out occasionally. In Lola's case, both girls had been suspended for a week and their parents forced to go through the humiliation of writing undertakings that they would be of good behaviour going forward. However, the message went out loud and clear: Lola may be quiet but she was no push-over and could hold her own, as Tessy had found out, much to her shock.

As Sally backed away, Lola linked her arm in Siyonna's.

"Don't let that one get to you," she said. "Just walk with me."

"Thanks, Lola. I really don't know what Sally's problem is. She's just relentless!"

"Don't sweat it, Siyonna. She's just jealous. Don't read too much into it."

When they came to the small courtyard that held the sixth form classrooms, the two girls hugged. Lola then crossed the courtyard to get to Form 6B, while Siyonna went up the stairs to Form 6A. The rest of the day was a blur as the lessons rolled thick and fast, one after the other. Our Lady's prided itself on the academic excellence of the girls and some had even gone on to universities, either in the UK or the US on academic scholarships. So, the school pushed the girls hard.

Straight after lunch, Siyonna endured a marathon two-hour lecture in Maths and by the end of the day, she felt so exhausted, she couldn't wait to go home and get some rest before digging into her homework. On the way out, she couldn't see her friends so she walked alone knowing that Mr Sunday would be waiting for her in the car park. However, just as she rounded the form block, Miss Ajose, the school's lead Administrative Assistant called out to her and said Mr Bellamy would like to see her.

Siyonna walked to the tutor's offices. Mr Bellamy would be sharing an office with Dr Obi who taught English Language. As she walked in, she heard both men laughing. There was something akin to happiness in Dr Obi's smile as he joked with Mr Bellamy. Up until now, he had been the youngest of the teaching staff. He was single as well and always seemed to be the odd one out.

"Ah Siyonna," said Mr Bellamy. "Sorry to pull you in but I want to give you something to read which I thought would help you grow? It is a brilliant book from one of Africa's most promising writers. Let's talk about it when you're done?"

Siyonna nodded as Mr Bellamy handed her a copy of Binyavanga Wainaina's 'One Day I Will Write About This Place.' She thanked him profusely.

She started reading the book in the car and was so captivated by it that she read it all through dinner, finally finishing it close to midnight. Just before she fell asleep, she picked up her necklace from the bedside table. As she held it, it felt heavy and cold to touch and as she looked at it, she could have sworn it glowed and then dimmed again. Strange, she thought, as she put the necklace in the little trinket box in her wardrobe then went to sleep, thinking nothing more of it.

On her way to school the next day, she cursed her decision to stay up so late, reading the book. She had done none of her private study, nor had she started on her homework which was due in two days! She knew she'd have to work through lunch to stay on top of things but she felt it was worth it. The story was not necessarily the sort she normally liked reading. This book was not fiction and dealt with concepts and places she did not know and could only imagine. Yet she had connected with it and felt the story come alive for her. She had sensed Binyavanga's pain as he struggled to find a purpose in life and cried at the passing of his mum. She felt the tug of his passion for writing and she celebrated the excitement and complete joy when he finally made it as a writer. She even found herself envying him his connections. He knew Chimamanda Adichie! Oh, how she yearned to be a writer! As she got closer to school, she couldn't wait to discuss the book with Mr Bellamy and thank him for introducing her to this particular genre of African literature. She knew she shouldn't but she was bursting to ask him for more books.

As soon as Mr Sunday pulled into the car park, she said a quick thank you and a good-bye to her dad, grabbed her rucksack and ran towards the assembly hall. As she flew down the path to the hall, she thought it odd that Mother Joseph had not been there to wave them to the hall. She also couldn't see any of her friends and surmised that they probably had come in early and gone on to the assembly. As she came to the hall, she found Mother Joseph in a stern huddle with the deputy head and a few of the senior teachers. The atmosphere in the assembly hall felt decidedly subdued as girls came in and quietly took their places.

Siyonna saw Amina and slipped in next to her, playfully tugging at her hair.

"What's going on? This place is so sombre today and Mother Joseph wasn't there to rush us to assembly. What's happened?"

"I think one of the teachers just died," said Amina, shrugging her shoulders. "I am not sure which one."

"Oh good grief," said Siyonna, as Amaka and Bunmi joined them.

"Good morning girls," said Mother Joseph. "I have some awful news which I wish I did not have to tell you." She paused for a moment and then continued. "Yesterday, Mr Bellamy spent his first full day with us here as a tutor and I hear he hit the ground running. Unfortunately, on his way home the car he was travelling in was hit when a lorry lost control and ploughed into them. Mr Bellamy died on the way to the hospital. He was just 25 years old. Our prayers are with his family. Please go back to class and try to carry on as normally as you can. I am sure that's what he would have wanted. In the interim, Dr Chidi Obi will pick up Literature for the 6th formers. Thank you."

Siyonna felt as if her whole world had just collapsed around her. The shock and sheer incredulity of the situation numbed her as she sat rooted to her chair, clutching Binyavanga's book to her chest, while the rest of the hall emptied. Mother Joseph noticed her and walked up to her, gently touching her shoulder.

"You must go to class, dear child and remember he was a good man. God gives life and God takes life. Go on, that is what he would have wanted you to do. I will arrange for grief counsellors to come and speak to you and anyone in the school who has been affected by this as soon as possible, dear child. Be strong and I will see you as soon as the counsellors get here."

"He-he lent me this book to read yesterday and wanted us to discuss it when I was done. I finished it and was going to discuss it with him today," Siyonna stuttered as tears poured down her face.

Mother took the proffered book from her.

"I will return it to his family, along with his other possessions," she said.

The rest of the day was a blur at Our Lady's, as pupils and staff struggled to come to terms with the news of this shocking death and how it was that someone so young could die after only one day in the school. It made very little sense. The school's proprietors sent counsellors to talk to the girls, especially those who'd been in his literature class. It was at one of those sessions that Mother Joseph walked into as the counsellor was talking to Siyonna. First, she cleared it with the counsellor that it was alright to speak with Siyonna.

"I have spoken to Mr Bellamy's parents in England and his mum said he had spoken to her just after his lesson with you and spoke very highly of you, child. She has asked that you keep the book as a reminder of her son and hopes it inspires you to do well. She also asked that if you were ever in England, it would be their pleasure if you could visit," said Mother Joseph, handing the now precious book back to her.

4

When Will I See You Again?

Siyonna could not believe just how long she'd slept for. She finally opened her eyes because she was just so hungry. As she groggily got out of bed, wondering why she felt the way she did, she remembered she had gone to bed the previous night without dinner. She sighed audibly. What a silly thing to do! All because she had convinced herself she was fat and needed to shift a few pounds!

Siyonna went into her bathroom and twirled in front of the mirror. No, she was not fat, not in the least. If anything, she could do with some flesh around the waist. Her mum still sometimes called her '*Ikpekere*', the stick waiting to break anytime there was a strong wind. Siyonna winced. That really wasn't the name for a young lady! But who was she kidding? Her mum would call her that until she either tired of it or thought Siyonna no longer looked like a stick.

Speaking of mums, Siyonna thought, where was mine? She probably had gone to the new supermarket she was setting up but Siyonna was surprised she'd gone without waking her up and loading her with chores. This was the first day of her week-long half-term break and she knew there was no way it was going to be chore-free.

She showered and dressed up quickly in a pair of jeans and a comfortable tee shirt, then headed down to the kitchen to grab some brunch. She quite fancied dodo and omelette, then she'd be ready to take on the day. She'd already lined up a nice collection of African authors whose books she planned to dig into and between that, catching up with the girls and chores at home, she really had a busy week ahead.

As she got to the foot of the stairs, she heard voices from the kitchen. She didn't think it would be the cook, who wouldn't be preparing lunch already. She opened the swing doors and walked in to see her mother and Ebele at the breakfast bar, deep in conversation. She went over to her mum, hugged and kissed her good morning and hugged her sister, tight.

"Eby-Eby," she said. "You did not tell me you were coming or I'd have been up at the crack of dawn to wait for you!"

"Ha!" sniggered her mum. "Sleeping beauty up at the crack of dawn on a school vacation day, without prompting? First, pigs must fly!"

Siyonna smiled and turned to her sister with a 'well, what's new?' look on her face.

"I have news," said Ebele, smiling. "You know how I've been applying to hospitals abroad for somewhere to do my residency and specialization training?"

"Have you?" said Siyonna, looking baffled. "I don't recall you telling me about going anywhere?" she added with a small frown.

"I did Siyonna!" countered Ebele. "I probably just mentioned it in passing because I wasn't sure I'd get it. Now one of the hospitals in the UK has made me a conditional offer after I sat my last West African surgical board exams. When I passed, they confirmed the offer and want me to train at their hospital. I have to be in the UK in two weeks to start work."

Obiageli beamed with pride and raised both hands heavenward.

"It is tight but we will make it happen, my daughter. God will help us meet this timetable."

"Amen," chimed Siyonna and Ebele in unison.

Siyonna felt it seemed the appropriate thing to say after her mum's prayer but she really couldn't understand what the issue was. You needed to go to England, you bought your ticket and you went. Simple. But there was also the question of where Ebele would live and she also knew a few people had applied for visas to the UK and been refused, so yes, one could surmise that it really wasn't as simple as just going when you wanted to. There were quite a few hurdles to overcome. However, the news was unexpected and she was still reeling from the suddenness of it.

Siyonna and Ebele had always been close, despite the age difference between them. As the other siblings all left home to pursue their dreams, Ebele had never been too far from home. While at the University of Lagos, Ebele would attend lectures from home as often as she could. Even when she started work as a House Officer at the Teaching hospital, she would often come home and only stayed at the hospital on the nights she was on call. Last year, however, the Teaching hospital had offered her a flat of her own and she had finally left home.

Siyonna looked at her older sister and realised for the first time just how much she would miss her. The thought filled her with such sadness that her eyes welled up with tears. It was always to Ebele she turned when she hit a roadblock. It was always Ebele who had time for her, understood her and advised her as she navigated her teenage years. Now, Ebele was leaving for the UK.

"Oh, come now Siyonna, don't cry. I'll only be six hours away and you can visit whenever you like. It'll be another place to spend your holidays."

Siyonna turned and hugged her sister and held on tight. She knew it was not going to be the same anymore and she knew that to some extent, her world had changed. She felt slightly lost at the thought of her sister leaving Nigeria. How would she ever cope, she wondered. She held onto Ebele, inhaling the rich scent of her perfume between her silent sobs and hoping the pain of missing her would go away soon. Ebele rubbed her back and whispered it was all going to be all right. Obiageli got up and came to her youngest daughter, prying her away from Ebele and consoling her.

"I have asked Cook to make *dodo* and omelette for you. Thought you'd like that. Now go get your food from the microwave and sit with us whilst we plan your sister's trip."

Siyonna smiled at her mum, wiped her tears and headed for the microwave where her platter was waiting. She warmed her food and sat down at the breakfast bar next to Ebele who had already produced a list and was ticking things off as she talked to her mum.

After her brunch, Siyonna stayed in the kitchen with her mum as the planning with Ebele went into full swing. They talked about clearing out her flat and giving notice at work. Siyonna asked if Ebele had told their dad yet and Ebele said yes, she'd called him this morning, the moment she got the email and also told her Supervising Consultant at work. The Teaching hospital had been magnanimous with their offer, allowing her to leave immediately. She had to be out of her flat by tomorrow though and dad was sending people over to help her move.

"I could use some help, Onna-mma. Will you come back to the flat with me and help me pack?" asked Ebele. "You'll have to stay the night and come back with me tomorrow."

"Yes!" said Siyonna, smiling.

She ran back to her room to pack an overnight bag. As she packed, she tried to sort through her feelings. This thing of Ebele's had come as a huge shock to her. Yes, Ebele had always talked about training and specializing 'someday' but one never fathomed that the day would come so soon. She could however not help but feel happy for her sister. It seemed to her that for the first time ever, she would really be on her own. All her siblings were away from home, all leading adult lives and she would be alone with her parents from now on. Well, for a while anyway. It wasn't so bad really, she reasoned. It had always been that way to an extent and even when they'd been at home, her siblings had mostly left her to her own devices because she was so much younger than them. Ebele, however, had been different. She was always the sister to play with, play pranks on, argue with, and steal make-up from. Even though they were mostly in different places in their lives, Ebele had done her best to be the typical immediate older sister to Siyonna, keeping her as close as she possibly could.

When Siyonna came downstairs, she found her sister and mother waiting for her in the big living room. As they walked out to the car, her mum promised to come around to Ebele's with dinner for the girls that evening.

Ebele's car was a 2-door Toyota her dad had given her as a present when she started her job at the hospital. She loved the car and loved the attention she got because of just how bright and distinctive it looked. It was striking red and their brother who also loved cars had put black stripes running across the car from the boot to the bonnet, giving it an even sportier look.

The drive from Victoria Island to Ebele's flat in Yaba took just over 40 minutes.

"I now see why you needed help with the packing," said Siyonna smiling, as they walked into the flat.

Ebele, it seemed, had already started packing. She had boxes open in the living room of the small, single bedroom flat. The place had come unfurnished, so her dad and her brother, Ikechukwu, had arranged for the flat to be repainted and furnished. Siyonna looked around at the tasteful furnishings.

"What will you do with your furniture?" she asked.

"All sold," said Ebele. "My colleagues bought everything, including the carpets. In two days, they will come in and strip the place. Whatever's left I'll give away. I really liked this place. It was my first home," added Ebele, wistfully.

Siyonna hugged her and said nothing. Both sisters stayed hugging for a while until Ebele finally broke away.

"We'd better get started otherwise we won't sleep tonight!" she laughed.

Packing soon became a bonding experience for the sisters as they worked together, side by side, placing clothes in suitcases, sorting out utensils and other bits of memorabilia that go towards making a home. Both girls were amazed at how much Ebele had accumulated in the short period of time she had lived on her own. The clothes alone filled three large suitcases with Ebele bemoaning the fact that she had never worn half of them.

As the girls finished with the bedroom and started packing the kitchen, Obiageli called to say there'd been an accident on the third Mainland Bridge. The traffic was horrendous. Lagos was notorious for its traffic jams and if you got caught in a bad traffic incident, a relatively short journey could easily stretch out for hours. So, when there was a report of an incident and the road had ground to a halt, one really had to assess one's journey and decide if it was worth continuing or not. Obiageli reckoned it made more sense for the girls to get a takeaway of sorts locally tonight and she'd see them tomorrow.

Ebele suggested they should pop down to the Pizza place not too far from the hospital, but Siyonna said she'd rather have fries. They were still trying to decide which option to go for when the doorbell rang. Ebele let out an excited shout when she opened the door, because standing there were her old classmates, Tunde and Charles. She hadn't seen them since graduation as they had both gone to other hospitals for their post-graduate training programs. Charles had gone north to the Teaching hospital in Abuja and Tunde had gone on to the military hospital in Port Harcourt, in the South-East of Nigeria. This was the first time she had seen either of them in two years.

As Ebele made the introductions, Siyonna mischievously relayed that she remembered Tunde coming to the house to visit Ebele when they were both in medical school.

"Ah yes," said Ebele, with a smile. "Tunde, you were quite a fixture at my house, back in the day!"

Tunde smiled. He had spent quite some time chasing Ebele but the sheer volume of work in medical school had made sustaining any serious romantic attachment impossible. They had settled into an easy friendship until they both left for their compulsory national service program after graduation and then on to training contracts in different hospitals.

"What's a guy to do?" asked Tunde, throwing his hands up in mock exasperation. "Siyonna, I worked so hard to win your sister's heart but she was just not having it."

"Ah-Ah, Tunde!" interjected Ebele. "That's not fair. Trouble was that between medical school and all the other girls chasing you, there really wasn't any time for little old me!"

They all burst out laughing, remembering Tunde's reputation as a bit of a lothario, always with a girl on his arm. His feeble attempts to change the subject and put the spotlight on Charles didn't work either, as everybody in the room concluded that he was the playboy, not Charles.

"Ok, ok, you got me. Now Siyonna is going to go away believing I am a bad boy," said Tunde, again in mock exasperation.

Siyonna giggled and hid her face in her hands.

"So," continued Tunde. "Charles and I were on our way to dinner when we ran into Dora who told us you were leaving the country and we thought we'd come surprise you. Are you guys hungry? Would you like to join Charles and me for a bite to eat? We were on our way to a restaurant at Ikeja."

"Yes, that will be lovely," said Ebele, answering for both of them. "Siyonna and I were just wondering what to do for dinner. Give me 2 secs, I'll throw on something comfy. Onna-mma do you want to change?"

Siyonna turned and walked with her sister into her room.

"I didn't bring anything for going out. Do you have a top I could wear over my jeans?"

"Of course, yes," said Ebele. "Here, try this. It'll go perfectly with your jeans."

Ebele handed Siyonna a lovely pink Polo shirt and she popped into the bathroom to try it on. She paired it with her navy jeans and a pair of black, tasselled suede pumps. As she finished dressing, she reached into her handbag, brought out her blue necklace and gingerly put it around her neck. She wasn't really one for makeup and was almost certain she wasn't allowed any, so she was quite pleased that the face looking back at her in the mirror was unblemished and adequately pretty. She smiled at her reflection and headed back to the bedroom where Ebele was now dressed in a pair of jeans and silver pumps, with a lovely top, embroidered around the neck and cuffs.

"You look so pretty," said Siyonna to her sister.

"Thanks, and so do you Siyonna. Look at you, no makeup and you can still stop traffic! You are so pretty and that necklace of yours, Ma Mabel certainly gave you a hell of a gift. How come it seems to go with whatever you wear?"

Siyonna smiled. Then she stopped and realised Ebele had a point. It did not matter what she wore, the necklace always seemed to go with it. She instinctively reached up to her neck and caressed the beads which felt cool and comforting against her skin. She felt safe and complete wearing her necklace. So she simply shrugged and walked over to Ebele's open suitcase and vanity bag, chose a perfume and raised it questioningly to her sister.

"Just a tad, Onna-mma. Don't bathe in it now!" said Ebele, with a smile.

Both girls walked out with Tunde and Charles to Tunde's Range Rover.

"Yours?" asked Ebele, surprised.

"I wish," replied Tunde. "It's Dad's, of course. He kindly loaned it to me for the weekend whilst I'm in town."

Ebele smiled to herself, remembering how wealthy Tunde's father was. A renowned businessman, Tunde was his fourth child and the only one who had shown any promise. So, his father never spared any expense in showing just how proud of him he felt.

Tunde and Charles climbed into the front and the girls sat behind. The trip to Ikeja was occupied with conversations about their individual experiences. Charles was deep in the grip of exams as well and like Tunde was looking for a training program in the United States. They were both in Lagos because they had sat exams the previous day. Charles had always been soft-spoken and in his measured way, declared that the lack of equipment at the hospital where he worked often left him frustrated. He didn't understand how he could be expected to save lives if he was unable to train with the most modern techniques and equipment.

"I feel you bro," said Tunde. "Pretty much the same where I am."

"Funny that," said Ebele. "I thought military hospitals had everything? Not that I've ever been in one! I almost did my national service at the military hospital in Ikeja but got sent to the General hospital at the last moment."

"Not really," replied Tunde. "The military hospitals face the exact same challenges as all the other hospitals."

As the discussion continued and each of the friends tried to rationalize why they were all looking to leave the country, Siyonna again thought about what life would be like without her older sister. She also wondered about herself. She knew she wanted to write, so whatever she ended up doing would have to lead back to her joy of writing. But would she ever want to live outside Nigeria? She really did not know. She wasn't sure her parents would want to let her go. More than anything else, she wasn't quite sure she'd want to go. Well, at least not today. The future may well hold a different promise. At that moment, Ebele reached out and took her hand.

"You ok, sweetie?" she asked.

"Yes," said Siyonna and smiled.

"We're here," announced Tunde as they pulled into one of the fashionable new hotels in Ikeja.

He parked and they all got out and went to the restaurant area. Tunde was well known and they were seated in minutes even though they hadn't a reservation. Dinner was lovely and for dessert, Siyonna enjoyed a delicious Nutella cheesecake. As the adults laughed and joked about their time in medical school, Siyonna listened and marvelled at just how much fun university seemed to have been. She really couldn't wait to go to uni herself! The evening ended and as they got back in the car, the necklace around Siyonna's neck suddenly felt like it was hugging her, or at least that was how it seemed. She touched her neck and found herself caressing the beads for the second time that evening.

With the adults still chatting away, Tunde turned the keys in the ignition and nothing. Tunde and Charles exchanged looks. Tunde turned the ignition again, still no spark coming from the car.

"That's strange," he said. "This car's new and hardly used. Most unusual."

"Cars are strange things," said Ebele. "Let's give it some time and try again?"

Tunde agreed and they all settled back and continued chatting about their jobs and future plans. The three colleagues must have lost track of time but Siyonna felt they'd been in the car for about ten minutes.

"Do you want to try the car again now? I think it may just start," she said instinctively to Tunde.

"Well let's hope so," said Tunde. "Dad isn't going to be impressed that I left his Range Rover at a restaurant overnight."

He turned the ignition and the car roared to life.

"Hmm. How peculiar," he said. "How did you know it would start this time?"

"I just knew," said Siyonna.

As they headed out of Ikeja, they saw a small crowd gathered around a couple. The lady looked shocked and distraught as the gentleman, who appeared to be in his fifties, sat on the roadside, shaken and confused. Tunde pulled up and stopped, rolled down his window and asked one of the onlookers, a young man on a motorbike, what had happened.

"Armed robbers," said the guy, wiping the sweat off his brow. "They just snatched their Range Rover. According to the woman, the car's only a year old. I guess they're lucky the robbers only took the car. It could have been worse."

Tunde shook his head and muttered something about how unsafe Lagos was getting.

"I know," said the biker. "It was only about 20 minutes ago, so it only just happened."

Tunde thanked the guy and rolled the window back up as he headed back on the road towards Yaba.

"Guys," he said. "That was 20 minutes ago. Had the car not stalled, it could have been us. The car stolen had the same profile as this one."

Everybody stayed quiet for a while.

"Well, it wasn't," said Charles suddenly. "Thankfully our car has a soul and kept us out of trouble tonight! All hail the safest car on earth! Tunde you should talk to your father. Perhaps this car can make the journey to the US with you?"

That broke the mood as everyone burst out laughing. Suddenly, Siyonna noticed the necklace no longer clung to her skin. She instinctively touched the beads for comfort and again welcomed their coolness on her skin.

Tunde and Charles dropped the girls back at the flat and they all promised to keep in touch. Once inside, Ebele and Siyonna went straight to bed.

The next day was manic, as the removal people arrived, picked up Ebele's things and took them back to the family home in Victoria Island.

As Ebele had several logistical errands to run in the days that followed, Siyonna saw little of her leading up to her leaving. Siyonna had also been busy, spending a whole day with her friends and also going over to her brother's home to spend a day with his family.

On the eve of Ebele's departure, all the family gathered in the family home for a special meal. What with Ikechukwu and his family, all Siyonna's cousins and Chieme and her husband Dele, there were easily about 30 people gathered around the dining table for dinner. Siyonna's dad said a prayer and asked God to look after Ebele and also help her find someone to share the rest of her life with. There was a cheeky resounding 'Amen" from the assembled family, then everyone dug into the sumptuous feast laid out by Siyonna's mum.

As the evening wore on, people started leaving and very soon it was just Siyonna, Ebele and their parents left. As they all said their goodnights, Siyonna thought her father looked drawn. She went over and hugged him.

"I am still here you know," she said. "I will look after you."

"I know you will Onna-mma," said Mr Nduka, smiling. "I know you will."

5

Amanda

Siyonna usually spent Sunday mornings ironing before getting ready for church and today was no different. She really missed Ebele and in the days following her departure, Siyonna found she had time to muse at how paradoxical life could be. When Ebele was in Nigeria they had sometimes gone weeks without seeing each other, while Siyonna happily got on with her life. However, with Ebele now in Europe, Siyonna felt a deep sense of loss as if part of her was no longer there. For the first time ever, she looked forward to Monday morning and school. She ironed all her uniforms and lay out her clothes for the week. She went through her timetable, then picked up her rucksack and packed the right books, checking her diary again to make sure she had no outstanding pieces of work that she hadn't done during the holidays. According to her diary, she was up to date.

After ironing, she quickly got herself ready for church. Mr Nduka could put up with a lot of things but being late for church was not one of them. St. Anthony's stood just a stone's throw from the house. They had worshipped there every Sunday and through all the holy days of obligation, from the time they moved into their current home. As far as Siyonna could remember, that was forever! This was the only home she'd ever known and had absolutely no recollection of living anywhere else.

Every Sunday morning without fail, she'd get up and be ready for 9.30, when she'd walk between her parents for the eight-minute walk to St. Anthony's. Her mum was not always very pleased with the whole idea of walking to church and would rather they drove.

"But it's just a short walk," said Mr Nduka, half-encouraging, half-protesting.

"It might be to you because you're not the one having to march for eight minutes in high-heels!" replied Obiageli.

Mr Nduka smiled and shook his head as he encouraged her to make the short walk with him. When Siyonna was younger, her parents would each take one of her hands. These days Siyonna would still walk between them but made no effort to hold their hands.

Church today was a blur. Father Benjamin really could go on and there had been many times during his sermons when Siyonna had questioned the very meaning of life! Gosh, how she had daydreamed all service long! Once in a while, she'd feel a pang of guilt and force herself back to the service but it never took too long before Father Benjamin lost her again. As they walked home, her father asked with a smile whether there was any need for her to come to church at all, since she spent so much of the service daydreaming?

"Of course, yes, daddy!" she replied with a frown on her face.

Obiageli made a derisive face and said nothing, while Mr Nduka just laughed.

Sundays were always fun. In the early days, all the children living in Lagos would come home for Sunday lunch. Now her brother Ike and his young family were the only ones left in Lagos and mostly did their own thing, coming around for family lunch just once a month or on special occasions. So today it would be just the three of them unless a cousin or one of her father's friends dropped by.

Lunch was fried rice and a delightful goat meat curry her mum had made, with salad and fried plantain for sides. Siyonna helped her mother serve and when they'd finished lunch, they cleared up together and Siyonna read the papers with her parents before retiring to get herself ready for school. She had just finished sleeking her hair into a bun when her phone started buzzing. It was her friend Bunmi who called to declare she really wasn't looking forward to school starting tomorrow.

"Why can't I just stay at home and wake up when I want, eat what I want, and play my music till I sleep off again?" asked Bunmi.

"Abegi! Go get ready for school, joh!" chided Siyonna with a smile. "Lazy cow. Endless vacation, how do you plan to feed yourself?"

"Hmmm, good point," said Bunmi. "I could always marry a rich man, or come live with you?"

"Ahh no-oo! I really cannot afford you!" screamed Siyonna and the friends burst out laughing.

"Anyhow, I have heard there's a new girl joining us. Her father is some big shot in an American company, posted here. So, she's joining us from some fancy school in America."

"Great!" said Siyonna. "I hope she's nicer than the other new girl we got."

Both girls laughed again at the veiled reference to Sally, who had only spent two years so far at the school and therefore was still the newest girl in Siyonna's year. The girls talked for a while about school and what they hoped the new girl would be like and were still chatting happily away when Siyonna's mum called her to come help serve dinner. Siyonna gasped at the time, said a quick good night to Bunmi and dashed downstairs for dinner.

After clearing up and washing up, Siyonna said goodnight to her parents, picked up the novel she was reading at the moment, 'Ghana Must Go' and dived straight into it. The book was on her chest when she woke up in the morning, with her bedside lamp still on and the alarm buzzing.

First days of school were always a flurry of activities with homework handed in and pupils beginning the reluctant process of getting back into their routines. Siyonna's class had a study period and she was working through some aspects of Pythagoras theorem when Mrs Cole, the Form Tutor walked in and broke the silence.

"Girls can I have your attention please, thank you," she said.

The girls all sat up as she gestured slightly to the girl standing to her right.

"This is Amanda Saul-Obi who has just joined the school. She has been assigned to this class so I am hoping you'll be nice to her? Amanda joins us from Washington DC where she lived and went to school until a week ago when she moved to Nigeria with her family. She does not know anybody in this school but I have assured both Amanda and her parents that she will be well taken care of here because that is the sort of thing we do. Am I right, ladies?" asked Mrs. Cole.

"Yes, Miss!" they all replied in a single, thunderous voice.

Amanda looked on, slightly bewildered.

As soon as Mrs Cole left the class, Alero who had a corner desk with no one beside her, quickly grabbed the new girl and offered her the empty desk right next to hers. By the time Amanda had sat down at her new desk, practically the whole class had gathered around her and started firing off so many questions, she could have been forgiven for wanting to head right back to Washington! Alero wanted to know what life was like in the big US of A. She had read so many books about America but had never been there.

"One visit and I am never coming back!" she declared dreamily to no one in particular.

Ola wanted to know what other countries Amanda had lived in, after all the rumour mill was awash with stories of how successful her father was and surely working for a big company like that, they must have travelled around a bit?

"Have you been to Hollywood, then?" asked someone else, just as Amanda was about to respond.

Amanda turned and met Siyonna's gaze with a plaintive look that said 'help'.

"Ok, ladies. We are meant to be studying," she said. "Leave Amanda be for now, will you?"

"Leave Amanda be-e-e?" Sally said, mocking Siyonna. "Who died and made you class prefect then?" She challenged, thrusting her chest out at Siyonna as she spoke.

Siyonna really did not want a confrontation with Sally, who for as long as she could remember, had been spoiling for some sort of fight with her. Siyonna would have walked away quite happily and left Amanda to her fate just to avoid the Sally-fight.

"You're right," piped up another voice. "She's not the class Prefect, I am. And guess what? I agree with Siyonna, leave the girl be. This is a prep period and we should all go back to studying. The time for catching up is at lunch and we still have two study periods before then. Please go back to your seats."

The instructions were loud and clear and all the girls returned to their seats. The voice belonged to Yvette Odogwu. Yvette was small for her age, the smallest girl in the class in fact. However, what she lacked in size, she more than made up for in intelligence. Extremely bright and always top of her class, Yvette also showed consistent courage by being outspoken and one of Mother Joseph's favourite pupils. When Our Lady's had beaten St Augustine Victoria Island to clinch the coveted Lagos State inter-school Quiz challenge, earlier in the year, it was Yvette who had answered the winning question in Mathematics. It had come as no surprise that she had been appointed Class Prefect by the Headmistress and Year Captain as well. If Yvette had any powers with her office, she rarely used them. However, on the few occasions she invoked her authority, everyone listened and at that moment, Siyonna was super grateful to Yvette for taking a stand.

The rest of the day passed very quickly and after school, Siyonna and her friends went out to the square where the boarders hugged the daygirls and said goodbye. Siyonna's family chauffeur, Mr Sunday, was already waiting and as Siyonna made for the car, Amanda called out to her and waved. She waved back and headed home.

First weeks back from vacation were always a challenge for the girls as they tried to fit into their routines once again. By Wednesday Siyonna was already dreaming of Saturday.

Saturday presented an opportunity to sleep longer and also catch up on the backlog of work, which all the girls complained was now beginning to mount up. As Bunmi, Siyonna, Amina, Amaka and Dupe sat together comparing notes on work they had to do, Amanda appeared.

"Hi Siyonna, mind if I join you guys?" she said.

Siyonna looked up at her in surprise. After Monday's little drama, Amanda had practically spent all of Tuesday hanging out with Sally and her 'happening' group of friends or, as Siyonna usually described them, 'The Flaky Sisters'.

The group built around Sally included Tinu, Sherry and a few other girls who wanted so desperately to 'belong'. With the pressure to look good and keep up with the latest fashion trends, Sally drove her girls hard. As they strode together and wore permanent sneers, they were revered and ignored in equal measure, with the school split between those who would love an invitation to join the group and those who saw the group as pointless and an abysmal waste of time. When Amanda started hanging out with *that* group, she was immediately written off as a snob.

So, as Amanda stood there in front of Siyonna and her regular friends and asked to sit with them, there was a faint gasp in the canteen as the rest of the girls wondered if this meant Amanda was now 'normal'.

"Yes, sure it's ok," said Siyonna.

Amanda smiled and sat down.

As the atmosphere settled and girls at every table analysed this swift change in social dynamics, Amanda asked what Siyonna and her friends were talking about before she joined them.

"First things first," said Siyonna. "Let me introduce you to everyone."

Siyonna went around her table and introduced Amanda to Amina, Amaka, Dupe and Bunmi who were all in different classes. Amanda smiled and said hello to each.

"We were just talking about the school Charity Day," said Dupe. "And what we could do this year. We all feel that it is so important to raise funds for the less fortunate and make a difference. Besides, it'll also be good to win the thing just once before we leave the school!"

"I agree," said Amanda. "In my last school, we did quite a bit to raise money for charity. We had bake-offs and sponsored events to raise funds for things, like cancer awareness and children's charities. I have some ideas and would be happy to share and help if you like?"

"Of course, we'd like you to help!" chimed the girls in unison. "We've never won the Charity Trophy and we're grateful for all the help we can get!"

"Good. It's settled then. Say, why don't you guys come to mine on Saturday afternoon for a planning party?" said Amanda.

"Planning party?" asked Siyonna.

"What's a planning party?" asked Dupe.

"Oh, just a normal eat, dance and 'look for inspiration for our event' kind of evening. It'll be fun, just us girls getting to know each other and working through ideas for our event. What do you think? It'll be fun, I promise," she declared in her American twang.

The girls all agreed at once, looking at each other and smiling. It was slightly trickier for Amina and Bunmi because they were boarding students. However, they decided to request extended day passes, so the school would let them out to spend the day with Amanda, provided Amanda's parents confirmed they'd be picked up and back at school on Saturday before 9 p.m. Amanda agreed to speak to her parents and make the arrangements. The girls all whooped with excitement as the conversation moved swiftly to Saturday and what the day was going to be like.

"I really like you guys," said Amanda, smiling. "Things are so much more relaxed with you."

They looked at each other and Siyonna covered her open mouth in mock horror as they all roared with laughter. As the teachers turned to glare at them, the girls all put their heads down, giggling uncontrollably as they finished their lunch.

If the conversion of Amanda Saul-Obi from a member of the Sally Bunch to normal was expected to go without a hitch, then Sally certainly missed the memo, because for the rest of the week she was never short of a catty comment for both Amanda and Siyonna. Most lunches were spent recounting the misdeeds of Sally and laughing at her jealousy-driven antics. A particularly distasteful incident happened on the Thursday when Tinu, possibly to remain in Sally's good graces, yelled at Amanda in the canteen for what was a very minor incident.

As the girls picked up their trays and walked down the line of serving ladies to receive the different dishes, they all had to make a sharp left turn to reach the bank of refrigerated water filters, to get drinks. The school always encouraged the girls to get their drinks and take a circular route back to their tables, rather than turn right round and risk walking into somebody coming in the opposite direction.

On this occasion, Tinu had her water on her tray and as Amanda made the turn, they almost collided, causing Tinu's water to spill on her tray but fortunately not on her food. As Amanda did the "oops so sorry" for presumably causing an accident, Tinu exploded in unfounded rage and yelled so loudly that Mother Joseph got up from her seat and invited both girls to her office.

Tinu was subsequently reprimanded for behaviour unbecoming of a lady and a pupil of our Lady's and all her privileges were withdrawn for the weekend. Now, for a boarder that was as serious as it got. It meant she couldn't be involved in all the leisure activities like movie night, club meetings and all the other activities the girls did on the weekend and of course, she also could not leave the school premises.

As for Amanda, Mother Joseph actually apologized to her for Tinu's behaviour and assured her that this sort of thing was not typical of girls from the school. Sally, however, was not done. Friday at the canteen saw a subdued Tinu and Sally spend the entire afternoon scowling at Siyonna and her friends. Amanda did her best to stop herself from looking in their direction and seemed pretty subdued herself.

"Are you ok?" Bunmi kept asking her.

"Yes, kind of. I just feel really bad at being the cause of Tinu's troubles. I don't even know the girl and you know she seems to have it in for me. Now this! It's all wrong," said Amanda.

For a minute Siyonna thought she was going to burst into tears. However, before anybody could say anything, Amanda got up and said she needed to go to the bathroom.

"Guys, shouldn't one of us go with her?" said Amina as she left.

At that point Siyonna noticed something.

"Guys," she said. "Look over at Sally's table."

The friends all looked and saw exactly what Siyonna saw: the table was empty except for Tinu. Without a word, the friends jumped up and headed to the restroom.

Our Lady's restroom was always impeccably presented. Some girls would even joke that it was almost as inviting as the restrooms in the Lagos Sheraton! Siyonna always felt that the analogy was a bit of a stretch but did admit that for school restrooms, our Lady's was up there with the best. As they ran into the passage, they found it eerily quiet. They pushed into the restroom to find Sally's friends holding a petrified Amanda, just as Sally raised a hand to slap her. Siyonna immediately grabbed Sally's hand and as Sally whirled round at her with her free hand, Siyonna jerked her hand up, bent her knees and slammed Sally hard on the toilet floor.

Sally sat up, stunned. Siyonna had never so much as spoken back to her in the two years they had been in the same class, never mind raise a hand at her. She had always dreamt that one day she would corner Siyonna in a deserted area of the school and give her a thorough thrashing. To find that the demure Siyonna was not a pushover was such a shock that Sally just sat there on the floor. Siyonna turned to the other girls holding Amanda who were also so mesmerized, they stayed rooted to the spot.

"Let Amanda go, now," said Siyonna, with a quiet vehemence.

The girls released Amanda and made for the door, at exactly the same moment as Ms Ojo walked into the restroom.

"Everything all alright in here?" she asked.

"Yes Miss," replied the girls in unison.

"In that case please return to the canteen and finish your lunch. You're all due back in class in 15 minutes and Sally, do get yourself off the floor and for the sake of everything that's dear, close your legs young lady, thank you!"

The girls looked at her and giggled nervously.

As they left the restroom, Amanda took Siyonna's hands.

"Thank you, Siyonna. For a moment there I thought I was a goner! God knows what would have happened to me had you not shown up."

Siyonna smiled and put an arm over Amanda's shoulder.

"Come on, Rambo, let's go feed those muscles!" said Bunmi, placing Siyonna's other arm across her own shoulders.

The friends all laughed as they went back to the canteen.

6

Ladies' Night

Preparations for the evening at Amanda's house got underway and all the girls were excited by their invitation. Siyonna's dad had mumbled a non-committal yes when Siyonna asked if she could go. When she asked how she'd get there, he raised his eyes from his newspaper and was about to deliver a sarcastic one-liner about the need to be independent, then thought better of it.

"You'd better go ask your mum if Bayo can take you."

Bayo was her mum's chauffeur and they had an understanding that as the junior driver, he could be called upon to run those errands considered to be beneath Mr Sunday, who had been with Siyonna's dad for longer than Siyonna had been alive. She thanked her dad, hugged him and rushed off to ask her mum to book Bayo for her, for Saturday evening.

Saturday arrived at last! Siyonna woke up early and set about doing her chores to make sure she did not give her mother any excuse to change her mind at the very last minute. These things can happen. Siyonna thought to herself as she wrestled with the injustice of being up and dressed and vacuuming at 8 o'clock on a Saturday morning. But her early start paid off because she was done by 10. She ate a bowl of cereal and went back to her room to study until early afternoon when excitement got the better of her and she threw open her wardrobe doors to assess the clothes' situation. She groaned in disappointment at her collection of jeans, tee shirts and more jeans. Her mum had always told her she dressed like a tomboy and she'd always waved her off.

Tonight, they were having an early dinner with Amanda's parents before the planning party. When she spoke to her friends, she got the feeling they were all going to make a bit of an effort beyond the usual tee shirt and jeans look. Siyonna looked at her clothes in despair then flew out of her room calling for her mother. Oh, how she missed Ebele. Had she been around, this was one of those days Siyonna would have run to her for help and advice but with no Ebele, mum would have to do.

Obiageli was in the smaller living room downstairs and on the phone to her sister Ify when Siyonna came flying in. Zach had gone off to Ikoyi club for his mandatory Saturday golf session, while she made her calls and checked in on what Siyonna called 'Oby's empire', the myriad of little businesses and medium-sized shops she had set up all over Lagos Island. These ranged from the fabrics' shop in the market to the medium-sized supermarkets she ran on the Island. In the midst of all that, Obiageli still managed to run a home. This meant that she really wasn't one to waste her time on frivolities. From the moment she woke up till she crawled back exhausted into bed at night, Obiageli was busy, tending to her various interests. So, as she sat on the phone and discussed different options for catching the 'rat' responsible for pilfering endless cans of coke from Bene's, her latest supermarket in Lekki, she was in no mood to be interrupted. As Siyonna bounded into the room, Obiageli's face fell, knowing her few minutes of catching up with Ify were just about to end.

"Siyonna what do you want?" said Obiageli at the same time as Ify asked who was interrupting their conversation.

"Is it not Siyonna, my second husband, barging into my conversation as if she paid dowry on my head?" she replied as Ify burst out laughing.

"Well, as her father is out, perhaps she is playing husband in his stead!" said Ify, teasing her sister.

Obiageli sighed audibly and turned to Siyonna again.

"Madam, I said what do you want oh?"

Siyonna was used to her mother's quick temper and testy tongue, so she simply ignored the irritation.

"Mum, I need help. I really cannot find anything to wear to Amanda's party."

"Ify, you see my life now?" said Obiageli into her mobile phone. "See big woman like Siyonna cannot find clothes to wear without bothering me. When will this end? Will I mother this child until she has her own children? Or maybe mother her and mother her children too? Siyonna, why don't you come and suckle since you won't grow up?" Obiageli said, half to Siyonna and half to Ify on the phone, at the same time shoving her bosom towards Siyonna.

"Mummy please come help me. Auntie Ify will understand if you call her later."

Obiageli looked at her, shaking her head.

"Ify, sorry oh, please let me go attend to my permanent baby. I will call you later. She has confiscated my car and driver as well so I'm stuck here until her father gets back from golf. I will call you later."

Ify agreed that Siyonna's emergency needed addressing and arranged to speak with her older sister later that evening.

"Show me what you have?" said Obiageli.

"No mum," Siyonna started. "I only have jeans and tops, no real dresses. Is there anything in your wardrobe I can borrow?"

Obiageli studied her daughter and apart from the fact that she was now curvier and slightly heavier than Siyonna, they looked exactly alike. Same build, same long legs and slender neck. She had just the thing for her daughter, a lovely simple blue dress she had made a year or so ago, complete with a blue scarf. She had never worn this dress because she felt she had put on weight and as she waited to find the will and energy to tackle her slightly-expanding waistline, the hopes of shimmying into it grew further away with each passing day.

"Come with me," said Obiageli.

Siyonna went with her mum to the huge master bedroom she shared with her dad. Siyonna immediately plonked herself on the bed and marvelled again at the size of the room. She always felt her parents' bedroom was large enough to qualify as a flat. They had a mini-sitting room and a walk-in wardrobe her dad jokingly referred to as 'Oby's grotto' because her mum had practically taken over the entire space. Obiageli came out of the wardrobe with the silky blue gown and asked Siyonna to try it on. Siyonna changed into it and twirled around in front of her mum. It was a perfect fit, accentuating her young body beautifully. The lace and silk mix shimmered slightly and the long neck set off Siyonna's own slender neck even more. Obiageli smiled. Gosh, she looks like I used to look, she thought to herself. Still smiling at her youngest daughter, she asked her to get the blue shoes she had bought to go with the dress and the accompanying clutch bag. Siyonna hugged her mum, thanked her and ran off to her room to get dressed.

It took her just fifteen minutes to change and be ready for the evening. By the time she came downstairs, her mum was back on the phone with her sister and gushed with delight at how pretty she looked. She broke off her conversation long enough to take a picture and send it to her sister. Siyonna knew the gushing would take a while, so between the 'you-look-lovely' and 'be-a-good-girl', she beat a path to the door and ran out to the waiting car.

Amanda's house was in one of the newer developments in Ikoyi. It wasn't too far from Siyonna's, but the Lagos traffic certainly meant it took far longer than the 20 minutes anticipated. When they arrived at the estate, Siyonna had to give the guard her name and the home she was visiting. The guard confirmed it was all right for her to be let through, then gave the driver directions to the house.

From the gate, it took another 10 minutes to get to Amanda's. The house stood in a cul-de-sac, hidden from view by the tall gates and shrubbery which covered the wall. The driver buzzed and the gates opened into a huge compound with several cars parked. Bayo stopped the car and assured Siyonna he would wait for her. Siyonna promised to be out before 8 p.m. and made her way to the door. Just as she got to there, Amanda flung it open and gave her a hug then stepped back.

"Wow," she said. "You look fab, Siyonna," just as Amaka and Dupe appeared and joined in the hug. "Come on, let me introduce you to my parents."

Amanda dragged Siyonna through the beautiful waiting area into an exquisitely furnished sitting room, then out to the deck at the back overlooking a private swimming pool, where her parents were sitting.

"Mum, dad, this is my friend Siyonna Nduka I told you about."

Her parents smiled and her dad reached out a hand to shake Siyonna's.

"Nduka, did you say? I had a friend from secondary school called Zach Akachukwu Nduka. We called him AK. Brilliant athlete! I lost touch with him when we left secondary school. The last I heard he had gone to the UK to study Engineering just about the time I left for the States. It's not the same Nduka, is it?"

"Yes, sir," gasped Siyonna. "My dad is Zach Nduka."

Mr Saul-Obi beamed and nodded his head, waving his hand expansively.

"What a surprise! Small world we live in, don't you think?" he said, looking at his wife who nodded, smiling at Siyonna. "Welcome to our home. You girls go have fun and let us know if you need anything. And give my very best to your dad. Tell him I'd like to reconnect with him now we're back here?"

Siyonna promised to deliver the message and clutched the card he had just handed her. The girls giggled and Amanda hugged Siyonna even closer.

"Our dads were secondary school buddies! Oh boy, this was meant to be!" she giggled excitedly as the other girls arrived.

There were frenzied hugs and kisses and Amanda led everyone outside to a small annexe, built in the style of a boathouse, except the space downstairs had been turned into a well-appointed living room. Dinner had been set for the girls there and Amanda hit the stereo to get the mood going. The girls ate and danced and before long, they were all having a good time.

At about 7 o'clock, Amanda's older brother Dante walked in. Amanda introduced him to the girls who all instantly fell in love with him. Dante was on vacation from university in Washington where he was majoring in Electronics and Computer Science. He had spent last summer working for a charity in East Africa, drilling boreholes, so Amanda had drafted him to help the girls find a charity and event to support.

Dante was tall and smiled a lot. Like Amanda, he spoke with a distinct American accent and when Siyonna asked him where his name came from, he smiled and explained how he was named after his maternal grandfather, Dante Rostein. He had been a Doctor and had travelled the world working with charities and solving problems in the places no one would go to. He had lost an arm in an explosion in Afghanistan but that hadn't stopped him. As soon as he was healed, he had been on the next plane out to Yemen to help. He had now retired.

Siyonna could tell Dante idolized his grandfather. There was so much affection in his voice as he spoke about him.

"Do you still see him often?" asked Dupe.

"Oh yeah, at least 3 or 4 times a year when I'm in the states. He lives on a ranch in California and I thoroughly enjoy spending time there."

Dante steered the conversation back to the charities the girls were looking at and asked them to discuss different ideas they were interested in. He said that by open discussion they would find something they all agreed on. As they went through different charities and discussed what they all needed, they became increasingly overwhelmed by the sheer number of options out there. It was becoming harder to settle on one.

"How about raising money to get things for a motherless babies' home?" said Dupe. "Orphanages always welcome help."

The girls sat in stunned silence for a moment then almost simultaneously jumped up and hugged Dupe.

"Fantastic," smiled Dante. "I like it. It is simple and straightforward and you guys can do this. So, what is the first thing you should be thinking of?" he asked, in his casual manner, with that smile playing on his incredibly handsome face.

Siyonna was finding it hard to concentrate with him in the room and tried her best to keep a straight face. She had heard of crushes and read about infatuations but just could not understand why she felt like she needed to sit down every time he looked at her. As if reading her thoughts, he turned and looked right at her with those intense off-blue eyes of his.

"Well, Siyonna, what do you think? Where should you guys start?"

Siyonna glanced at him and then stared at the floor.

"Well, erm, I guess we should get in touch with the home and tell them what we're doing and ask if they are happy for us to raise funds on their behalf. We should also ask what they would like us to get for them."

She raised her head tentatively to find a big admiring smile for her from Dante.

"Good! You guys have got this. I think my job here is done. Go for it!"

He stood up and the girls all followed him across the room with their eyes as he walked towards the door, turned and said goodbye to the group, holding Siyonna's gaze a little longer than the others, smiled and was gone.

After Dante left, the girls were quiet for a while soaking it all in. Amanda sat back and watched her friends, amused. Dante had always been a big draw, even back in the States. He had always been so handsome and pursued tirelessly by girls wherever he went. His incredible eyes didn't help. Her mother had four other siblings and they all had children. But between them and their cousins, only Dante had inherited their grandfather's incredible faded blue with a tinge of green eyes.

"Ladies," she said, turning to her friends. "We need to get a move-on or we'll never finish this."

"I agree," said Amaka.

They decided Siyonna should write to the home they had identified, introducing the girls, asking if it was all right to raise funds for them and what they'd like the group to buy with the funds raised. They also decided they'd make cookies and bake cakes on the school charity day and offer these to parents and visitors on the day. They agreed to use Amanda's kitchen for the baking. The Boathouse had a kitchen and working from here, they'd be in nobody's way. As the charity day was only a month away, the girls agreed to start work as early as Monday with sourcing ingredients, writing letters and finding a stand for the charity day.

Amanda clasped her hands together and praised how much they had achieved. Amaka got up and paired her phone with the stereo. She picked a d'banj song to play and very soon, the girls were dancing and prancing around the living room in absolute delight.

They were still dancing when Cook arrived with a cart set with their dinner. The girls thanked him and settled down to a meal of wild rice and curried goat, with a lovely cherry cake dessert. By the time they had downed their third or fourth malt drink each, they felt completely stuffed and Amaka, the designated DJ for the night, turned up the volume on Tekno's 'Pana' as the girls all jumped up and started dancing and singing along to the catchy lyrics.

Amina loved to dance and the reserve she always displayed in school, completely disappeared as she lost herself in the spirit of the song, gyrating and winding her body to the tune. As she swayed rhythmically, expertly mimicking popular Afrobeat dance moves, her friends cheered and the girls got louder. Amanda who was not that familiar with Nigerian music and dance moves, looked completely intrigued by what she was seeing. Before long, she found herself at the centre of the small circle the girls had formed, dancing, twisting, and doing her very best not to be outdone by her friends. She was rewarded by their joyous whoops at her more inventive moves. They all agreed that what Amanda lacked in African dance skills, she more than made up for with enthusiasm.

The evening was an absolute success and as the music blared on, Amanda's dad popped his head round to say it was time for Bunmi and Amina to be taken back to school, in line with the terms of their pass. Dupe and Siyonna also thought they should head off as well so it wouldn't be too dark when they got back. It had been an unforgettable evening. The girls all trooped out, thanked Amanda's parents for having them, hugged Amanda and said their goodbyes.

As Siyonna walked over to where Bayo was parked, Amanda joined her and linked hands.

"Watch out, you have an admirer," she whispered.

"Who?" she asked, slightly confused.

Amanda whirled her round and pointed upstairs to Dante's bedroom where there was the faintest of movements behind the curtains. Siyonna looked at her friend and smiled coyly.

"Good night Amanda, and thank you so much for having us. I had an absolutely unforgettable time," she said, as Amanda hugged her one last time.

Then she stood back as Siyonna got into the car and watched as she was driven away and stayed watching and waving until the gate finally shut behind the car.

7

One Good Deed

Charity Day was fast approaching and the school buzzed as the girls all worked on their various projects for the day. Charity Day at Our Lady's had always been seen as a big event when the school held a carnival of sorts to raise money for local charities and give something back to society. However, it also had a serious side because the girls were meant to learn an important lesson in life- skills as part of the Charity day process. The girls had to do something on this day, to raise money for the charity of their choice, giving back to society in their own little way. The school encouraged them to be inventive in what they did but also put a cap on how much they could spend on the event. Since the whole essence of charity day was to encourage the girls to be socially conscious and hardworking at the same time, parents were not allowed to take over the show and do the work instead of their daughters, nor were parents allowed to make large donations to their daughters' charities. The girls had to do as much of this on their own as possible.

At the end of each Charity Day, the School's Chairman of the Board of Governors, Mr Titus Yakubu, would attend assembly at Our Lady's and announce the winning team. Siyonna had worked hard at Charity Day every year she had been a student at Our Lady's, largely because her father had encouraged her to believe in giving back and doing something for those less fortunate in society. She had never been part of a winning team and again her father had told her winning was not important. It was not a race or competition and what mattered was she had done something to change somebody's life. So, every year, Siyonna would pour her heart and soul into different Charity Day projects, working hard to make a difference to someone's life through her efforts. This Charity Day was no different. The girls had planned the menu for their cake and patisserie stand and wanted to make sure they provided a variety of small cakes and cookies to keep people coming back to their stand. Dupe and Siyonna were very good cooks and also baked regularly, so they were put in charge of baking for the event, with Amaka helping. Amanda, Amina and Bunmi would help with buying the ingredients, decorating the stands and leading on sales for the day. The girls all contributed money for the ingredients and agreed to start baking on Friday after school, so the cakes would be fresh for Charity Day on Saturday.

The week breezed past and on the Thursday the girls all sat down for lunch and went over their plans for Friday and Saturday. It turned out that Amanda was quite good at organising things so the girls all agreed she would be the Project Manager for their enterprise. As they finished lunch, she produced a neatly typed up list of tasks, showing what stage each of them had reached with what they had to do.

"Amina," said Amanda. "Have you applied for your pass for Saturday?"

Amina put her hand over her mouth in wide-eyed horror. She had forgotten to apply for her pass!

"I'll do it now," she gasped and ran out in search of her dormitory Matron.

The other girls shook their heads and whispered 'Amina!' in collective acknowledgement of her usual forgetfulness. Siyonna smiled and remembered the first time she had become friends with Amina. They had met at a PE session in Form 1 when Amina had forgotten her PE shorts. As she searched frantically for them, the PE Teacher Mr Duncan had glared at her in consternation. Siyonna had quickly whipped out the spare shorts her mother always insisted she kept in her bag, saying 'here, these are your shorts. You lent them to me for basketball last week, remember? Thank you and I am sorry I forgot to give them back.' Amina had taken the shorts from her, mouthed thank you and turned back to Mr Duncan who, satisfied that the girl had her shorts, had moved on to seek another hapless victim.

At the end of the lesson, Amina had walked up to Siyonna, thanked her and promised to wash the shorts and return them to Siyonna before the next lesson.

"That was a very kind thing you did for me there. You are a really nice person. Thank you so much. My name is Amina Bakari," she said, shyly thrusting her hand out to Siyonna to shake.

"Pleased to meet you," said Siyonna, taking her hand. "I am Siyonna Nduka. Do you like basketball?"

"Not really," replied Amina. "But I'm willing to give it a shot if you'll teach me?"

"Come on then," said Siyonna, laughing. "No time like the present."

And so began a wonderful friendship, which got even stronger when Siyonna found out that Amina's dad, Dr Bakari, was her father's very close friend from his youth. They had remained friends only finally losing touch as life had taken them down different paths. On their next visit to Lagos, the Bakaris had joined Siyonna's family for dinner, reconnecting after all those years and the girls eventually started spending time in each other's homes on vacations. Abuja was in the centre of the country, due north and visiting the Bakaris was the only time Siyonna ever went there.

Amina and Siyonna were roughly the same build and over the years, after Siyonna had introduced Amina to her love of Basketball, Amina had become so good that both girls made it into the school's senior basketball team. Just like Siyonna, Amina was brilliant, with a keen mind. However, outside of academia, she was so absent-minded that everyone always wondered how a girl could be so bright on the one hand and so forgetful on the other. All her friends were used to her and loved her the same. On many occasions, Amina had run off with her hand on her head as she remembered either an uncompleted task or an item of clothing forgotten on the laundry line.

This time, as Amina rushed off to negotiate her time off, the other girls continued with their planning for the day. Amanda went to great pains to state that all the tasks were important and when she offered to help with the decoration, Siyonna and the others refused, insisting she concentrated on her role as project manager which was crucial to their winning. Just as they were wrapping up the meeting, a jubilant Amina showed up waving her green leave slip.

The excitement around the school grew as the girls prepared for Charity Day. From Monday the groundsman and other contractors had started work tidying the garden, which to the untrained eye, barely needed it. The groups involved with selling goods were allotted stalls, given on a first-apply, first-serve basis. Siyonna's team had taken 'Busy Hands' as their group name and Amanda, following Siyonna's advice, put in an application for a stall promptly. By Wednesday when the school announced stalls, she was happy to tell her teammates they had been allotted a stall in the front row facing the guests' gazebo. This was one of the most highly-prized spots because the guests would invariably go past it as they made their way to the other stalls. The girls hugged each other and danced with joy at this brilliant news, then huddled up again and went over the list of things they needed to have ready before baking started on Friday. The mothers had all agreed to provide the ingredients and arrange for them to be dropped off at Amanda's by Thursday evening.

The other thing the girls needed to sort out was the stall decoration. Initially, they had thought about colouring it like the Nigerian flag, green, white and green but abandoned the idea when Amaka informed them that the Hibiscus team, led by Siyonna's friend Lola Abiodun in 6B, were theming their tent with the Nigerian colours. The girls decided to do a raffia theme on their stall, combining a raffia roof and sides with soft lace buntings, reflecting pre-colonial local architecture interspersed with the softer touches of white lace. As Amaka drew the designs, the girls updated the list of what they needed. Siyonna's mother had raffia chairs they could put in corners of their stall and Siyonna also knew that the market in Yaba had stalls that sold raffia fronds and other things. She would speak with her mum and see if she would agree to help her pick up a few things.

Friday came and was a blur! After school on Thursday, Amina had come home with Siyonna and the two girls spent the rest of Thursday reviewing what Siyonna's mum had bought and helping get them over to Amanda's. The raffia pieces were fronds for the roof and two-free standing walls and Siyonna's mum had arranged to have them delivered to the school and set up on the stall on the Friday when Amanda and the other girls who would be decorating the stall would be at school. Amaka had produced several designs of what their stall would look like when it was finished. She hoped to study Architecture one day and was a very talented artist. She would work with Amanda and Amina to have the stall ready and decorated on Friday whilst Siyonna and the rest of the team baked.

Siyonna was in the middle of the most pleasant dream about dancing ice cream cones when Amina shook her awake.

"Wake up Sisi Onna!" Amina said, using her special pet name for Siyonna. "It's 7.30 and your alarm's been buzzing since 7. We need to get going."

Siyonna jumped up, smiled a good morning at her friend and headed to the bathroom to get ready. Then the girls wolfed down breakfast as Siyonna's mother hurried them along. Mr Sunday, Mr Nduka's driver, would drop them off at Amanda's and then come back for him. The girls piled into the car and headed for Ikoyi.

Amanda's annexe looked like a scene from Master Chef with ingredients and utensils stacked neatly in the kitchen, next to aprons and chef's hats. Siyonna quickly went over and inspected everything. Satisfied that all the things they needed were there, she brought out 4 printed copies of the recipes for the cakes the girls had agreed to make and started mixing her first batter. The girls had decided to make half a dozen chocolate cakes, sponge cakes, strawberry cakes and a significant number of cupcakes.

As she put together the mixes for the different cakes and carefully labelled them, her friends Dupe and Bunmi came in and gasped at how much work she had already done in the hour or so she had been there. Dupe saw an opened bottle of brandy and turned to Siyonna in mock amazement.

"Girl, you drinking at 16?!"

Siyonna laughed.

"It's for the brandy chocolate cakes, silly," said Bunmi, playfully pretending to smack the back of Dupe's head. "It makes the chocolate cake rich."

"Won't people get drunk on it?" asked Dupe, looking bewildered.

"No hon," said Bunmi. "The amount is so little you'd never know it had been added, trust me. Besides, we are also making plain chocolate cakes with no brandy. The plan is to sell the brandy-infused cake to the adults and charge more for them," continued Bunmi, in the most maternal voice she could muster.

If Dupe noticed the sarcasm she certainly did not let on as she proceeded to tie her apron and dive into helping clear and wash up the utensils that were now beginning to pile up by the sink.

The annexe had two ovens, each holding two cakes. Siyonna asked Dupe to prepare the frosting, so she could decorate the cakes when they were ready. They also knew that they simply had too many cakes to bake and the ovens at the boathouse would certainly not be enough to accommodate all the cakes in the time they had. As if on cue, Amanda's mum popped in to see how they were getting on.

"Hello ladies!" she called from the door of the boathouse.

"Hello auntie!" they chorused.

Mrs Annette Saul-Obi was very beautiful and elegant. Siyonna thought her skin looked almost translucent, bronzed and unblemished. She wasn't very tall but Siyonna did not think she appeared short either. This morning she had on a pair of white baggy trousers, a sleeveless patterned red shirt and red pumps, looking simply radiant.

"How are you all getting on?" she said, looking around the kitchen and giving the girls a comforting smile.

Siyonna explained that they were doing ok but could use another oven as they were running out of space in the boathouse. Suddenly, Mrs Saul-Obi started laughing. She threw her head back and laughed until she was bent over. This reaction confused Siyonna. What was so funny about asking for more oven space? She tried to recall her mother's advice about the ways of Americans but nothing came to mind. As she turned to look at Bunmi and Dupe, she saw they were also trying hard to stifle their own laughter. She turned again to Amanda's mum.

"Come, my dear," she said, taking Siyonna's hand. "Let me show you why we're all laughing."

She took her into the bedroom and stood her in front of a full-length mirror, with the other girls close behind. Siyonna gasped in horror. It was like looking at a ghost. Her face and neck were white with flour dust. With the opening and mixing of flour bags, the flour had somehow landed all over her.

"Don't worry, you look like a real baker now!" said Amanda's mum, smiling and hugging her.

Her friends, of course, laughed and took pictures of her on their phones, while Annette took a wet towel and cleaned

Siyonna's face and neck, still chuckling. When she was done, she wheeled Siyonna around to face the mirror.

"There, you look your pretty self again!"

Siyonna smiled, thanked her and gave her a hug.

"Now about the oven, I will ask Cook to let you use the big oven in the kitchen as well. I'm off to see how Amanda's doing at school and will see you girls in a bit.

"Thank you, Auntie!" the girls sang out as she left.

When cook came to the boathouse to see what the girls needed, they showed him the mixes to go in the oven. The main house had two large ovens so they were able to get a few more cakes in, to start baking at the same time as bringing out the chocolate cakes from the ovens in the boathouse.

By late afternoon they were done, cakes all baked, with Bunmi and Dupe putting the finishing touches to the icing and decoration. Siyonna felt exhausted and lay herself down, flat out on the living area floor. Amanda and the others had also come back with pictures of the decorated stall which looked exactly like the drawings Amaka had made.

"This is beautiful!" gushed Dupe.

"Amaka, you really have an impressive gift here, you know," said Siyonna.

"Very impressive," said Dupe. "Unlike some peeps over here who can't even draw a straight line!" she added as an obvious taunt at Siyonna's non-existent drawing skills.

"What-e-ver," drawled Siyonna and all the girls laughed.

Amanda's mum called out that the girls' rides had arrived. They all arranged for Amanda and Siyonna to bring the cakes to the stall tomorrow, in time for the event, starting at midday and all the other girls would be in school to help.

Saturday was a buzz of activity as Siyonna and Amina got ready for school, dressed in their pristine skirt-suit uniforms and knee-length socks. The girls looked very smart indeed. Obiageli had already arranged for a van to pick up the cakes and drive to school to arrive at the same time as the girls.

As the girls were all saying their goodbyes, Mr Nduka came downstairs.

"Ah Onna-mma, were you going to leave without a goodbye for your father?"

"Of course not, Daddy! You know I never would!" she laughed as she walked into her father's embrace. "Promise me you'll make our event, dad?"

"You try stopping me!" said Mr Nduka, looking at her in feigned shock.

Our Lady's had turned into a hive of activity as all the girls worked hard to set up their stalls and be ready by the time the guests arrived. There was also the added challenge of making sure their uniforms stayed spotless even as they worked. One thing certain to set Mother Joseph off was a girl in an untidy or soiled uniform. Two years before, a girl had had the brazen effrontery of showing up to Charity Day with a massive soup stain on her shirt. She'd hoped her blazer would hide it and it succeeded for a while until in her excitement she forgot herself and raised her hands to beckon to a friend with her blazer undone. Mother Joseph had ordered her back to the dormitory to change immediately and she served a stiff detention the following Monday, with loss of privileges for a whole week as a result.

By noon, the girls stood to attention ready to compete. Once the sale started, it soon became obvious that theirs was the stall to beat. The chocolate cakes flew off the table. One of the mothers snatched up the brandy-infused cake and the last large chocolate one caused a bidding frenzy as two ladies went for it. In the end, the successful bidder happily confessed it was her son's birthday the next day and it would make a perfect birthday cake. Siyonna's parents showed up and to everyone's surprise, accompanied by Amina's parents who had flown in specially to support Amina at the sale. The reunion of Mr Saul-Obi and Mr Nduka gave rise to a wonderful scene, of much shouting, hugging and backslapping between the two men as they tried to fill in the gaps on what had happened to them throughout so many intervening years. They both introduced their wives and all went off talking, happily.

When Amanda realised they still had quite a few cupcakes left, she cut up a couple and put them on plates as taster samples. By early afternoon, the girls had sold everything. Pupils and younger guests, who couldn't afford to spend much, ended up grabbing most of the cupcakes, as word spread and more customers rushed in to buy them. Having finished in record time, the girls packed up their stall and went to explore the rest of the fair, visiting other stalls and eating ice cream. They had enjoyed such a successful day and knew they had done more than enough to raise funds for their chosen charity.

Charity Day always ended with counting the takings, announcing how much each team had made for their charity and the presentation of a small trophy to the winning team. This year had seen a good number of interesting events and stalls. Siyonna had especially liked the stall the fine art students had put together, selling their paintings and quick pencil portraits but she silently prayed her team would win. The bidding war for the large chocolate cake had pushed their earnings just slightly over those of the artists and Mother Joseph declared it a close-run thing.

As the girls gathered to hear the results, you could feel the tension in the air. Lola, a good friend of Siyonna's and head of the artists' group, snuck up next to her and linked hands.

"Good luck, Sisi Onna," she said. "You know I'm rooting for you."

Siyonna smiled at her friend and just as she opened her mouth to respond, the Chairman cleared his throat, adjusted his *Agbada* and embarked on a long-winded speech about the importance of giving. He was a retired Barrister and gossip had it that in his entire career in corporate law, he never got the chance to argue a case in court. People said he was making up for a lifetime of legal liabilities, contracts and so forth, with monologues and soliloquies interspersed with old English quotations, completely lost on his audience.

The yawning and perplexed looks never deterred him. He continued gamely for half an hour, a record even for him. Finally, he congratulated all the girls for a job well done. He announced the Bronze prize, which went to the girls who had made exotic crafts and earthenware, adorned in bright Nigerian colours. Then he announced the Silver, which went to Lola and her team. Lola smiled and hugged Siyonna as she went to join her team for the prize giving.

When the Chairman announced that the first prize and Gold Cup had gone to Siyonna's team for the impeccable cakes they'd baked, Siyonna nearly fainted with delight. He thanked them for their hard work and invited the girls to talk about their charity. Amanda, the nominated leader of the team, gave a brief description of their charity and why they had chosen to support it. She spoke of how the entire team had been touched by the challenges confronting the orphans and how the children still smiled in the face of an uncertain future. She hoped that the money raised would be useful and make a real difference to the home. When she finished, everyone stood up and applauded. She felt so proud because she had never given a speech in front of a crowd before. The girls accepted their cup and the cheque from the Chairman and left excitedly to compare notes with their friends.

The rest of Saturday went into carnival mode. Everybody enjoyed the huge amounts of food and drink on offer and danced to the music provided by the band. Once again, Amanda did her best to come to grips with Nigerian dance and presented an amusing sight to her friends who said teasingly that she danced like an 'oyinbo'.

At about 7, the guests started leaving. Siyonna's mum prodded Mr Nduka, who had spent the entire time reminiscing with Amanda's dad and they all got up to leave. The girls hugged and Amina came with Siyonna. Amina and her parents would be staying the night at Siyonna's and the Bakaris would be going back to Abuja in the morning after breakfast. Amina, of course, would be going back to school with Siyonna on Monday morning.

"Zach this was an amazing day, don't you think?" said Obiageli, as the cars pulled out of Our Lady's. "The girls worked really hard! Absolutely amazing! Who knew they had it in them?"

Siyonna's dad didn't answer. He was fast asleep.

8

Little Grace

Siyonna and her friends did their homework well when deciding which charity to support. They found out that in Nigeria, most of the homes for abandoned children and orphans were run either by missionaries or private individuals, many of them relying heavily on donations and contributions from organizations and kind members of society. They also discovered there was a difference between orphanages and motherless babies' homes. While orphanages catered for children who had lost both parents or were abandoned, motherless babies' homes were meant to be facilities for very young who had lost their mothers. However, for the most part, the two terms were used interchangeably with the result that all facilities that catered for unwanted, orphaned or children who lost their mothers, came under the generic term Motherless Babies' Homes.

Little Grace was one such home. The proprietor, Mrs Grace Apkabio, had embarked on this project late in life. A larger than life character, a big woman in her sixties with a broad smile and known to everyone as Ma Grace, she had raised six sons of her own and her husband had been a Colonel in the army. As her sons grew up and left to go to university, she and her husband often discussed what they would do in their retirement years.

The Colonel had lost his own parents when he was young and had spent time in state-run orphanages, always saying that they were places where a child could not find love. The Colonel believed that the army saved his life. It was in the army he had learnt to be disciplined, it gave him an education and eventually, a career. He thought that without the army in his life, he probably would have ended up on the wrong side of the law and been dead by the time he was 21. Sadly, however, he did not make it to retirement and died just before leaving his military career.

Ma Grace grieved and put it down to the will of God. She raised her children and as soon as they left to pursue their own lives and careers, she remembered the plans she and the Colonel had to run a home for orphaned and unwanted children and this led to the creation of Little Grace. She had already acquired a sizeable portion of land on the outskirts of Lagos Island, years before and decided to develop the property into a home for abandoned children, giving them as much of herself as she could and helping them transition into adulthood. Always with the memory of her husband's experience at the back of her mind, she vowed to make sure the home she built never left the children wanting of love. She had little but intended to make sure it went into giving love and succour to these children.

Over the years that Ma Grace had run the home, it went from housing ten little children to over a hundred, purely from her own resources and donations from friends. Her husband's friends, her children and even their colleagues were very generous and the community of neighbours and church contacts also helped with donations and scholarships for the children. One of the older children had gone from the home to an apprenticeship in a bank, which was now paying for him to train as a banker. However, it was always a struggle and Ma Grace consistently went with very little just so the children in the home had love, a secure environment and warm meals.

Through the passing years, she had sold practically everything she owned and ploughed the proceeds back into the home. Her sons who had gone on to become quite successful in their careers continued to support their mother as much as they could, with loans that would never be repaid.

Ma Grace was very religious and resorted to prayer at all times. She cut an impressive figure, attending church every day. She wouldn't miss the morning Mass for anything. As her fledgling home survived, year in year out and help continued to come from the most unexpected sources, she became even more prayerful and committed to the indelible help of Christ and the Blessed Virgin Mary, who, in Ma Grace's view, continued to intercede tirelessly on the home's behalf.

Even though Ma Grace had been told that Our Lady's School was coming to make a presentation to the home, she did not know what they were going to be presenting the Home with. She had entertained young people in the past who had been moved by her work and felt compelled to make a donation, so she did not think this was going to be any different. In her usual hospitable manner, she harried her staff and made sure the meal of jollof rice and chicken they were having for lunch that afternoon could be extended to their guests. The poor kids were not going to come all this way and not be fed, in her opinion.

Ma Grace also went around the dormitories to make sure her wards were all well turned out to receive the girls. The Home had two large dormitories, one for the boys and one for the girls. Over the years, the dormitories had been extended and another floor added to each building to accommodate the growing number of children in the Home. The babies and younger children would usually stay in rooms with matrons until they were old enough to join the other children in the dormitories.

Right now, she had a boy who was completely attached to her, little Deji. The little one had been found wrapped up in a blanket and crying, abandoned at a bus stop not far from Little Grace and had been brought to her. The doctor who examined him put his age at the time at a few days old. She had kept him and cared for him and now Deji would not let her out of his sight, not for a minute. So today, Deji was tied to her back with a wrapper and he drifted in and out of sleep contentedly as Ma Grace went about her chores.

Siyonna, Amanda, Amaka, Dupe, Amina and Bunmi all wore the formal Our Lady's uniform. The girls had met up at school today for the 40-minute trip from the school to the Little Grace Home and would be accompanied by Mr Ese Ogunde, the Deputy Head Teacher. Mother Joseph turned up to see them off and congratulate them again on their fundraising. She also informed them that some of the parents had come together and started a scholarship fund for the Little Grace Home, guaranteeing that the ten brightest children from the home, after successfully finishing secondary school could go on to University, all expenses paid. Mother Joseph handed Amanda the letter and asked her to give Ma Grace the good news. She apologized for not being able to accompany them on such a special trip but wished the girls Godspeed. Then they all piled into the school bus, followed by a smiling Mr Ogunde who was looking rather distinguished in a white shirt, blue blazer, chinos and a burgundy tie. The girls all commented on how smart he looked. He smiled and thanked them as they set off.

Across town, just as the girls set off for the home, Jeremiah, patient number 202, walked out of the Western Lagos mental hospital. Jeremiah was schizophrenic but usually all right when medicated. When not medicated, he presented a danger to both himself and others. Over the years he had tried to kill a plethora of family pets and his parents finally decided to have him institutionalised when they had woken up to find their son standing over their bed with a butcher's knife. Jeremiah's father had tried to talk to him but had given up when Jeremiah lunged at him with the knife. Both parents made it to the bathroom, locked the door and called the police.

For some reason today, the superintendent had left the ward door unlocked, so Jeremiah had just walked out. The gate also stood open, so he simply kept walking, unchallenged. As he wandered the streets, he became increasingly agitated and started talking loudly to himself. He wanted to get home but simply did not know how to. As he wandered, he found a knife lying on the floor of an open-air canteen kitchen. He grabbed it and as the canteen's manageress accosted him, he waved it menacingly at her and ran off.

Jeremiah wandered off the main road as if drawn by an unseen force towards a metal gate. As he came near, he heard the sound of an approaching vehicle and ducked into the low-cut shrubs to stay out of sight.

The traffic was not particularly oppressive today, perhaps because it was a Saturday and the girls had a fairly clear run from Ikoyi and through VGC and towards Aja on the outskirts of Lagos where the home was. Amanda had never been this far out of Lagos since she'd been back to live in Nigeria, so Siyonna acted as guide explaining all the sights on the way. Eventually, the bus left the main road as if heading to the new Lagos free trade port and just there on the right stood a metal gate with the sign for Little Grace Home. The bus drew up by the gate and the driver gave a slight hoot of his horn. A few minutes later, a gateman came out, verified who they were and threw the gates open. They came into what seemed like a big compound and parked up.

Ma Grace came out of one of the buildings with Deji on her back and a wide smile on her face as she strode towards the bus to receive her visitors. A few of the children from the home, curious at the sight of the bus, also came out and fell in behind Ma Grace.

"Welcome, welcome my dear children! Welcome to the Little Grace home for children! We are all so happy to see you!" proclaimed Ma Grace as she came to the bus door.

"Good afternoon, Ma," said Amanda and Siyonna, the first off the bus and curtsied in the respectful fashion of the Yorubas.

Mr Ogunde greeted Ma Grace, introduced the girls and explained what had brought the girls here. When he finished, Ma Grace thanked him and asked them all to come with her. They were all so busy meeting each other, that nobody noticed the lone figure of Jeremiah who had entered the compound behind the bus. He quickly darted into the garden and disappeared behind one of the buildings.

As they walked in the baking sun to Ma Grace's office, the children from the home joined them. One of the little girls who Siyonna later learnt was called Maria, quietly slipped her hands into Ma Grace's and walked with her as she looked at the strangers with large, curious eyes. As their eyes met, Siyonna smiled at her and Maria blinked and quickly looked away. Siyonna smiled. The child seemed about five years old and looked quite skinny, not in a malnourished way but in the way of children who needed a little persuasion to get them to eat. Siyonna smiled again as she recalled the stories of the pain she used to cause her mum when she was little as she had to be cajoled into eating her meals. How times changed. These days, she needed little persuasion. Perhaps that was because nobody was now chasing her around to eat.

At her office, Ma Grace invited the girls to sit down and asked them what they knew about the home. Dupe who had suggested they raise money for the home explained that the girls had done some research online, and felt that Little Grace was doing an amazing job of providing a home and love for these children and that nothing would be more worthy than to support this work. Ma Grace beamed, thanked the girls and gave them a brief history of the place. Then she suggested they come with her on a tour of the premises.

As they went through the dormitories, more children fell in behind them. There were children as young as 6 in the dormitories and as old as 16. The older children usually attended the local secondary schools and would stay in the home until either they finished full-time education or were adopted. Ma Grace explained that a few of her children had gone on to good families and one of the older children had left for a banking apprenticeship.

She introduced the girls to Yetunde, a bright 18-year-old who was hoping to start university in the next school year. Ma Grace explained that she had managed to secure funds to support Yetunde through the first two years of University, but since Yetunde was going to University to study Pharmacy, they needed funding for five years. She was still hoping for a miracle before the next school year when Yetunde must either accept her place at University or lose it.

Mr Ogunde said that he felt their visit may help ease that concern.

"Every little helps, thank you," said Ma Grace, not realising the extent of the funding they had achieved.

When they returned to the office, Mr Ogunde asked Amanda to tell Ma Grace about their gift for the Home, so she stood up and told Ma Grace and the matrons about the Charity Day at Our Lady's, how Little Grace Home had been chosen as their team's charity of choice, and how they'd won. Amanda then presented two cheques: the first was a cheque for 2 Million Naira, raised from the bake sale and matching donation; the second was the letter confirming that a foundation had established to send up to ten qualifying children from the home to university every year. This meant that Yetunde could go to university immediately and Ma Grace no longer needed to worry about her.

When she heard this, Ma Grace sank into her chair and covered her face with her hands as tears of joy poured forth. A lot of the children who until then had crowded in the doorway now flooded the office and all tried to hug her at the same time, as she laughed and cried out with joy at the love and contentment within her little community and the little miracles that meant she could simply keep going, changing lives every day.

"Please girls, Mr Ogunde, come, come, let's all have lunch," said Ma Grace between all the hugs and laughter. "What a wonderful, blessed day! We have lunch prepared and served in the dining room and the girls can also sit with our children and get to know them. Thank you so much for your gifts! It is so hard to put into words just how special and thoughtful they are. It means these children can go on to change their lives and God willing, help other children like themselves! Thank you, thank you!"

All the adults seemed to have tears in their eyes and the children, especially the younger ones, who couldn't possibly know what the excitement was all about, joined in the crying, hugging and laughing celebration. The call for lunch though extinguished all immediate crying as the children guessed that the presence of guests would mean that today might be a day for jollof rice and chicken, normally a Sunday lunchtime treat. They were not wrong. The jollof rice had been steamed to perfection in a spiced tomato paste and waited to be served in the dining room. Because of the care taken in making jollof, the children saw it as a delicacy, reserved for special occasions like birthdays, Sundays and Christmas. Today was definitely special and when they stood in line at the dining room and the dinner ladies dished out portions of hot jollof rice and chicken pieces, there were delighted smiles on their young faces as they made their way back to their seats at the tables scattered around the simple dining room. Ma Grace waited for the matrons to bring in the babies and younger children and then stood up.

"Let us pray!" she announced in her rich voice.

The children immediately bowed their heads and clasped their hands as Ma Grace thanked God for the food and the hands that made it. She thanked God for the gifts they had received and asked God to bless their guests and Our Lady's school. After a universal Amen, the children sat down and tucked in.

The girls sat at the same table as Yetunde and another girl, Antonia, who was in her early teens. They talked as they ate and got to know a bit more about the home. Antonia thought she was 13 or 14, she couldn't be sure. She had come to Little Grace as a young child and didn't remember much about her earlier life before the home. She had been found wandering around Tejuosho Market, the famous market in Yaba and taken to the Police Station by a market trader when she couldn't explain who she was or where she came from. The Police had kept her for a week as they made efforts to contact her parents then asked Ma Grace if she would take the child. She had remained here ever since.

In the beginning, she had been angry and got into several fights with some of the other children in the home. She could not understand why her parents had abandoned her and felt ashamed for many years. Ma Grace had spent a lot of time talking to her about the complexities of life and the importance of contentment and dealing with grief. She advised her to try to find peace and maybe someday, she could be reunited with her family. Ma Grace had also taught her to pray and to believe in God. She was more at peace with her circumstance now and though she still felt sad, especially when she was teased at school for being an unwanted child, she was grateful for the security of the Home and the love she got from Ma Grace who had been like a mother to her for the past ten years. Yetunde agreed that the home had provided a sanctuary for them. Ma Grace was strict and the rules were not to be flouted under any circumstances. It was tough for Ma Grace keeping the children and seeing them through school but she was determined and kept faith with all her children. There were many sacrifices everyone made at the home but they always had a warm meal. Amaka asked Yetunde what sort of sacrifices they made.

"You can't be choosy about what you eat," said Yetunde, smiling. "You eat what you're given. And you can't choose what you wear either. Ma Grace can't buy designer clothes for everyone here," she said, waving a hand round the room and the girls laughed. "So you wear hand-me-downs and you find joy in helping others, helping the matrons with the younger children and babies."

"Don't you miss all those things, the clothes and other things?" asked Amanda.

"Not really. This is the only life I've ever known. As I got older, I became aware of a totally different world and what other people have but I am also grateful for the upbringing I've received here. I think it will help me as I get older, build a career and have a family of my own."

The girls all ate in silence after that as they went over in their minds what Yetunde had said. Siyonna thought, even though they were almost the same age, Yetunde seemed so much more mature.

"Do you want to see something special?" Antonia asked as they finished lunch. "Come on, I'll show you."

They gathered their plates and took them to the kitchen where some of the teenage children on kitchen duty were washing and drying the dishes and putting them away. The boys all smiled and waved as they took the plates from the girls.

With Antonia leading the way, they weaved through the grounds and came to a lovely, well-tended vegetable garden and at the end of it a small chicken coop with a few hens. On the other side of the chicken coop, they saw a beautiful canary in a small cage. As it flapped its wings and sang, all the girls smiled in amusement.

"I call her Whitney after Whitney Houston," said Antonia. "I found her with a broken wing a month ago and built this cage for her and nursed her until the wing healed."

"How did you know what to do, to heal the wing?" asked Siyonna in amazement.

"The internet!" laughed Antonia. "There are so many articles on how to help birds heal and I just followed the instructions. I think I want to be a vet when I grow up."

"Ah, Antonia! A vet now?" said Yetunde, rolling her eyes. "Last week it was a pilot, the week before a Nun and last month, the Army. I wonder what tomorrow will bring?"

Antonia laughed and everyone joined her.

"Hello?" said a quiet voice and they all turned around to see a boy of about 12 standing shyly by the chicken coops.

"Hey Chris!" said Antonia. "Everyone, this is Chris. Chris is our house Magician!"

Chris walked up to Siyonna, shook her hand, opened his hand wide to show there was nothing there, then stood on tiptoe and retrieved a coin from the back of her right ear. The girls whooped in delight and asked him to do more. Chris showed off his tricks with cards, with pebbles and many more. Meanwhile, Jeremiah had been watching with growing trepidation from his hiding place behind the chicken coop. The voice in his head kept telling him that the teenagers knew the directions to his house and that he needed to force them to take him home. He'd never liked teenagers anyway. His parent's neighbour's teenage children had always tormented him and made his life a living hell.

And now he had no choice but to obey the voice in his head. Just as one of the little boys ran up to say that Mr Ogunde was looking for the girls because it was time to go, Jeremiah sprang out, seized the boy and put his knife to his throat. The youngsters were terrified!

"Take me home now or I'll cut his throat," he said, looking directly at Chris and Yetunde.

Yetunde stared back at Jeremiah in absolute panic. Chris on the other hand, ran off to raise the alarm just as Jeremiah's hand moved to a cutting position.

Siyonna suddenly felt very tranquil.

"Hi," she said, stepping forward. "I'm Siyonna. Please let the boy go and I'll take you home."

Suddenly the others started screaming but she simply held her hand up, signalling for them to keep quiet. As she walked towards Jeremiah, she could see the doubt in his eyes and he tightened his grip on the boy, moving the knife closer to his victim's neck,

"Please let him go, sir. He doesn't know where you live. I do, and I promise to get you home. Please, sir?"

Jeremiah paused. He thought there was something calm and sincere about this teenager. She wasn't quite like the others and the voices in his head went quiet for once. He surmised they must also agree with his judgment. He would take her instead and with that, he let go of the boy and grabbed Siyonna's arm.

"Please sir," she said, looking down at his hand on her arm. "I will need to walk on my own so I can point you home."

Again, the voices in his head seemed to agree so he knew it was safe to let go of her. She marched towards the exit with Jeremiah in tow. As they approached the gate, the gateman came up to accost them and Siyonna immediately asked him to step aside and unlock the gate. He did as he was asked just as people started pouring out of the buildings, Chris having raised the alarm.

Siyonna walked Jeremiah out of the Home, feeling the comforting weight of her necklace on her bare skin, tucked away under her uniform. She wasn't really sure where they were going but she just kept walking and Jeremiah walked silently behind her. She was roughly fifteen minutes away from the Home, on the main road, when she saw a minivan full of psychiatric orderlies drive past, stop, swing around and start coming towards them. Jeremiah noticed it as well and his face suddenly contorted in anger and gripping the knife he came at her menacingly. Siyonna felt a calm she really couldn't explain and sticking her hand in her collar, she clutched her necklace and felt it sitting comfortingly around her neck, as she waited for Jeremiah to strike her.

He stopped mid-strike and seemed perplexed by the necklace, almost transfixed where he stood, knife raised at Siyonna. The hospital minivan drew close and six orderlies jumped out, disarmed him, put restraints on him and bustled him into the van.

"Are you all alright my dear? Did he hurt you?" asked the Warden.

Siyonna shook her head and burst into tears. The warden comforted her, explaining that Jeremiah had escaped during a changeover of shifts in the hospital and they had spent the last half hour looking for him. Then he hailed a cab, paid the driver and asked him to take Siyonna back to Little Grace.

Back at the Home, both Ma Grace and Mr Ogunde were beside themselves with worry. Nothing like this had ever happened before and neither could even bear to think of how they'd explain themselves to Siyonna's parents if anything terrible happened to her.

"That's it," declared Ma Grace, suddenly. "We're going to do what we should have done in the first place. We're going to look for her. Come on," she said to Mr Ogunde. "My car is parked near the gate."

After passing a protesting Deji to one of the matrons, she marched purposefully towards her car, with Mr Ogunde in tow. Just then, the gate opened and the cab with Siyonna drove in. As she stepped out, everybody ran to her and hugged her. Was she hurt? Why had she sacrificed herself so easily? Was she not scared? What if he'd stabbed her? How brave Siyonna was, they all exclaimed. Siyonna looked at all of them, her friends, Ma Grace, Mr Ogunde, the children, and just shrugged. She did not know why she did what she did and certainly did not feel brave now she'd done it. All she knew was that she had felt an absolute compulsion to stop Jeremiah hurting anybody and had felt safe enough within herself to distract him. Simple really.

As the girls made their way back to the bus, they hugged Yetunde, Antonia and Chris, exchanged email addresses and promised to keep in touch. At the bus, Ma Grace gave them bear hugs and thanked them again for their kindness. Even little Deji, back in the familiar comfort of Ma Grace's back, managed to gurgle and smile at the girls for the first time. Then Ma Grace took Siyonna's hands in hers and looked deeply into her eyes.

"God bless you my child and thank you for averting disaster here today. Look after yourself and may the angels watch over you."

Siyonna smiled and curtsied a 'thank you ma' then joined the others on the bus. The children and Ma Grace waved until the bus was out of sight. Amina had tears in her eyes and the girls all turned and hugged her. It had been an enjoyable and very emotional day for all of them.

9

About the Boy

As half-term approached, a frenzy of activity took place at Our Lady's, with the girls working extra hard to complete their homework and make sure nothing came between them and a peaceful, school-free week. Those less-discerning pupils who left their assignments and course work half-done, usually found themselves spending the week's holiday in school under the supervision of Mother Joseph!

The girls saw Mother Joseph as stern and austere. She rarely left the school's grounds and her only luxury appeared to be her annual retreat to Lourdes in France, undertaken every summer when school broke. Those unfortunate enough to spend the half term in school reported being given classical texts to read and discuss with Mother Joseph, on top of the work they had left undone! It was little wonder then that as half-term approached, the girls were frantically working through their subjects and list of assignments to make sure they had nothing left outstanding.

Excitement filled the air. The girls who lived in Lagos usually planned to catch up with each other during the holidays and it wasn't any different for Siyonna and her friends. Apart from Amina who would be going home to Abuja for the week, all the other girls remained in Lagos. Amaka would also be turning 16 this week and her parents were throwing her a Sweet 16 party, something else for the girls to look forward to. Siyonna and her friends had just finished lunch and were discussing what Amaka's party was going to be like when Amaka announced that her father had hired a well-known DJ to play music on the day and she was hoping to give him a list of all her favourite tunes.

"Why don't we put a playlist together?" said Siyonna.

The friends all agreed to come up with music ideas, to be discussed the next day at lunch. They had free study periods for the rest of the day and decided to spend it in the library. Siyonna had a meeting with Mr Ayodele, the Maths Tutor for the last period at 3. Amanda and Amina also announced they would go with her, so they all headed out to the library. The library was in the newer section of the school, which also housed the chapel. The interior was wood-panelled and had high ceilings. Serene and very quiet, it provided a perfect place for research and study. It also had a reputation as one of the best school libraries in the country. Mother Joseph guarded it jealously, bluntly refusing to allow other schools access to it.

To reach the library, pupils had to skirt through a long winding corridor between the dining hall in the old building, and the small park that separated the old building from the new building. As the girls walked through the corridor and rounded the corner, just before they got to the park, they saw Miss Udoka, the Biology Tutor. Miss Udoka was young and had joined the staff just two years ago, first serving with the school during her National Youth Service year and staying on after the service as Biology Tutor for the junior classes. She also doubled as unofficial mentor, friend, advisor and confidant to many of the girls and because she was one of the younger tutors and open, all the girls liked her.

"Hello Miss!" sang out Siyonna and her friends.

"Well if it isn't the Premier Squad," said Miss Udoka, smiling.

She had taken to describing Siyonna and her friends as the Premier Squad and it always made them smile.

"Where are you girls off to?" she asked.

"The library, Miss," replied Siyonna for them.

"I wonder if you could spare me a few minutes of your time? I need some help labelling up the practical projects for next session. It shouldn't take long."

"Sure," they chorused and followed her into the science lab.

Miss Udoka pointed to a box of newly delivered lab items and asked them to help her number and match them to beakers and other lab equipment, to assist with dissection experiments in the new session. As the girls donned lab coats and got to work, Siyonna noticed a large glass case, set into the wall that she had never noticed before. From where she was sitting the case looked like a huge painting, displayed in an alcove.

Siyonna soon got lost in her work. She loved Biology and had once wondered what life would be like if she took a career as a Marine Biologist, travelling the world and working in all the great oceans, studying and cataloguing the amazing wildlife that lay at the bottom of the ocean. She resolved again that if she ever changed her mind about studying literature, Marine Biology would be up there as a strong contender.

As she worked on, labelling Petri dishes and test bottles, she was drawn to a movement in the box on the wall. She turned and stared and let out a sharp scream that brought the attention of all the other girls and Miss Udoka.

"What is in that box, Miss?" asked Siyonna.

"Oh, that's Titus, the African Rock Python," laughed Miss Udoka. "He's only little and could grow to be about 5 meters long. He's been with us for about six months and we will probably send him to a zoo in the next year or so when he gets too big for his cage."

"Is it safe having him in here? What if he breaks the cage?" persisted Siyonna.

"Unlikely. The glass in the cage is reinforced. Titus will not be leaving until we're ready to rehome him. Come, take a closer look?"

The girls walked to the cage to stare at Titus. He was about 1.2 meters in length and curled up with his head lying on the curl. He appeared completely uninterested in the gasps and chatter from the girls and did not move all the time they stood staring at him.

"Do you guys know anything about these snakes?" asked Miss Udoka.

"No," replied Siyonna. "Apart from the fact that they strangle their prey and swallow them. Some say they can eat a full-grown man.

"Not sure about the man bit. They do swallow their prey whole after constriction and stretching but it would be a particularly large snake to swallow a man. They tend to eat mice and other rodents and the occasional livestock in the wild," said Miss Udoka. "Come, let me show you something."

She led the girls over to the television set on the wall, connected her laptop to it and chose a program. Moments later, a large python showed up on the screen in a nature program. It was in the middle of constricting a small antelope, still trying feebly to free itself from the firm muscles systematically squeezing the life out of it. As Miss Udoka talked the girls through the process, the antelope stopped struggling and very soon, the python started swallowing it whole.

At this point, Miss Udoka stopped the video saying the entire process could take several hours. The girls asked a few questions about how the food digested in the snake's body and how often it fed. Miss Udoka told them it all depended on the size of the meal and the size of the snake. A meal like the antelope, for instance, would keep the python going for several weeks or even a month. The girls finished their tasks, thanked Miss Udoka and headed off to the library.

Just as they left the lab, Siyonna's phone buzzed. She thought that strange since nobody ever called her at school. She picked up her phone, a Samsung hand-me-down from Ebele and said a cursory hello as she struggled to hang onto her bag and folders.

"Siyonna!" said her father.

"Hello, dad."

"Darling you'll have to make your own way home today. I have a late meeting with the state government representatives and I need Mr Sunday to take me there. So, get the bus to first gate and make your way home, ok?"

Siyonna said that was fine and said goodbye to her dad.

"Sorry folks gotta make my way home. My dad can't spare his driver today," she told her friends.

There followed 'ohs' and 'ahs' and an offer from Amanda to drop her halfway home but Siyonna said her 'thank yous' and 'goodbyes' and started her journey home.

She walked out of the school gates onto Alexander road. The bus stop was already busy as children from neighbouring schools gathered there. Siyonna knew full well that Nigerian buses did not run to a timetable. Some were operated by the government but the privately owned minibuses known as 'danfos' offered stiff competition. They obeyed few rules, picking up passengers wherever they found them and stuffing as many people in as possible. As Siyonna waited, one of the minibuses pulled up.

"Oniru!" shouted the conductor at the top of his voice.

She made a beeline for it and found a window seat in the second row. As soon as it was full, the bus lumbered off. The conductor half-sat, half-stood by the window, making catty comments at anything that moved, from cab drivers to mammies with wares on their heads. As the bus driver did not want to pay the toll to cross the Ikoyi Bridge, he took the scenic route, dropping passengers and picking up new fares as he weaved his way towards Lekki peninsula.

It started raining and Siyonna pulled her window shut. The bus had grown quite stuffy, made worse by the fact a particularly large woman had taken the seat next to her. She had a huge basket on her lap and the conductor suggested he would charge her double for the journey because she was taking up the space of at least two regular-sized passengers. Everyone in the bus laughed as the woman put up a stout defence, blaming what she described as 'big bones.' The conductor grinned, telling her he had been referring to the huge basket on her lap, which brought more laughter from the other passengers. As she protested, the lady pushed more towards Siyonna, so much so that less of Siyonna remained on the seat, than was firmly wedged against the window. Siyonna winced, as she sat squashed, convinced that she was unlikely to breathe comfortably for the rest of the journey. The conductor picked up on her discomfort.

"Ejoor oh!" he said in Pidgin English. "Stop squeezing the poor girl on your left! Na because of the extra fare? Abeg oh! I no wan kill person for this bus oh!"

This brought on renewed laughter from everybody, including the driver. The woman protested some more but did move, giving Siyonna a bit of a respite and she smiled a silent thanks to the woman.

As the bus wound its way through Falomo to Victoria Island towards Lekki, Siyonna thought about Titus the snake. She had always been drawn to the environment and had a strong interest in ecology and the preservation of species and ecosystems. However, she was not a huge fan of snakes and when she had considered a career in biology, she really hadn't given any serious consideration to the thought of handling snakes of any kind. She really could not imagine being face to face with Titus outside its cage and felt herself shudder at the thought.

Her reverie was broken by a call from her mum, asking her to stop by Bene's to pick up a bag of sugar and oats for her dad's breakfast. She thought about telling her mum she was on the bus but decided against it. The 'and-so-whats' that would accompany such an unwise comment far outweighed the effort to get to Bene's. Besides, Bene's was a short stop from the market and she could walk from there.

The rain began to subside as they got to Oniru Market. Busy and with a lot of traffic, the road was damaged and quite dangerous in the rain because of the open-drain gutters on either side of it. These drains were mostly clogged with debris and overflowed whenever it rained heavily, making the area practically impassable. Today, fortunately, the rain had not persisted. As the bus stopped, the big lady got off with her outsized basket looking relieved that she had not been charged double the fare, despite threats from the conductor.

Siyonna paid, said thank you to the conductor and was just setting out towards Bene's when she saw the big lady trip and fall into one of the drains. As people shouted, a few men went to her aid but could not pull her out as one of her legs seemed to be trapped beneath the surface. Water was pouring into the drain at a rapid pace and it began filling up very quickly.

Siyonna quickly ran over to where the men were struggling to get the lady out and just as she got there, a fresh wave of water gushed through the drain and was now up to her chin. The woman had a wild look of pure terror in her eyes and screamed incessantly in Yoruba, calling on Jesus to help. The men, now numbering about six, struggled to pull her out but made very little progress largely because her foot was firmly trapped by something beneath the surface. Some people suggested trying to swim underneath the water to free her but the water was murky, dirty and so filled with debris that no one would dare climb into it. As her necklace warmed familiarly around her neck, Siyonna gently walked closer, skirted round the men trying to help the woman, chose the man closest to her and grabbed his hand lightly. As the man started to protest, he looked at Siyonna and stopped, then he simply shifted his weight slightly, got his hands under the woman's elbow and heaved. The woman rose effortlessly and the other men helped her back onto solid ground.

As everyone patted the man on the back for his heroism and the woman rained blessings on him, he turned to look for the girl whose touch had dramatically transformed him and given him almost superhuman strength for that moment. He had felt the difference and been overwhelmed by both purpose and inexplicable strength at the time. Only now that the task was accomplished did he want to know how she did it but she had vanished. He turned and asked a few people around whether they had seen her only receiving blank stares. Amazing, he thought, so Angels do exist.

Siyonna walked as quickly as she could to her mum's supermarket where the assistants were glad to see her and teased her endlessly about the length of her skirt. She smiled, picked up the things for her mum, paid and made a quick escape only after promising to visit soon. She liked going to *Bene's*. No one knew where her mum got the name from but she had obviously liked it enough to name her premier supermarket Bene's.

She had to admit, going there today had provided a welcome distraction from the thought of Titus, not to mention the incident with the big lady from the bus. As she stood waiting for a bus or *'Okada'* motorbike taxi, to cover the remaining journey, the supermarket manager drove out on his way home and gave her a lift to her street and she walked the rest of the way home.

Titus grew further from her mind when her mum informed her that there were dinner guests coming that weekend. That meant if she still wanted to make Amaka's party, to make sure she finished her Saturday chores early. Her mum expected her to help with cleaning and tidying the house and also help make some of the starters for the day. Siyonna wolfed down her dinner as her mother delivered instructions about her expectations for Saturday. She nodded, quickly kissed her father on the cheek and ran upstairs to get her work and her private study done. Over the years, Siyonna had surmised that the only guaranteed way to keep her grades and keep on top of her work was to maintain a strict routine of study and homework then play afterwards. Anything short of that, she knew, would leave her falling behind at school. Suddenly, it dawned on her that she really did not have as much time as she thought she had.

The next day was the last Friday before half term. It was usually easy and school broke just after lunch. Amaka's party was the next day! Amina's parents had decided to let her attend the party on Saturday and then fly home Sunday, which meant Amina would spend the weekend with Siyonna. Both girls excitedly picked up Amina's valise from the hostel, said goodbye to their friends and headed to Siyonna's waiting driver.

Ebele called on Friday evening and both Amina and Siyonna filled her in on school. Siyonna also told her about Titus and they both screamed as they thought about the likely implications of Titus breaking out of his glass cage. "God forbid it!" they both said in unison, laughing.

"I guess this puts paid to a career in Biology, huh?" teased Ebele.

Siyonna admitted she never quite gave a lot of thought to snakes being in the family of the living in need of studying. Amina left to get a drink and Siyonna quickly told Ebele about the big woman on the bus. Ebele listened quietly.

"Did you give the man the strength to pull the lady from the drain?" she asked and received no answer. "Siyonna?"

"Yes," she blurted out. "I guess I did. I didn't think about it. I just felt drawn to help the woman, just as I felt drawn to get the mad man away from Ma Grace's home. I don't know why I just felt a compulsion to do."

"And were you wearing your necklace on both occasions?" asked Ebele gently.

"Yes."

Ebele was silent for a moment.

"That necklace is magical," she said finally. "Do not discuss the powers it gives you with anybody, not even our parents, you hear? Keep the necklace and your abilities a secret."

Siyonna was just about to question her sister, when Amina came back into the room and Ebele quickly changed the subject to her work and how busy her training kept her. She told them how she had initially wanted to specialize as a gynaecologist but had since developed an interest in public health and would specialise in that after qualifying in gynaecology. Siyonna asked what the difference was, and Ebele patiently explained that as a Public Health specialist, she'd be working more in disease prevention and epidemic management. She felt she would also get the chance to do more in the developing world by combining the two disciplines.

"Wow Eby," said Siyonna. "You are something, you know that? You are so brilliant! Anyway, you know what dad would say. *Husband nkoh?*

They both laughed at Siyonna's poor effort at imitating their father's baritone.

"There is somebody actually," said Ebele. "We've been seeing each other since I got to the UK. It's steady but I don't know if it's serious yet. Don't tell Dad yet oh! Anyway, you'll meet him when you visit next summer."

"I am visiting you next summer?" shrieked Siyonna in excitement.

"Yes, the parents and I have discussed it. You'll come and spend the summer with me. I have got my own place now and I could use the company over summer. You'll come?"

"Sister," said Siyonna. "Try and stop me." Then she stopped to think. "But dad did say he was owed a large sum of money. I know he has put some company cars up for sale and has cut down on his golf days. If he is struggling, I really wouldn't want him worrying about my ticket on top of everything else."

Both girls agreed. Ebele had been told their dad's business was owed some money but hadn't quite realised just how bad things were. They both agreed to watch this space and see what happened before finally saying their goodbyes. The conversation was somewhat marred by what was happening with her father and Siyonna knew she might not make it to London this summer. Amina hugged Siyonna, reassuring her that all would be well.

Amina really did not see what the big deal about London was but said nothing to her friend. The weather was pretty inclement and it always felt cold and wet. Her older sister had been at the King's College London and had described London as the 'greatest city in the world'. Amina just couldn't see it. The shopping was nice but it seemed to rain all the time. She remembered going to Hyde Park with her father to see the Princess Diana Memorial Fountain. It had been a lovely, pleasant August afternoon when she had left the family's flat in Knightsbridge to make the short walk to Hyde Park. Baba had also promised her ice cream and a visit to Bond Street to look at the shops. Just as they got to the fountain, it had all changed and the persistent, slow London rain started. Her father had thrown his hands heavenward in exasperation and they had both laughed as they ran to the lido Café, just south of the memorial fountain. It had turned out to be one of the best moments she ever shared with her father. It had been just the two of them, which was rare with her dad, always working and always surrounded by people.

"You're wet," he said when they got to the Lido café.

"So are you, Baba!" shrieked Amina.

His blazer was sodden and hung off him like a wet blanket. His usual impeccable appearance was drenched and gave him a vulnerability she hadn't seen in a long time, not since she was five and used to slide off his knees. These days, their relationship was much more formal. Her father had laughed and gathered her in his arms.

"I love you, you wet not so little Amina!" He said and Amina laughed.

One of the ladies at the Lido offered them lots of sheets of serviette to help dry themselves off. Then they ordered large mugs of cocoa and some blueberry muffins and looked out at the Serpentine Lake as they waited for the rain to stop. That for her had been the best part of that visit to London and she'd give anything to recreate those moments, spending time alone with her father.

As she tried to find the words to tell her friend about London's temperamental weather, Siyonna's mother called them to dinner.

That night, as Siyonna lay on her bed waiting for sleep to come, she thought about what Ebele had said. She had always suspected a certain peculiarity about her necklace but had never for one moment thought of it as being magical. However, the things that had happened around her these past few months, made her believe it could be. The feats of extraordinary selflessness always happened when the necklace was with her and at those times, she felt driven, almost guided to act. She shuddered. If only she could speak to Ma Mabel. Was she in danger? Would the necklace always be there to protect her? How far could she go? As she nodded off, she could still hear Ma Mabel's voice saying, *"keep the necklace close to you, it will bring you luck."*

Saturday started with a blur as Siyonna, with Amina's help, woke early and started off on her tasks of dusting and vacuuming the house. The house was quite substantial and whenever she entertained, Obiageli wanted the place to be spick and span. They cleaned the guest toilet and mopped the long marble porch as well as the corridor leading to the living room. Just when they thought they were done, Siyonna's mum came in, ran a finger across the large mirror in the hall and turned to Siyonna with beaded eyelids.

"Don't make me ask again," she hissed.

Siyonna looked at Amina, both girls shrugged, took out fresh cloths and set to work cleaning the long mirror. When they were done, Siyonna muttered to Amina that the mirror was now so clean that she could see all the way to her soul, never mind just her reflection. Amina laughed which got Siyonna's mum to query from the kitchen that she hoped all the cleaning was done? People weren't meant to be laughing when they were meant to be cleaning! They both giggled and went off to put the cleaning products away.

Once they were dressed and ready, the girls got a ride to Amaka's party from Mr Sunday, Siyonna's dad's driver. He would come back for them at 7 that evening. Both Siyonna and Amina wore colourful *Adire* tops and skirts. Siyonna liked it, particularly because it was the tie and dye cotton fabric used by many Nigerians for making colourful, casual clothes set off by tasteful accessories like beads and bangles. Siyonna was wearing a yellow and black number with yellow pumps that accentuated her long legs. Amina had chosen something in turquoise and also looked very pretty.

Amaka lived in a tasteful estate not too far from Siyonna's Lekki home on the Island. They came across some traffic but soon turned off the expressway and drove into the familiar new gates leading into the estate. Siyonna saw other girls from her school making their way in as well. Amaka's home was a detached house sitting on a corner plot, which gave it slightly more space than the other houses around it. As the girls got out of the car and thanked Mr Sunday, a black jeep pulled up and slotted into the car space across from them. And just as Siyonna and Amina started walking towards Amaka's front door they heard a familiar voice coming from the jeep.

"Wait up you guys!" shouted Amanda.

Both Siyonna and Amina smiled. Amanda looked very smart in a lovely red and yellow Abada blouse and a pair of black jeans and patent black shoes. They all ran and hugged.

"Nice, now where did you get that blouse? Can't believe your mum arranged this?" teased Siyonna.

It was a standing joke among the girls that Amanda's American mum did not know her *Ankara* from her *Abada*.

"Yep, she did choose it," laughed Amanda. "She has become really good at the whole African style thing. She is so good now that she is even helping create designs. This is one of hers. Like it?"

Both Amina and Siyonna dropped their jaws in surprise. This was really something. In less than a year Mrs Saul-Obi had transitioned from being an interested bystander in African design to a designer. That was impressive and the girls all made the right noises to let Amanda know just how impressed they were. Suddenly, another figure emerged from the parked jeep.

"Dante," said Siyonna, almost to herself, and had to lean on Amina to keep her balance.

Amanda smiled her mischievous smile.

"Oh yeah, forgot to tell you. He flew in yesterday and insisted on bringing me when I told him you were going to be here," she said to Siyonna.

Siyonna wasn't listening anymore as she fixated on the tall, lean figure walking towards her. Gosh, he's so fine, she thought to herself. She had never felt this way about a boy. Scratch that, she had never felt anything for any boy. As far as she was concerned, up until this point, they were pointless and rough. She had little experience of them save for her brother and father who were both much older than her and her cousin Odera, who was an infernal pain. He played pranks on her and teased her endlessly and as far as she was concerned if all young boys were like him, they could all go take a hike.

However, here she stood, speechless and with feelings that were entirely alien to her about a boy she had only met once. She really hadn't the foggiest idea what to say or do when this boy got to her and right now, he was striding confidently across the path to where they were standing. He looked bronzed and confident, tall and very masculine. At 19, a lifetime of American football had made Dante lean and athletic.

"Hello Siyonna," he said in that deep voice with the foreign twang and pushed back his bushy curls.

"Hello," Siyonna just about managed to reply.

Amanda and Amina looked at the two of them in utter amusement as they all stood on Amaka's drive with people walking past them to get to the front door.

"Come on, these two can find us inside when they're ready," said Amanda, grabbing Amina by the arm.

"You look nice," said Dante, now they were alone. Then he smiled a little shyly.

"Thanks, you don't look bad yourself," said Siyonna and they both laughed. "So, you came back yesterday? Wouldn't have thought this was your kind of party?" teased Siyonna, suddenly finding her voice.

"Oh? So, what is my kind of party then?" asked Dante.

"Well you know, big boy parties with busty hostesses and plenty of champagne!"

Dante laughed till tears came to his eyes.

"No, I think not," he said. "This will do and besides, you're here and I get to talk to you, so that's a bonus," he added, again looking shyly at his feet.

Siyonna smiled as she cocked her head and looked at him as if she was seeing him for the first time. He was so good looking, with Amanda's half-moon face but with beautiful faded blue off-green eyes. His skin was bronzed-brown and as far as Siyonna was concerned, he looked every inch a black-Greek hero.

Why she felt so comfortable with him in a way she had never felt with any other boy was beyond her but she simply welcomed the moment and accepted that she liked Dante. At that moment she also realised that she was only 16 and really hadn't the foggiest idea about what it meant to be in a relationship.

"Shall we go in, or would you rather walk?" he asked.

"Let's walk at least for a bit," she replied.

They walked back out of Amaka's drive and headed for the park in the centre of the estate. It was a lovely green space and well looked after, with benches and shade provided by the branches of short acacia trees. They sat and talked about friends, ambitions, schools and what each of them wanted. Siyonna reminded Dante that they were in different places in their lives, with Dante a college guy and she still in secondary school. They were close in age but at this stage, it felt like a lifetime.

"What are we doing Dante?" she asked, verbalizing her fears.

She felt out of her depth and even now talking to Dante, could not quite believe she was with him.

"Siyonna, I know this is complicated but I really do like you. Why don't we be friends for now? What do you think?" he asked.

"Ok," she replied and shrugged.

Truth be known she felt relieved. She was happy to keep in touch with him and be friends. She knew that at 16 she was way too young to consider any other kind of relationship with him and was grateful he felt that way too. They talked some more about everything and laughed together a lot. She felt comfortable with him and very safe. It was almost as if she'd known him all her life. She talked about her brother and sisters, her nephew, her cousins, her world and Dante told her more about the adventures with his grandfather and his dreams of working with jet engines when he graduated.

Siyonna eventually suggested they go back before everyone started wondering where they were and Dante agreed. They returned to the party to strains of Michael Jackson and Justin Timberlake belting out '*Love never felt so good*' on the stereo. People were dancing and singing along and they joined in. The rest of the evening was a blur as the two danced, laughed and spoke to no one else but each other.

Just before 6, Amaka's mum came in with the cake with sixteen candles. As all the guests gushed and gathered around, her siblings also arrived and joined in singing happy birthday. Amaka was the youngest of 3, with an older brother and older sister and like Siyonna, she had been born late to her parents. Her brother had finished University and was already working at one of the banks in Lagos. Her older sister was in the final year of an Architecture degree. They had both been home during the party but the older siblings had sat with their parents in the smaller family room. They had been trying hard to watch a Premier League match with their father, despite the noise of the party downstairs. Amaka's dad was a diehard Arsenal fan and his team had won the match that day so he was in a great mood. He was so happy that even as his wife turned and glared at him muttering something about the idiocy of supporting people 'who don't even know you exist' he still wore the satisfied look of a grateful devotee. If he had heard her, it certainly did nothing to diminish his joy. So, when summoned to come and wish his youngest child a happy birthday, he got up with gusto and a spring in his step.

After Amaka cut her cake, everyone went back to dancing.

"Hello again," said Dante, turning to Siyonna.

Siyonna laughed. She had never had this sort of attention from a boy before. Then again, she had never felt this way about anyone before. They danced some more and it was a bit of a relief to see that Dante really wasn't as confident a dancer as he seemed to be at everything else. Siyonna laughed a lot as she tried to teach him the intricacies of *Azonto* and *Etighi*. Dante gamely carried on, mostly making his own interpretations of the moves Siyonna was making. He really couldn't care less. He was having a ball and he was with Siyonna. That was all that mattered.

When it was time to go, Siyonna went over and said good-bye to Amaka's parents and hugged Amaka. Then as Dante took her hand to walk her to the car, she smiled and gently pulled her hand away. It wouldn't do for Mr Sunday to see that and tell her parents. Mr Sunday looked at the two of them and if he noticed anything, he certainly wasn't letting on. He had watched Siyonna grow from an audacious 5-year-old to the young and beautiful 16-year-old of today. He had always felt a bit protective of her and Siyonna knew it. When they reached the car, Dante said hello to Mr Sunday. Then he held the door open for Siyonna and promised to call as soon as he got home. Amina got in behind and the girls waved Amanda and Dante goodbye. As the car left, Siyonna turned and took one more look at Amaka's house. Dante was still standing in the drive, watching until she was out of sight.

10

Odera Moves West

Siyonna and Dante had spoken often since the party and on one occasion she bumped into him at the Palms Mall where she had been hanging with her friends. They had since managed to go see a movie together with Amina coming along too. On another occasion Dante had joined them when Siyonna and her friends hung out at Amanda's house, spending the day in the annexe watching old movies and eating popcorn. Siyonna had enjoyed being with Dante and her friends. She told her sister Ebele about him when they had their usual talks.

Ebele said she was pleased for her but thought she should tell her parents what was going on so they were not surprised. Siyonna promised she'd think about it and Ebele encouraged her not to take too long about it. Dante was leaving to go back to the States at the end of the week and with her own return to school looming, Siyonna knew it was unlikely she'd get to see him again before he left. She just could not bring herself to discuss Dante with her parents and frankly did not know how they would react, so despite her promise to her sister, she decided not to mention him for now. He'd be gone in less than a week and life would settle back to normal until he returned for Christmas.

Siyonna was back to school and the first week flew by. Friday had been unusually busy. On top of her lessons, she had also been drafted onto the editorial team of the school's quarterly magazine and sat through her first meeting that Friday. It was tough and she would quite happily have given up were it not for the fact that Mother Joseph would see it as a huge dereliction of her responsibilities. The magazine, innocuously called The Flute, was a major part of the girls' lives. Acting as a reporter or editor on The Flute was a status symbol. Reporters had to be interviewed and hired by the editorial team, which itself had members appointed by the school's academic staff. Remaining on the team depended on the quality of your schoolwork as well as how well you performed on the magazine. It remained a highly sought-after post.

Siyonna had contributed articles to the magazine in the past. She wrote an insightful piece on 'Charity as a Duty' after the visit to the Little Grace home after the Charity Day. Her paper had questioned society's dependence on charity to meet the needs of the less fortunate and what role the government had to play. She really believed the government had much more to do in reducing the need for charity and providing fit-for-purpose services, to address welfare gaps in society. It had been such a strong paper that Mother Joseph mentioned it in the assembly as being the sort of deep philosophical thinking on issues of the day she wanted to see in the magazine. Although Mother Joseph's opinion had been that government could not possibly close all the gaps of society, she did acknowledge that there was a middle ground to be found so charity could be more effective, whoever was performing it.

Siyonna's invitation to the editorial team however only came about because the girl she was replacing had done badly in her midterm tests and Mother Joseph felt she was not coping well. This particular morning after assembly,

Mother Joseph simply announced that as the next quarter's pieces were being pulled together, Siyonna was going to be joining the editorial board to replace Elsa Peters whose term on the board had ended.

The meeting took place just after lunch during a study period and Siyonna disagreed with a piece Sally had submitted because she felt it was likely to be offensive to a group of students whom Siyonna felt were the subject of the article. Siyonna felt strongly that the reporters should not write articles picking on specific students and possibly bringing unwanted attention to these girls. Some other girls on the team felt the humour more than made up for whatever embarrassment the subjects would endure. Siyonna disagreed, arguing that the school magazine should not be used as a tool to humiliate students. Eventually, she won the team over and they agreed that the article should be pulled. Sally was sent an email asking her to write another article.

That afternoon both girls met at Literature and from the spiteful look Sally gave her, Siyonna assumed she had seen the email and had concluded Siyonna was the reason her article had been pulled. Oh well, Siyonna thought, whatever. After the run-in they had last term, she doubted Sally would want to confront her again over anything. Literature was a pleasure as always and this term the girls were getting to grips with Wole Soyinka's '*The Man Died*'. Written during his incarceration amid the Nigerian civil war, it explored both the injustice of his incarceration as a political prisoner, fearing for his life and the desperate need for company as he sat in solitary confinement. Siyonna found this book intriguing but challenging and was glad that Mr Abibi was taking her class in literature this year. Mr Jake Abibi was a student of Soyinka and could guide them through the complexities of the writer's thoughts and read between the lines of the somewhat complex musings which made up the book. It was not an easy read, but Siyonna was so intrigued by the subject of why Soyinka had ended up in jail that she lapped up the book and kept working at it.

The lesson ended with the quote: *"The man dies in him who keeps quiet in the face of injustice."* Mr Abibi asked the girls to think about the quote in the light of the book and its impact on social awareness and justice, then they were to write an essay before the next class arguing pro or against the quote. In his words, 'there are no right or wrong answers, just persuasive arguments'. Siyonna smiled. She liked Mr Abibi. He carried a wild afro like Soyinka and was skinny. He also had an affinity for tight, gaudy clothes and could never pass for fashionable. If anything, he was quite the opposite, especially for someone so young. He had that rakish disregard for fashion you'd associate with a revolutionary or a socialist. He had once described himself as 'minimalist' and Siyonna could find no better adjective for him! But he was smart. He could quote lines from books with ease as if he had just put the books down. His classes were always such fun and high tempo as he whizzed through texts and detailed analysis of books. He pushed the girls to read more and they responded to his coaching and cajoling, with gusto.

As Siyonna packed her books to leave, Sally suddenly showed up in front of her.

"I know you pulled my article," she said. "None of the other girls on the editorial team would have done it. I was pretty upset initially but I guess I sort of see why what I wrote could have been offensive. I will take it away and rework it. With all the other work I have to do, it might take me a while to get this done, but I will do it."

With that, she turned and left. Siyonna slumped back in her chair in sheer disbelief. She had guessed that Sally would be upset at her article being pulled and also knew that Sally was likely to confront her about it. But she had not expected Sally to see things her way and actually accept that she may well have crossed a line with her article. Sally? Siyonna thought, what a turnaround. Who would ever have thought? And it wasn't even a blue moon!

"Come on, class is over. I'm sure your grandpa driver will be growing a wrinkle waiting for you," said her friend Lola, as she gathered herself and stood up to go.

Siyonna laughed at Lola's description of Mr Sunday. He was getting on and she also wondered sometimes as Mr Sunday said "Yes sir" to her dad, if he was really younger than her dad. She knew she dared not ask. Mr Sunday had been with the family so long and was held in such high regard by her parents that not even her big brother Ike dared cross him. So, she would walk to the car as demurely as she could, say hello to him and ask how his day has been so far. She liked him. He was more like an uncle than an aide and growing up she had relied on his good counsel more than once. So, grizzly or not, she quite liked Mr Sunday and knew she'd better hurry otherwise she'd have to explain why she was late. She fell in beside Lola.

"So," said Lola. "I saw the little witch Sally hovering over you. Is everything Ok?"

"Yes," said Siyonna, smiling.

When she gave Lola a quick update of what had transpired between Sally and her, Lola shook her head in disbelief.

"Well, well, what do you know? There's hope yet!" she said and they both laughed. "That's my ride, baby girl. See you Monday," she said, giving Siyonna a hug before running off to get into the car with her mum.

Siyonna walked over to her own car, said good afternoon to Mr Sunday and got in for the ride home. As they pulled up at home, she saw the usual familiar cars in the compound. Ebele's old car was parked at the far end of the big drive, waiting for the day Siyonna would learn to drive. Ebele's last act of sisterly love before she left for England was to gift the car to her younger sister. Siyonna had pledged to take lessons and get behind the wheel of her new car but thought it best to do that during the summer break. Right now, there was just too much going on at school to add the complexity of learning to drive. Besides she had no immediate need to drive. If she were to attend a local university next year, she could not see her parents letting her keep a car there. The lovely red Toyota would either remain parked and 'warmed' by others, or sold soon.

She shrugged as she took in the other cars, mostly her father's company cars. Then she saw the black jeep and her heart jumped into her mouth. Black jeep. Dante's car. What was he doing here? Mr Sunday must have seen the perplexed look on her face and shrugged as if to say 'don't ask me, I know nothing of it'. Siyonna walked tentatively into the house, her heart pounding so loudly she could hear it in her ears. What was she to say to her mum? If there was precedence for dating in this family, it must have happened long before she came along. She imagined a long weekend of recriminations ahead of her, not to mention her father's long disapproving looks! As she walked through the sitting area, she heard voices coming from the kitchen and headed there.

Dante was on a bar stool with his back to her, while her mum sat on the settee by the long bay window with none other than Mrs Saul-Obi beside her.

"Good afternoon" murmured Siyonna, timidly as all eyes turned on her.

Dante smiled his usual disarming smile and as confused as she felt at the moment, Siyonna was struck again at just how handsome he looked.

"Onna-mma, welcome home," said her mum in an unusually warm greeting.

Mrs Saul-Obi also smiled a welcome.

"Aunty Annette here came around to discuss a possible collaboration with our stores," said her mum to Siyonna's puzzled, inquiring look. "Selling a new range of clothing design she's working on. Very impressive."

Obiageli looked at Mrs Saul-Obi and both ladies smiled. Their conversations had always been warm and this was the first time they'd actually been alone without their husbands. It was clear there was a mutual appreciation between them and the two practically ignored Siyonna and Dante as they got into a deep conversation about strategy and sales projections. Siyonna's mum was quite a businesswoman. She had married young and studied for a business degree from the University of Lagos, whilst raising her young family. However, rather than taking a job after she graduated, she had started a series of petty businesses that fitted around her needs as a mother. Over time, these different concerns had grown and she now ran two market stalls that sold fabrics, as well as 3 Supermarkets dotted around the Island, the newest and biggest of which was Bene's. Her mum was keen to develop Bene's into the sort of mini-market that stocked everything from food to clothes and even pharmaceuticals, and when the store's building had come up for sale, she had convinced Mr Nduka to invest in it as a means of growing the business.

As the two women became more engrossed in their conversation, Siyonna looked at Dante and inclined her head, subtly asking him to follow her. As he got up, Obiageli turned to look at them.

"Ah good. Siyonna take Dante to the anteroom and get him something to drink. Dante will also have something to eat, yes?"

Dante shook his head to indicate he wasn't hungry but as a typical African mum, Obiageli ignored the gesture.

"Siyonna warm some of the pepper soup for him. I'm sure he'll like that."

Siyonna nodded and headed for the anteroom off the living room with Dante in tow.

"Are you alright?" he said, smiling as soon as they were out of range. "I wanted to see you before I left tomorrow. I offered to bring mum. You looked as if you'd seen a ghost. I didn't mean to make you uncomfortable."

"It's ok really," she smiled. "I just wasn't expecting you and wouldn't want my mum getting the wrong idea about us. I really couldn't live it down! Let me get you a drink now. What would you like, a soft drink perhaps? Or a malt?"

Dante was still getting used to the Nigerian habit of describing sodas as soft drinks. He guessed all the sugar in them made them soft, perhaps softer than the lagers and spirits that were equally popular in Nigeria. He opted for a Coca-Cola and Siyonna went off to get it. She came back quickly with a tray with Coke, ice and a glass and a small bowl of pepper-soup, the chef had made in the Nigerian way of mixed-meat, garnished heavily with chilli and served piping hot. He smiled and thanked Siyonna as he tucked into his pepper-soup. It smelled delicious and even though he knew it was likely to be too hot for his palette, he craved it all the same. First taste and he was pleasantly surprised. It wasn't too spicy. Result! Dante thought.

"Thank you, Siyonna! Did you make this yourself?" he asked cheekily.

"What's the right answer, oh master? Should your little lady say yes? Would that make *nna'nyi* happy" Siyonna teased him back.

When his face contorted into an embarrassed 'oops didn't mean that', Siyonna laughed, got up and touched him on the head.

"Relax, I'm just messing with you. Yep, I make a mean pepper-soup but no, I did not make this one. This one's the Chef's special and my dad absolutely loves it. Would you give me a minute? I need to get out of my school uniform."

"Ok. I'll be here," Dante replied.

As Siyonna changed, she thought about the events of the day and the shock at Dante's visit. She had to admit that it hadn't turned out that bad after all. She was happy that her mother did not appear to read anything into the visit. She changed into a pair of jogging bottoms and a tee-shirt and put her uniform shirt, skirt and socks in her laundry bin. Then she slipped her feet in a pair of leather slippers and ran downstairs to Dante.

He was still gushing about the pepper-soup so Siyonna asked if he wanted more.

"Oh no, I couldn't possibly," he said, which Siyonna read to mean 'yes, please', so she simply went and got him more from the pot in the kitchen.

Her mum and his mum were still talking and barely noticed her. She went back and a grateful Dante took the bowl from her and tucked in. She also brought him another bottle of coke and some ice. As he ate, they talked. His flight was tomorrow afternoon but he would be back at Christmas. He'd be spending Christmas in the family country home in Ogidi. He hoped he would be back in time to see Siyonna before heading off there.

Soon his mum came out and he got up to go. He hugged Siyonna and they all walked out to the car.

"Thank you, Annette, I believe this line will do well," said her mum as the Saul-Obis climbed into the car. "We'll give you all the support you need and then take it from there."

They waved them goodbye before walking back together into the house. They'd only just locked the door when the bell buzzed. That's weird, Siyonna thought. Dante's mum must have forgotten something and they'd come back. That meant another opportunity to see Dante! Siyonna rushed to the door, threw it open and the smile froze on her lips because standing there with his suitcase in hand was her cousin Odera.

Odera's father, Uncle Obi, was her dad's older brother. After their father died, Uncle Obi had looked after her dad and Uncle Udozor. He had worked many jobs before he eventually started a transport business and ended up as a government contractor. He had retired and lived mostly in Umuabado, though he also had a home in Enugu. He was very close to Siyonna's dad, and so were their children, apart from maybe Siyonna and Odera. They were closer in age in the extended family than anyone else and enjoyed a definite cat and dog relationship. They fought often and Siyonna did not have many fond memories of her cousin. Now, here he was at her front door, luggage in hand. As the two stared at each other, Siyonna in shock and Odera in sly amusement, Siyonna's mum came up behind her.

"Odera!" she cried. "Nice to see you, son. How did you get here? I thought you'd call from the airport to get picked up?"

"Hello, auntie. No, I decided to make my own way and not make a fuss. I got a cab," he replied, grinning.

"Come in, come in!" said Obiageli. "Come to the dining room and I'll get you something to eat. Look at you; you're all bones and legs. Don't they feed you at school?"

"Oh Auntie Oby," he laughed. "You are funny! Of course, they feed me and I also cook. I just decided to lose some weight and get fit."

Siyonna made a face. Her cousin caught her and winked. Siyonna stared at him and had to admit he looked different. He was an undergraduate at the University of Nigeria in Nsukka and seemed to have a newfound confidence in himself. His body was beginning to firm up and he looked like he worked out regularly.

"So why are you here? And that suitcase, you don't look like a guy on a two-week visit." Siyonna blurted out.

She really was keen to get to the bottom of why her cousin was here and seeing that her mother was never going to get to the key question, she thought it best to take the bull by the horn, so to speak. As his food arrived, Odera sat down and thanked Eunice, the housekeeper.

"I am here for my industrial attachment, which I shall do at Uncle Zach's firm, so they decided it was best for me to stay here. Yep, that's right, my attachment is for an academic year so I'll be here for a year."

Odera knew just how uncomfortable and angry his younger cousin was feeling and relished her torment. Obiageli laughed and got up to leave, asking Siyonna to help Odera settle in after his lunch. He would be taking Chieme's old room. With that, Obiageli left to get ready and head to her office at Bene's. She wanted to be there when they did the stock-taking this evening.

After eating, Odera gathered his tray and took it to the kitchen with Siyonna in tow. He washed his dishes and cutlery and put them on the rack by the sink. Then he dried his hands.

"So where do I pack my bones then Siyonna?" he asked.

She mimicked the 'where-do-I-pack-my-bones' as she turned to go upstairs. Odera laughed and followed her. He would be in Chieme's old room, right next to Siyonna's. It was a big room and very tidy, reflective of Chieme's fastidious tidiness. It hadn't been lived in since Chieme got married, and as her husband and parents-in-law lived in Lagos, she hardly stayed at home anymore. When she did visit, she preferred to stay in the guest room.

Siyonna and Odera stared at the room for a while, another reminder of just how life had changed and people moved on. Siyonna always wondered how her parents coped with the fact that all their children, save for her, had now left home. Did they miss the kids? Did they mind that the house was now quieter? Whatever they felt, it wasn't a conversation they shared with her. Life certainly changed quickly, Siyonna thought, at least for her. She had always been the only one home, for the most part, as the others had come and gone. At least she always had Ebele, until now, she too had left home, big time.

"I'll go get the beddings," she said to her cousin as she turned to leave the room.

"Thank you," said Odera, starting to unpack his suitcase.

Siyonna came back and helped him make the bed. She was surprised to see his clothes were all ironed and put away tidily.

"So, who washed and ironed all your clothes?" she couldn't help but ask him. "What poor person did you con into doing your laundry?"

"Me," he said, laughing. "I did the laundry, ironed and folded my clothes. I have changed you know, Siyonna. I am no longer the child you used to know."

Siyonna rolled her eyes in disbelief and told him she was off to do her work and she'd see him at dinner.

"If you need anything, just knock on my door," she said on her way out.

Odera smiled and threw her a mock salute as he continued unpacking.

Her mum came back just in time for dinner. Zach Nduka hated having his dinner without his wife, so wherever they were, they always made sure they returned home in time to have dinner together. Siyonna was just finishing off her chemistry homework when her mum called her for dinner. She came down, hugged her dad and asked how his day went.

"Alright, I guess," he said and gave Siyonna a brief update on the challenges the business was currently facing.

Ikechukwu or Ike as everyone affectionately called him, now effectively ran the company, as Siyonna's dad was semi-retired. The company was going through a difficult time as one of the state governments owed the company a significant amount of money and insisted on dragging their heels on the issue. Zach Nduka explained to his family that he was working tirelessly with Ike to avoid redundancies. He had already sold his coveted Mercedes Benz to raise funds and told Siyonna that unfortunately, some company cars would have to go, including Ebele's. Siyonna was fine with this. Though Ebele had promised her that car, she was nowhere near ready to start driving. She felt no particular affinity to the car. What she cared about though, was her father's wellbeing. She told him that as long as it made life easier for him, she was happy for him to sell the car. Zach had never cried, at least not in front of Siyonna. But that evening, she could have sworn she saw tears in his eyes.

Thankfully the conversation soon swung around to Annette and Dante's visit and when Obiageli teasingly declared that Siyonna fancied Dante, Siyonna's dad raised an eyebrow.

"Funny," he said cheekily. "Nobody brought me any palm wine with all these goings-on."

"Dad!" gasped Siyonna. "I am only sixteen! No one's bringing you anything on my behalf, thank you. I am still a child and have many years to go before I even begin to consider marriage. Dante and I are just friends, don't mind mum!"

"Ok oh!" said Mr. Nduka, airily.

Siyonna smiled as her dad went back to his plate of rice and stewed beef, with *moi-moi*. Typical mum, she thought. She should have known that her mum's show at being a perfect hostess masked a suspicion that there was something going on between Siyonna and Dante. Mum! Siyonna thought.

"Boyfriend, eh?" giggled Odera. "My, my, I didn't see that coming. We have to vet this chap, make sure he's good enough for one's precious cousin," he said with a twinkle in his eyes.

"Oh Lord please give it a rest!" said Siyonna and went back to her dinner.

Her parents looked at each other and smiled. The house will be warm again with these two. Zach Nduka certainly missed the sights and sounds of a big family since all the kids grew up and left home.

Siyonna woke up the next morning to two things: glorious sunlight streaming into her room as a reminder that she had forgotten to draw her blinds last night; a noise that sounded like someone being strangled from next door in Chieme's room. Odera! She jumped out of bed, grabbed her housecoat and ran next door only to find Odera under the single-seater sofa that usually sat by the window. He was using it as a dumbbell as he lay down on the carpet naked to the waist and pushed the sofa up and down. As Siyonna stood open-mouthed by the door, Odera gently set the sofa down and got up, dripping with sweat.

"You Ok?" he asked.

"I should be the one asking you that, shouldn't I?" she replied. "Are you ok? I heard a sound from my room like you were being strangled, only to find you using the sofa as weights! Who does that?" she said, genuinely perplexed.

"Makes perfectly good sense," grinned Odera. "I needed to do my morning exercise. Works perfectly well in the absence of a gym."

Siyonna sighed and went back to her room as Odera resumed his routine. By the time she had showered and come downstairs, Odera was already at the dining table with her parents.

"Morning mum, dad," she said airily as she took a plate and put a slice of toast and egg on it.

"Morning Onna-mma, haven't you forgotten your cousin?" said her dad.

"We already saw each other this morning. He was using the sofa in Chieme's room as a dumbbell and woke me up with his grunting!"

Zach Nduka stopped munching on his toast, regarded Odera for a while.

"Ingenious," he declared. "Nothing like devising exercises that utilize everyday implements. Good thinking OD."

"Thank you, uncle," beamed the annoying Odera.

Even Siyonna's mum, Obiageli nodded approvingly as if the man had just discovered a new source of renewable energy. Siyonna shook her head and muttered 'good grief' as she sat down for breakfast.

Breakfast done, her dad picked up his golf bag and headed out to the car. Mr Sunday was off today so he would have to drive himself to his game at Ikoyi Club. As he left,

Siyonna asked her mum if she could go over to see Dante off with Amanda.

"Yes," she said. "But there is nobody to take you. I have to go to my shop in Balogun Market to receive a delivery and have to rush back to the Island immediately afterwards. So Bayo can't take you, unfortunately."

Oh no, Siyonna thought, and then Odera piped up.

"I can take her. We can use Ebele's car and also give the engine a run at the same time. I'm not doing anything else today."

Obiageli turned to Siyonna as if to say 'well?' Siyonna said yes, that would be fine and also said thank you to her cousin. Not like she had any choice. It was either that, or she missed the chance to see Dante off. Obiageli agreed but asked Odera to use one of the other cars instead, as Ebele's car was being picked up by the new owner today. Siyonna cleared up breakfast with Odera's help and then went to her room to read. They would be heading off to the airport late afternoon and hopefully, she would catch Dante before he crossed into the departure area.

When she came down at about 3 that afternoon, Odera was ready in his trademark tight blue jeans and trainers and a black *Adire* shirt. Her cousin was turning into quite a handsome young man, Siyonna grudgingly admitted to herself as they headed for the blue Honda. They got in and Odera gently eased the car out of the drive and onto the road. Soon they had joined the traffic heading out of Lekki towards Ikoyi through the new Lekki toll bridge and Odera drove carefully through Lekki towards Ikoyi onto the Third Mainland Bridge. The Third Mainland Bridge was long and provided the main access route from Lagos Island into the mainland. Once Odera got on the bridge, he opened the Honda up and put his foot down.

"I'm not sure this car has ever gone this fast before," said Siyonna.

"Don't worry," he laughed. "I'm not doing more than 70, honest."

Siyonna muttered that it didn't feel like it and lapsed into silence again as Odera connected his phone to the car and started playing Jazz, drumming his fingers on the steering wheel as he hummed softly to the tunes. Amazing, Siyonna thought. How could somebody so young like Jazz? It must be a provincial thing, she concluded.

They arrived at Murtala Muhammed International Airport just as it was getting busy. Odera let her off and told her he would keep circling till she came out again, and to call if she didn't see him. She ran in past the security guards and caught sight of Dante's tall frame talking to Amanda. She came up behind him and poked him lightly.

"You came!" they said in unison as Siyonna smiled.

Siyonna and Dante hugged and said their goodbyes. He promised to call when he got back. Then he went through immigration and was gone. Amanda hugged her friend and the girls left the airport together. Amanda got in her car and promised to come and see Siyonna tomorrow. After a while, Siyonna found Odera as he came around in another circle. She must have looked miserable because as they drove away, Odera decided to be quite nice to her.

"Right young lady, let me cheer you up. Why don't I take you for a lovely ice-cream?"

Siyonna looked at her cousin with new admiration.

"You'll do that for me?" she asked.

"Of course," he laughed. "You're not my favourite cousin for nothing. So come on, where's a good place?"

"Let's do the Ice Cream Factory at the Lekki Peninsula. It rocks!" she said and settled back happily for the drive back to the Island. Lovely, she thought. Nothing like a big bowl of ice cream; perfect for setting the blues aside.

11

Christmas at Umuabado

Every other year, Uncle Obi would decree that everybody come back to Umuabado for Christmas. Siyonna loved Christmases at the village because it was the only time the entire family was ever together in one place. All her cousins came home, her sisters and their families and her brother too. Everybody would come home to the house.

Up until her sister, Chieme got married, her dad's house would host all her immediate family and there had been enough room for everybody. However, with the family growing through marriage, her dad had extended the house in the village, adding an extra floor with a suite of rooms. Ike and his family would stay upstairs along with Siyonna's oldest sister Adaobi, who had two children of her own. They were twins and couldn't have been more than two-years-old the last time Siyonna saw them. She couldn't wait to see them again. Nnamdi, Adaobi's husband, was much older than her and everybody called him brother Nnamdi. It seemed quite inappropriate to simply call him Nnamdi. He was a big man and her mum said he was very intelligent. He was a Professor of Chemistry in Canada and always brought Siyonna beautiful gifts whenever he visited. He was quiet and smiled a lot and Obiageli and the girls teased him endlessly.

As Siyonna sat in class, she dreamt of Christmas in the village. Her parents called it the *'mass return'*, probably because so many people returned home from wherever they lived and some of them probably never visited the village except at Christmastime. She was still in the middle of her reverie when Mr Baffo, the Maths tutor startled her.

"Miss Nduka," he asked. "What is wrong with the equation on the board?"

Siyonna jumped and stared at the board.

"The equation is right, sir, but the factors applied are wrong."

Mr Baffo smiled. He liked Siyonna. Very bright, he thought. Even when she was distracted, you could always rely on her to pull it together. What a tidy mind, he thought. He nodded and proceeded to work on the equation.

The mood at Our Lady's was busy. The girls were all preparing for their end of term exams and the results would be out before they broke for Christmas. Girls who did not do well might find that their presents reflected just how poorly they had performed, so everyone put their best into it. Amanda thought the number of exams she sat at Our Lady's was simply too much. She'd lived in the States all her life except for a stint in Dubai whilst her dad was working there. She always maintained she never had to do as many elsewhere. Siyonna just shrugged. This was the only life she knew. You studied and prepared for exams, constantly and if you did poorly, everybody heard about it. She believed it best never to be the one in the unenviable position of being the butt of the class joke.

At the end of Maths, Mr Baffo rattled off a series of chapters the girls were to work on as an assignment and submit to him in two days' time. Their next lesson would be the last before their exams. Mr Baffo was Head of Maths. He always reminded Siyonna of Einstein. A black Einstein, more like. Tall and with a thick moustache, he was incredibly bright and intensely in love with Mathematics. He had co-written several books on the subject and one of his had become the workbook of choice in many secondary schools. But Mr Baffo was also incredibly impatient with what he liked to describe as 'academic indolence'. His belief was that the pupil must participate in the exploration of the question and achieving the final answer. He couldn't abide a student who didn't try to at least articulate what they didn't understand. He wouldn't win many popularity contests at Our Lady's but he was well respected. Students in his class understood his exacting standards and worked hard to keep up with him.

As the girls left the class clutching his most recent set of assignments, Amanda fell into step with Siyonna and Amina.

"Guys," she said. "You have got to help me. I think I may be falling behind in Maths."

Siyonna looked very surprised and felt shocked that Amanda had waited till now to say anything, with the exams just a week away.

"What is it you need help with?" she asked.

"Everything," groaned Amanda. "Binomial expansions, Logarithms, the lot! Dad tried to help me and I think he made things worse. You gotta help me, girls!"

She looked desperately at Siyonna for support. She always seemed strong in Maths and understood the topics covered quite comfortably. Siyonna figured that by helping Amanda, she'd also be revising her own Maths and preparing for the exams.

"I tell you what," said Siyonna. "Why don't we catch up at study period and I'll work you through some of the principles and we'll take it from there? We can go to the tutorial room in the old block. There's no one there and we can work without bothering anybody?"

"Splendid!" beamed Amanda, as they all set off to the lab for Chemistry.

After Chemistry, the friends headed to the old section of the school, which had a string of offices and classrooms, mostly used as private study rooms by the students. Room 002 was Siyonna's favourite because it was right at the end of the corridor. It was quiet and private and hardly ever attracted any attention from either teachers or curious students. While Amina went off to the library to start on her homework, Amaka joined Amanda and Siyonna and all three went to room 002.

When they arrived, they found two other girls huddled together whispering and scribbling furiously. They gave them a furtive look then continued scribbling. Siyonna thought she recognized one of them, Dobi Mekpa. Dobi usually had a small smile playing on her face. She had a reputation as a girl who knew how to fix most things. Siyonna had always known her in passing but wouldn't really say they were friends. Today though, Dobi shifted defensively as the three of them walked in and kept glaring at them until they sat down.

As Siyonna and her friends went through examples and Amaka and Amanda started picking up the concepts Siyonna was explaining, they all decided to take a crack at the homework Mr Baffo had set them. Just then Dobi and her friend got up and walked out of the room. The girls looked at each other.

"Strange," said Siyonna. "What's with those two?"

Amaka and Amanda shrugged and they went back to studying.

As the week drew to a close Siyonna forgot all about the episode. She worked with Amanda who was soaking up everything she told her as well as asking her parents to get her a tutor. Mr Baffo was most definitely going way too fast and losing her. Amanda was hell-bent on a career in finance and felt she needed to be not just good, but perfect in Maths. She had her heart set on one of the big American Universities for her degree and knew she needed impeccable grades to have any hope of getting there.

The exams kicked off on the Monday with Literature and Spanish and according to their timetable, would end with Mathematics on the last day. All the sixth form exams would take place in the school auditorium, mimicking the school certificate board exams. The girls were placed randomly around the room, in rows. Sitting right next to Siyonna was Dobi. She sat there staring straight ahead. Siyonna gave her a curious glance and went back to looking at the question paper in front of her.

Finally, the invigilators asked the girls to start. As Siyonna worked on the Maths questions, she noticed Dobi becoming distressed and looking furtively around the hall. Siyonna ignored her and got on with her work. She really couldn't afford not to finish. She considered that the most important thing of all. At the end of the exam, their papers were collected and as she left the hall she noticed that the teachers had detained Dobi and two other sixth formers. Amanda, Amina, Dupe and Amaka caught up with her as they excitedly talked about the exam and how they found it. When the conversation got to the topic of Dobi being detained, Siyonna told them about Dobi's muttering whilst they were sitting the exam and all the girls agreed that this was quite peculiar behaviour.

The conversation soon changed to their plans for Christmas. The term had finished. Students would come in the next day to watch the nativity play and have their Christmas lunch and by one o'clock they'd leave school. Girls who did not live in Lagos would be taken by school bus to the airport and handed over to their designated airlines for their journeys home. A euphoric, satisfying feeling of freedom and joy pervaded the whole school at the thought of the four-week Christmas holiday.

Siyonna hugged her friends and made her way to where Mr Sunday had parked, waiting patiently for her. She got in the car, said hello to him and sighed audibly.

"*How ya exams take be?*" Mr Sunday asked her in his trademark Pidgin English.

Siyonna smiled as she turned to look out the window at the familiar sites of Ikoyi as they drove towards the bridge. Mr Sunday would speak nothing but Pidgin. She could say he was singularly responsible for teaching her the popular West African slang language.

"E good o, thanks Mr Sunday. Many of the tings I prepare na im they come bring for the exam," she said.

"Good, very good. E better to dey prepared all the time. Well done, my daughter," said Mr Sunday, nodding his head in approval. This Siyonna na good pickin, he thought. Oga Nduka dey lucky well well with im pickin dem.

As they drove through Gerrard Road and into Alexander Road, Siyonna admired the new buildings springing up everywhere as the old colonial-style homes were torn down and replaced by modern multi-unit apartments. They looked beautiful and Ike was always talking about how lovely these new flats were. Perhaps one day he'd buy one so he could move Nnedi and little Afam to the Island.

Soon they were on the new bridge across to Lekki and Siyonna found the traffic surprisingly light for a weekday. They pulled into Siyonna's drive and she thanked Mr Sunday, gathered her things and headed indoors. As usual, she was alone. Her dad was most likely at the golf club where he seemed to spend most of his time these days and her mum was likely to be at one of her Supermarkets. Siyonna did not mind the solitude. As the youngest child and with siblings much older than her, she had learnt a long time ago to enjoy her own company. She went upstairs into her parent's room. The door to the bathroom in their suite was open and as she looked at the sunken bath, she suddenly had the urge to take a soak. She quickly ran the bath, went back to her room and undressed, wrapped herself in her bathrobe and headed back to her parent's room to relax in the bath.

As she lay there letting the soft, soapy suds wash away the stress and pressure of the past few weeks of preparing for her exams, she thought about Christmas in Umuabado and smiled. She loved the village especially when everybody was around. With all the families visiting and the house full, there was always a carnival feel to the season. Siyonna was also looking forward to seeing the masquerades that came out at Christmastime and would come to their family's compound to entertain. They would shower praises on all the Nduka men and dance in the compound. Her father and his brothers would give the masquerades and their helpers, food and drink and money as well and they would leave very happy. The masquerades were supposed to be imbued with the spirits of the ancestors, so they did not eat and girls were forbidden from getting too close to them. Siyonna and Odera would still sneak out of the compound and follow them at a safe distance. Eventually, the masquerades would notice they were being followed by the uninitiated and turn and chase them a few feet, with their long canes swishing menacingly through the air. The cousins and others in the crowd would run, only to come back when they felt the threat had passed. You never really wanted to be caught by those canes and the smaller masquerades tended to be quite nimble and capable of getting away from their minders as they chased down luckless girls or members of the public to flog.

Siyonna smiled as she thought about just how lovely Christmas at the village usually was. She really couldn't wait for Christmas.

As Siyonna lay there daydreaming, she heard the door to her parent's room open and her mum walked in, heading for the bathroom.

"Siyonna when did we start sharing this bathroom, eh?" Obiageli asked her daughter, using her full name. "Abeg use your own bathroom madam." She said, walking out before Siyonna could respond.

Siyonna smiled. Famous last words, she thought. Use her own bathroom? Yes but the bath was no way as comfortable and inviting as this one. Oh well, she thought, dreaming time's over. She got up, rinsed herself and drained the water from the bath. It had been a good soak and well worth it. Wrapped up, she picked up her toilet bag and headed for the door.

Her mum lay sprawled on the bed, with the television on the wall tuned into CNN showing a program about endangered big game in Southern Africa.

"Hello mummy," Siyonna said with a demure smile.

She walked over to the bed, kissed her mother and clambered in next to her, hugging her. Obiageli looked at her youngest daughter and smiled.

"So, madam how was school today? Tomorrow's your last day, right?"

"Yes. School was ok. I have finished my exams and I guess we'll get the results before we leave tomorrow. We had the strangest experience at our last exams. This girl sitting in the row next to mine just kept mumbling all the time and when we were leaving, she got detained by the invigilators."

"Hmm. Most peculiar," said Obiageli. "You don't think she was having some kind of breakdown, do you?"

"That's interesting mum. I don't know. Perhaps she was. I just found the whole experience slightly worrying. Also, last week when we were revising for the test, the same girl had been in a room studying with her friends and when we came in, she had looked really uncomfortable with us being there, almost as if she did not want us to be there. She left soon after we came in."

"Hmmm," said Obiageli again, just as the CNN program focused on Lagos.

Both Siyonna and her mum sat up and looked at the screen as the CNN reporter panned on the business districts on the Island and talked about entrepreneurship and just how enterprising Nigerians were. Then it panned on the poorer outskirts of Lagos and spoke about people getting on with it even in the face of the most challenging conditions.

"It's hard to imagine some people live like this," muttered Siyonna, more to herself than anything.

"Yes, you're right," said her mother. "And very privileged, never forget that. Neither your father nor I were as privileged as you are. We have done as well as we did because we took advantage of most opportunities that presented themselves to us and thankfully, made a life for our children and ourselves. It is your duty to do the same too. Get a good education and change the world so you too can be a blessing not just to your family but to the wider world around you and people less privileged than you."

Siyonna thought for a while. She knew she was privileged. Granted, attending Our Lady's often felt like being in a different world cocooned from the realities of life on the outside. Most of the girls came from privileged homes or their families wouldn't be able to afford the expensive fees. There were a few less-privileged girls on scholarship from the school board but the majority of the girls were from privileged homes. Siyonna thought some more about poverty and what it meant. She could articulate the inability to buy all you needed but was also curious about the social impact of poverty.

"What does poverty really mean?" she asked her mum. "Beyond the ability to buy what you want when you want it. What does it really mean to be poor?"

Obiageli swung her long legs off the bed and walked to the big bay window overlooking the compound all the way to the East fence. She had always liked this view and to make sure it was unhindered had had flower bushes planted around the edge of the fence and a beautiful gazebo in the middle with a swing-chair. She had always dreamt of going out there and losing herself in a good book while enjoying the summer smells of bougainvillaea. However, with her busy schedule and the challenges of running both a home and a growing business, the opportunity never arose. So, she comforted herself with admiring the well-maintained lawn and flower bushes as well as the gazebo she had designed, from the comfort of her bedroom.

Poverty? How could she explain to her daughter how she and her sisters had to hawk wares on the streets of Enugu to earn enough money to help their parents with their fees? How her younger brother had almost been killed when he was knocked down by a car while hawking boiled peanuts and afterwards, as he scrambled to his feet, he'd been more concerned with the peanuts now scattered on the ground like petals to an uncaring bride, than his own health? And how meeting Zach Nduka had changed her life? He had half-teased, half encouraged her to look at education as a series of different events, all disparate in nature but leading to enlightenment and financial independence in the end. Like her, he'd been born dirt-poor. He had also had to do petty jobs to survive and had lived with his brother Obi who had effectively taken over his upbringing after their father died. Life then was a struggle. But Zach had always been strong and focused and saw opportunities everywhere. He was already an engineer and no longer poor when they met. Working for the government, he had been hoping to get a job with a large construction firm that had won a contract to build federal roads. The offer of the job finally came through and as soon as he had it, Zach proposed to her and took Obi to see her father as was required by tradition.

"To put it simply," she said. "Poverty is the inability to afford the basic needs of shelter, food, security and education. You see the effects of it every day in children who hawk things on the street to support their parents and people who live with serious illnesses but cannot afford to get the treatment they need. You don't have to be a multi-millionaire but you have had a good start in life and the rest is up to you."

Siyonna rolled over on her stomach and supported her chin on her hands as she listened to her mum. She sort of understood what her mother was saying even though she had never lived it. Getting up eventually, she hugged her mum, thanked her and left her parent's room.

The next morning, she got downstairs only to find that her dad had already left. She knew she wasn't late because this was the time they usually set off every morning. As she turned to go back into the house, she met Odera.

"Uncle Zach had to make the first flight to Port Harcourt for a meeting so couldn't wait for you. I'll drop you. Come on," he said, walking purposefully towards the cars parked at the side of the house.

"You have a car now?" asked Siyonna, running after him.

"Yep," replied Odera, unlocking the blue Honda Accord. "I have to help with a lot of our build projects in this region and need to be able to get up and go. Ike assigned me this car. Cool, isn't it?" he grinned.

She guided him to her school and as he dropped her off, her friends all gathered around her.

"Cheating on my brother already?" laughed Amanda. "Who's the hunk?"

Siyonna looked back as Odera threw her a mock-salute and gunned the Honda out of the drop off zone towards the gate.

"Amanda for the umpteenth time, Dante and I are just friends! And that, my dears, is my cousin Odera. All grown up and hunky but alas, still my cousin Odera," Siyonna responded with a smile.

"Hmmm," said Amanda. "What a dish. Introduce me?"

"No 'Manda dearie, he is super shy and not your type! Besides just like me, you are far too young to be dating a boy at university!"

They all burst out laughing.

"Get to assembly, girls!" came the familiar voice of Mother Joseph, prompting the girls to walk quickly into the hall.

When Mother Joseph came up to address the assembled girls that morning, she looked stern and business-like. She stated how she was proud of the girls and how they always comported themselves with dignity and respect for the school's rules. Then she went on to state how disappointed she had been to find out that a few girls in year six had cheated on the Christmas term exams. The school discovered last week that the exam papers for Maths had been copied from Mr Baffo's laptop, which had gone missing for a day and mysteriously turned up at the science lab the following day. The school had reset the papers without making any announcements. The cheating students were caught because they had prepared for the wrong questions and found themselves in a pickle when faced by the new exam paper. As a result, all three girls led by Dobi Mekpa had been expelled from the school and their parents informed. The school had standards to maintain and cheating simply went against the very moral fabric of Our Lady's. At the announcement that Dobi and the other girls had been expelled, a horrified gasp ran through the assembly. To be expelled in your final year just did not bear thinking about.

After Assembly, the conversation buzzed a little over the expelled girls but only for a while. From the hall, the girls went straight to the school Christmas carol service, which for the 6th formers would be their last one ever. After the carol service there was a break and then it was time for the nativity play, painstakingly put together by the junior forms. The production was great and left Siyonna wondering about her own performance all those years ago. She had to admit that this performance way excelled her class's version. Come to think of it, the nativity production seemed to improve every year, with each new class outperforming the one before. After the play, they enjoyed a delicious Christmas lunch, with roast turkey and all the trimmings. Then, that was it, end of school, beginning of Christmas holidays. The staff had already emailed the students' exam results to their parents and for most of them, the scene had been set for what sort of Christmas they would expect.

Siyonna, Dupe and Amanda accompanied Amina to her dormitory to help her pack, aware that without their assistance, she would quite likely leave half her stuff behind. Amina was coming home with Siyonna and would leave for Abuja early the next day. They decided Amina should leave the bulk of her things behind and only take some of her books, toiletries and laundry. She grabbed the small valise with the things she needed and left to catch her ride with Siyonna. At the car park, the girls all said their goodbyes and Siyonna and Amina joined Mr Sunday, waiting patiently for them.

As soon as the girls arrived home, Siyonna's mum rushed from the kitchen and hugged her.

"Your results came in. Straight A's. What a star! You got my brains!" she cried.

"I thought I had dad's brains?" she teased.

"Don't mind your father. Whenever you guys do well, you got his brains. Whenever you do something silly, you're your mother's daughter. So today, I claim you my darling. You got mama's smarts!" declared Obiageli and both Siyonna and Amina burst out laughing.

"Don't worry, I am sure your results will be just as good," said Obiageli, walking over to Amina and hugging her.

"Thanks, Auntie," she said in her usual quiet voice.

Both girls headed upstairs. Siyonna needed to start packing for the trip to Umuabado as well. She would be flying to Enugu with her mum tomorrow and continuing the journey south by car from Enugu airport. She was hoping all her sisters would be back for Christmas but really didn't know which ones would make it home this year. She was chatting with Amina and absentmindedly packing when she heard excited screams. She looked at Amina in alarm and ran downstairs to find Ebele and Chieme, standing right there in the living room! Siyonna screamed and ran to them, hugging first one, then the other and jumping up and down in excitement.

"I am so happy to see you guys!" cried Siyonna. "But why didn't you tell me you were coming? Ebele I just spoke with you last week and you said nothing about coming home for Christmas."

Ebele smiled, showing off the dimple on her left cheek

"I wanted to surprise you and I think I succeeded! Seriously though, I wasn't sure I could make it. Then my rotation at the hospital got changed and I suddenly had 10 days' holiday. I booked my flights and ran. Chieme routed her flight through the UK so we could travel together. She is getting on now so needs looking after," finished Ebele with a wink.

Getting on? Siyonna thought, what was Ebele on about? Then she looked at Chieme again and noticed the little bump under her blouse and screamed, ran to her and hugged her again, hard.

"Onna-mma," smiled Chieme. "Go easy before you squeeze the child out of me!"

Everybody laughed. Amina had joined them and also hugged Chieme.

That evening, as everybody gathered and the conversations whirled around, Siyonna smiled and thought how lucky she was to have such a big family. She wouldn't trade it for the world.

On Saturday evening, an exhausted Siyonna arrived at the family home in Umuabado. It had been a long journey with the drive from Enugu taking almost two hours due to so much traffic on the motorway, forcing them to make several detours and use minor roads to reach the village. Ike and his family travelled in another car along with Odera. Siyonna stared up in awe at her family home, it looked so huge and imposing with the new floor added. They trooped into the house and Siyonna couldn't resist going up to Ike's floor to see all the work that had been done there. The floor had been divided into two separate suites each with two bedrooms and a living area, then a further single suite with one bedroom. She put Chieme's things in the single bed suite, figuring that Ike, Nnedi and Afam the baby would stay in one of the double rooms. Then if her sister Adaobi and her family did show, they would stay in the other.

As she made her way back to the first floor, she thought they were in danger of having too many rooms but her dad always worked on the assumption that it was better to have too much space, rather than too little. She felt hungry but at this point, sleep was beckoning. She went to her room and made the bed. Ordinarily, Ebele would share this room with her but since Chieme and Ike had moved to the next floor, they could both have separate rooms. Before long Siyonna fell into a deep and welcomed sleep.

Very soon, she met Ma Mabel in a dream. Siyonna found herself in the quaint, old living room admiring Ma Mabel's family album and suddenly, she heard her dad say: "I'm off to see the Governor about the money his state owes the company." Siyonna looked up from the album just as Ma Mabel walked out of the kitchen, drying her hands on a tea cloth, and said "Go with him child, he needs your help. Go with him." As Siyonna started to call out to her dad, she woke up to sounds in her room.

She opened her eyes and saw two young kids, a boy and a girl, standing over her and talking excitedly. Siyonna sat up in surprise and at that moment heard a familiar voice from the door asking the children to leave the room. She got up and screamed with joy! Adaobi had come home.

Adaobi was the oldest of the Nduka's five children. She looked the most like their dad and was quite striking. She had a very determined streak and when younger, took her role as the oldest child very seriously. As a child, she had been the main protector of the Nduka brood, including Ike, her immediate younger brother, standing tall against all comers whenever her siblings were threatened. As she stood in the doorway ordering her twin children out of the room, Siyonna jumped up and ran into her arms. The sisters hugged and cried. It had been over eight years since they had last seen each other and at the time the twins had been mere babies. Now they were almost nine-years-old and tall. They looked like a careful mix between their mum and father Nnamdi.

"I guess Kenny and Kem have found you then?" said Adaobi. "These chaps don't do subtle. Go freshen up and come say hello to Nnamdi. We're all just settling in upstairs." Then stopping to look at the twins. "Out!" she said.

They giggled and trooped out of the room. Adaobi turned and winked at her sister as she shut the door.

Siyonna sat down on the edge of the bed. It was Sunday and her parents had no doubt gone to service at St. Matthews. She had slept all evening and all night! Wow, she must have been exhausted. By the time she had showered and tidied her room, everybody was downstairs. She went around the table to her parents just back from church and her brother-in-law Nnamdi, who gave her a hug in his quiet, stoic way.

"How are you, Siyonna? How's it going with you?"

"I'm fine," she smiled.

"Oh, she's doing very well," said her mother, jumping in with enthusiasm. "Straight A's this term and she also has a boyfriend. Tell them Siyonna."

Siyonna could not believe what she was hearing.

"Mum!" she yelled, mortified by her mother's seemingly endless appetite for embarrassing her.

If Obiageli noticed Siyonna's embarrassment, she certainly neither showed it nor appeared to care as she continued to regale the gathered family about tales of Siyonna's new-found love. As everyone laughed at the roasting of young Siyonna, Odera came in and the focus shifted to him. Like Siyonna, Odera was also the youngest of five children, in his case, all boys. They all lived abroad and rarely ever came home for the holidays, much to Uncle Obi's dismay. As the ladies prodded and guffawed at Odera's bulging biceps, the question also shifted to his love life and whether he was dating. As he smiled and tried to shake off the questions, Siyonna's dad came to his rescue.

"I hear the Central Bank is facing further calls to devalue the Naira again and we will hear an announcement by the New Year," he announced.

That did it, as the conversation now moved to the state of the economy and the currency. Siyonna and Odera sat quietly listening as the family went into a detailed discussion about the impact of any new devaluation. Chieme's husband Dele had also joined her in Washington and was currently interviewing for a job. He had left Nigeria partly because of fears and concerns about the economy.

"I don't know that it's that bad," said Ike. "We have never been busier. Our problem is cashflow. If the state government would pay what they owe, it would free us up to take on more work and reduce the amount we turn away because we really haven't got the money to complete them. Admittedly, most of the work we do currently is for private individuals and companies."

"Yes, that is true," said Mr Nduka. "Private enterprises are doing pretty well. But the rest of the polity is not necessarily reflective of that burgeoning private space. I think this is where policies need to change to find mechanisms for involving the entire population in economic growth."

Everybody agreed. The discussion went on until Uncle Obi appeared, the patriarch of the Nduka clan. The three brothers all had homes in this big Nduka compound and were very close, but Zach and Udozor all deferred to their older brother Obi who had raised them after their father died. As Obi walked in, everybody in the room got up to greet him. He waved them back to their seats and sat in the space made for him as Siyonna quickly gave hers up. When Obiageli put a plate before him, he smiled and said he'd already eaten. This was typical of Uncle Obi, never wanting to impose. His wife had died not long after Odera was born and he had refused to remarry, running his business and raising his children alone. Now in his late 70's, he was slowing down and Zach wanted him to stop trying to do so much for himself.

As he sat down, everybody in the room insisted he should eat, ignoring his protests. This was Siyonna's cue to escape and as she made her way to the kitchen the twins suddenly decided they were bored and joined her, with Odera close behind.

"And what would you young people like to do then?" he asked.

"Not sure why you're calling us young," said the girl, Kem. "We're almost as old as you."

"Yeah!" said Kenny.

"Oh, ok, my bad," said Odera, raising both hands in surrender. "So, do you know what you'd like to do? Can you swim? I can take you to the stream and you can swim to your hearts' content. What do you say?"

The twins thought about it for a second before deciding it was an excellent idea. They ran back to their parents to get their approval, leaving Siyonna and Odera to gather the things they needed for the swim.

As soon as the noisy kids ran in asking if they could go for a swim, their dad quickly pointed them in their mother's direction. Adaobi asked who was taking them and Siyonna popped in to say both she and Odera would be with them and they'd be back by early afternoon. Adaobi agreed and the twins whooped with joy as they ran alongside Siyonna for the trip to Uruku stream, just under a mile from the compound.

For the twins, this visit to the village felt like a huge adventure. They marvelled at the red earth paths, the trees and the constant company of the unassuming *Agama* lizards, the females all dark coloured whilst the males had a greyish body and prominent red head, which they nodded quite regularly as if acknowledging the humans who hurried along on the shared paths. The twins were thrilled and did their best to catch the elusive lizards. As they drew nearer to the stream, middle-aged women and girls with earthen pots on the head gave them the traditional *"nn'o nnu'oh!"* welcome, a courtesy that still exists in rural Eastern Nigeria and both Odera and Siyonna answered back in kind.

As this was December the *Harmattan* weather had turned most of the trees ashen brown. Everything appeared to be stripped of green. It hadn't been very windy this year but the effects of the *Harmattan* were evident in the patched earth and dried twigs all around.

When they arrived closer to the stream, they could hear the excited sounds of children squealing with joy as they played games in the warm water. In the distance, you could also hear chanting and singing from the Pentecostal Church of Pastor Jacob. Pastor Jacob had been a tailor in Onitsha until one day he'd suddenly claimed that he had received a call to devote the rest of his life to God's work. A few years ago, he returned to the village to live in a tiny room in his father's house. His wife and children had remained in Onitsha where she was a petty-trader and his church had been any street corner where he could attract an audience. These days he lived in a sprawling mansion with his family, and work continued apace to complete the Church he was building. It was larger than the local Catholic Church and attracted more followers every Sunday. The Pastor always referred to himself in the third person as 'Man of God'. Siyonna's father always hissed 'fraud' under his breath whenever his name came up, to which his wife would smack him and say "behave Zach! How can you speak ill of a *Man of God?*"

They got to the stream, which was slow-running and trickled into a river somewhere, or a larger stream, Siyonna did not know. But she did know the stream was big and divided into two sections for bathing and swimming and drinking water. Soon the twins had stripped off and jumped into the water. Odera also went in to keep an eye on them. They could both swim quite well and soon were in the thick of the games with the other children, giggling and squealing as they chased a little ball around the bathing pool. Siyonna felt quite the aunt sitting on a rocky outcrop at the edge of the stream watching the children. Odera was performing solid lengths up and down the swimming area, content to take his exercise wherever he could find it.

People came and went, some to fill up their big earthen pots, others with plastic jerry cans. Others chatted at the water's edge. A bevvy of young girls huddled in a group, giggling and laughing at the young men and boys coming out of the stream with shirts slung over shoulders, revealing bare, muscular upper bodies. Siyonna couldn't see anyone she knew, so felt happy to sit and watch the world go by. As some of the kids came up and jumped off the rock into the water, Siyonna promptly discouraged the twins from the notion and they quietly slunk back into the stream with their new friends.

As she watched them swim, she had to admit to herself that they were pretty good. Suddenly one of the little boys appeared to be struggling, then disappeared under the water. Odera went straight in to find him and after what felt like an eternity, he surfaced but without the boy. Siyonna dived in and was initially blinded by the silt in the water, then her eyes focused and she swam quickly under the surface beyond where Odera and one or two of the bystanders were still bobbing around searching for the boy. She went deep far beyond the shallow end of the stream and saw the boy lying on the riverbed. She grabbed him and headed up to the surface, propelled as if by an invisible force.

As soon as she surfaced, Odera grabbed the limp body from her and carried the boy to the riverbank. The boy's older sister was at the bank, screaming uncontrollably as Odera tried to revive him. Siyonna walked up to Odera and touched him on the shoulder just as he pushed lightly again at the boy's chest. The boy immediately coughed up water and opened his eyes. The boy's sister couldn't stop hugging Siyonna and Odera, thanking them for saving her brother's life. Other women at the riverbank also joined in thanking them and raining blessings on the next generation of Ndukas.

Siyonna smiled. There was something rather poignant about life in the village. Everybody knew everyone else. Without them saying a word, the people had known who her family was, quite unlike the anonymity of Lagos. She was soaking wet and knew it was time to go. Kem walked up to her and slipped her hand in hers.

"That was awesome, auntie Siyonna!" she said. "And I love your necklace. Do you think when I am older, I could get one like that?"

"Of course," she replied, smiling. "Come on kids, time to go. It's getting late."

The stream began to empty as the swimmers made ready to go home.

Siyonna pointed the twins to a bush where they could get out of their wet things. Odera came over, slung his tee-shirt over his head and waited till they were ready. Then they all started their walk back to the compound with the twins in front taking in the sights and giggling at everything new they came upon. Suddenly they heard a lot of shouting and quite a commotion ahead, which stopped the twins in their tracks. A few of the women dropped the baskets on their heads as they fled into the homes along the path.

"Masquerade!" said Odera. "Quick, let's get out of here!"

He gathered the twins and fled towards the bushes, with Siyonna following closely behind. They found one large enough for them all to hide behind. The Masquerade was an *Iga,* covered from head to toe in brown raffia. It raced down the path towards the stream, big cane in hand, daring anybody to stand in its way. This *Iga* was powerful and fearless, imbued with the spirit of the ancestors and only the foolhardy would dare to stand in its way. This was why he had an attendant whose job was to pull the rope around his waist and rein him in before he did any harm. However, this did not always work, because right at that moment an unsuspecting teenager on his phone got a rude awakening when the thud of the cane landed across his bum. He jumped and ran off, barely clutching his falling phone.

As the *Iga* danced from one end of the road to the other, the young handler kept tugging at him and once in a while the frustrated *Iga* would turn on its handler and chase him, mutter loudly about the sheer foolhardiness of the sons of mortal men who dared walk the paths he trod, as he danced to the melodious sound of the *ogene* coming from his other handlers. Then he ran down the road where he thought there might be unsuspecting people lurking.

As the party moved past and went into the compound of Akunne Odonyili, one of the titled men whose home was just off the road, Odera gathered everybody and they ran home. Just as they got into the compound, they heard shouts behind them that told Odera and Siyonna the *Iga* had noticed their audacious escape only too late.

The twins were hugely excited. This was the most fun they'd had in ages.

"The *Iga* was ten-foot-tall and ran faster than Usain Bolt," said Kem to her wide-eyed mother and adoring grandparents.

"And did you know that the *Iga* will flog everybody, even when they are not being naughty?" asked their grandfather.

"These two don't get flogged at all," said their mother. "Even when they are being naughty."

"Yeah but you keep telling us you will!" said Kem.

Everybody laughed, including baby Afam who just kept laughing throughout the excitement. Siyonna looked at her assembled family and smiled. The twins started telling their mother how Siyonna was as good at saving lives as any lifeguard and she saved a little boy's life today! Siyonna quickly slipped away to her room to change and shower before the questions started. Yes, this was a significant part of why she loved Christmases in the village.

Adaobi and Nnamdi left with the twins for Ogidi, Nnamdi's village, after lunch, promising to come back to Umuabado on Boxing Day. Nnamdi's elderly parents and family were also waiting to see them. Ike had his driver run them over to Ogidi, about 20 minutes away on the new road network, built by previous governments around the state.

After they left, Siyonna played with Afam until he slept then she went and found Odera binge-watching movies in the family room on the first floor.

Siyonna sat next to him but after 20 minutes, she was bored with the movie. She didn't get the title and only knew it was one of those 'shoot first and ask questions later' kind of movies Odera loved so much. He had a little satisfied smile on his face, watching in rapt attention as the screen exploded in blood every few minutes. Siyonna grabbed her book, stuck her headphones into her ears to drown out the noise and soon lost herself in the magic of Harry Potter. Legend, she thought. This beat meaningless blood-soaked violent movies any day, as far as she was concerned.

When the movie ended, Odera got up, stretched and yanked out the earphone in Siyonna's left ear.

"Auntie Oby asked me to go ask Mama Obele if she is coming here for Christmas lunch. You coming?" he said.

"Yes," she said and jumped up.

As they went downstairs, Siyonna could hear the adults chatting happily in the big living room. Her father's brothers were there, as well as Uncle Udozor's wife, Nneka. Siyonna hadn't visited Uncle Udozor's since she'd been back and knew she would receive a telling off for it from Auntie

Nneka. So, for now, she walked quietly and quickly behind her cousin as they made their exit.

"Where are you two off to?" called out Ebele.

When they told her she quickly decided she'd go with them too.

The journey to the old compound took about 15 minutes and everywhere you looked, people were getting their homes ready for Christmas. One of the compounds they had to pass was Nweke's. Nweke was in the same age group as Siyonna's dad but had never left the village. Siyonna's mum said he was more interested in what lay at the bottom of a beer bottle than what tomorrow would bring. Nweke loved Christmas. Both his wives had abandoned him a long time ago but no matter, because at Christmas he always found a willing, God-fearing neighbour to visit. This ensured he was well fed over the period and with some luck, would have enough to make up a doggy bag for later. Nweke was an enigma. He had not walled the compound he inherited from his father and most of it was derelict through years of neglect. His children were all grown up but had mostly been raised by their mothers and did not tend to come home often. His younger brothers were successful traders in Onitsha but had also moved away from the ancestral home, which belonged to Nweke as the first son. They had all bought land and built their own homes elsewhere. Their wives were rumoured to have banned the men from entertaining Nweke in their homes, so not even his brothers' homes were an option for Nweke.

As Ebele, Odera and Siyonna chatted excitedly on their way to Mama Obele's, they absent-mindedly walked through Nweke's compound. He was sitting on his front porch. Last night had been quite good. His first son Udoka had sent him some money for Christmas. He was a bank Manager in

Lagos and unlike his siblings, did what he could to support his ageing father, even though he hardly visited. His mother would forbid it, so he never told her about sending his father money on a regular basis. He knew his father fed his drinking habit with the money he sent, but still felt it best that the old man had money just in case there was an emergency.

So last night, flush with cash, Nweke had headed straight to *'Chop first'*, the drinking joint at Nkwo Market, one of the few places where he was still welcome and still good for credit. As he walked in, Felicia, the manageress rounded on him about his unpaid tab.

"Relax you small girl, ah-Ahh?" Nweke said. "I have money. What do I owe?"

Felicia indeed relaxed. A middle-aged, canny businesswoman, she knew a good deal when she saw one. She knew Nweke's first son sent money regularly, so she fed his need for alcohol whenever he wanted, and collected when Nweke's allowance arrived. Today was payday and by the time she was done, Nweke was as broke as he had been before his Christmas allowance arrived. That night, Nweke left the bar not only broke but totally inebriated, and only made it home because some good Samaritans at the bar were kind enough to dump him at his door. He had woken up on his porch and had stayed there ever since. He was idly scratching a mosquito bite when through his drunken haze he made out three young people walking along the path that ran through his compound.

"Who goes there?" he called out, trying to focus.

"Oh Lord, I forgot about him," whispered Odera.

As they stood there contemplating what to do next, Nweke struggled up to them.

"Ah, the Nduka children! How are you? And how are your most illustrious parents?"

"Fine, thank you, sir," they chorused, gagging at the combination of stale beer and bad breath coming from him.

"Good, good," he said. "Zach Nduka is my old, old friend. We are the same Umunna and went to the same school. I have not seen him for many years now. Tell him I will be coming for Christmas lunch at his, eh? Tell him! Friends and brothers must keep in touch. We cannot stop seeing each other simply because we're grown up. Tell him!" he said, between loud hiccups.

"Yes, sir. We will let our father know you'll be over on Christmas day for lunch," said Ebele. "Thank you, sir. We'll be on our way now."

Before Nweke could say anything else, she marched purposefully down the path towards the old compound, with Siyonna and Odera running to keep up with her. As soon as they were out of earshot, everybody opened up about how awfully Nweke stank of stale beer and bad breath. They were still talking about him when they got to the old compound.

Built in the colonial 1930s style, the old compound comprised two large bungalows with a wide courtyard in the middle. It always looked pristine and Mama Obele lived there with a few other relatives who had nowhere else to go and had come back to live in the village. Mama Obele was kind and well-loved, and took in most relatives who fell on hard times and came running to her. She was the only grandmother Siyonna had ever known and Siyonna loved her dearly. She was kind, consistent, and incredibly generous. As soon as they were in the compound, Siyonna announced her presence by shouting:

"Mama Obele, Siyonna'a'bia'goh" (Mama Obele, Siyonna has arrived).

"Onye'kam'kene'lu? Siyonna my daughter is here! Onnamma, Siyonna Chukwunyelu!" (*Whom am I greeting? Siyonna my daughter is here! Siyonna our gift from God!*) came the delighted response from within.

The three of them went into the living room, which always seemed to Siyonna to be frozen in time. Spotless, yes, but very dated with an old-style gramophone and dated TV set in the corner and a heavy-set table in the middle.

Mama Obele sat in an armchair, with a big smile on her face as she squinted at her guests. It was obvious her sight was failing. She instantly recognized Siyonna but struggled with Ebele and Odera. When Siyonna finally told her Ebele was in the room, she cried with joy and almost danced as she hugged Ebele.

She seemed to have aged more since the last time and this worried Siyonna. She asked how she was and in her usual manner, Mama said she was fine, just old age and nothing more. The Good Lord had given her a long life and she was grateful for it. They talked about all the local gossip in Umuabado and who was doing what. Then they told her about Nweke and she shook her head in disbelief.

"That man simply refuses to contemplate life outside the bottle," she said and Siyonna smiled, remembering her father saying exactly the same thing.

As they chatted Mama Obele asked after Odera's father and he replied, saying he was fine. Mama Obele offered to get them some food and they refused. She then offered soft drinks and again they declined. Ebele reminded her that they were not strangers here and she laughed. As they chatted, other cousins who lived in the compound popped in to say hi. Mama Obele did her best to introduce them and some Siyonna already knew, like Cousin Alfred's daughter and Uchendu, her Father's cousin. Having spent quite some time with her, they got up to leave and promised to come back to pick Mama Obele up for Christmas lunch.

The journey back took them through Nweke's compound again but this time they were ready. They ran as fast as they could when they got to his compound. Perhaps they shouldn't have bothered. Nweke had at last left the porch and gone back into the house.

Christmas day started with all the promise of a magical time. The family all dressed up and went to church. Dele had arrived on Christmas Eve and joined Chieme and the rest of the family. As with most Christmas services, it went on for over two hours and Afam got restless after the first half-hour. Nnedi and Siyonna took it in turns to mind him and Siyonna was relieved when the service was over and they could all go home.

Siyonna's mum had arranged for caterers to help prepare various dishes for the Christmas meal and by the time they got home, the table was being set for the big lunch. There was the *onugbu* soup made from bitterleaf soup with beef, lamb and chicken, served with *foofoo* or pounded yam. There was *nsala* soup made with different herbs and fresh fish and Siyonna's favourite soup, *egusi*. A yellow soup, it was made with ground melon seeds and various vegetables and tasted absolutely delicious. While all her uncles and her father loved bitterleaf soup, for Siyonna no soup compared to a well turned out *egusi*. There was also rice and fried plantain and carved turkey pieces. Siyonna knew she was going to overdo it with the food today and by the way Odera was eyeing the packed dining table, she figured she wouldn't be the only one.

That afternoon, Siyonna and Odera drove to the old compound and fetched Mama Obele who looked lovely in her festive lace *blouse* and *George wrapper* with matching *George headscarf*, and as soon as they got back, Nweke showed up. Siyonna was surprised at how well turned out he actually was. He had on a traditional *isi-Agu Igbo* shirt, with the woven woolly hat on his head. The shirt was not new but at least it was not dirty either. And he did not smell drunk!

There was so much to eat and Siyonna was hell-bent on sampling everything. There were also so many people around the big dining table that Siyonna, Odera, and Ebele took their food and disappeared upstairs. Later, Dele and Chieme joined them and as Uncle Udozor's children also popped in, they all ended up upstairs where the conversation quickly switched to movies. Between deciding who was a better actor, De Niro or Al Pacino, things were getting louder until they all heard the gong of the *ogene* and beat of various masquerade drums in the compound.

They rushed to the balcony upstairs and looked down on the most amazing sight. The whole courtyard was taken up by one of the largest masquerade troops Siyonna had ever seen. There were three smaller masquerades with painted faces and lipsticks on their garish masks. They shuffled around for a while and then broke into dance, in cadence to the beats of the drum and the melodious sounds of the *ogene*. The swaying took on a life of its own as the legs moved in such fast sequence it was hard for the eyes to follow. As the masquerades danced, jumped and somersaulted in response to the melody of the music, the singer kept calling to the men of the house to come out and greet the masquerades.

The entreaties were steeped in praise, enjoining the worthy and wealthy to come out and greet the spectacle that only went to those who deserved them in this life.

The three brothers, Uncle Udozor, Uncle Obi and Siyonna's dad were joined by Ike who towered over them as they walked out to greet the masquerades. Each masquerade danced up to the men, shook hands and then went back to the circle to continue dancing. The men joined the masquerades and did a few steps to great applause and then Uncle Obi welcomed them formally to the Nduka compound. Arrangements were made for food and drink for the attendants.

About half an hour later, there was a shout as the biggest and scariest sight Siyonna had ever seen approached the compound. This huge masquerade with no face to speak of, was covered from head to toe in *Ijele* cloth. As it approached the compound, the other three danced on their knees in utter supplication to the superior force that had now joined them. The masquerade was so big that it could hardly dance and moved to the beat of the music in short, deliberate steps. Uncle Obi was an *Ozo* titled man, an elder of Umuabado, so he came out to welcome the big masquerade to the compound as his brothers stood back. Over the next hour, many other masquerades came in. The Ijele and the three accompanying masquerades left as their followers thanked the Ndukas profusely for looking after them.

A little while later a fearsome masquerade with one arm and smoke billowing from its head made its way into the compound. Its followers simply watched in silence, and a loud gong announced its presence. As Siyonna gawked from her safe perch in the balcony, she felt a firm arm pull her back into the house. It was a stern Mama Obele.

"You never look that thing in the eye. Stay indoors. If you must look, find a crack in the window and stare from there," she commanded.

Siyonna had never seen her like that and quickly sat down. Mama Obele ambled over to one of the settees and sat down.

"Go on, go look from that window, my child," she said.

Siyonna nodded and went, just as Odera came up behind her and they both pulled the curtain back. All the other dancers had deserted the compound, leaving just this one and its two followers. Neither Uncle Udozor, Siyonna's dad nor Uncle Obi had come out to greet this masquerade. As they stood, the smoke puffed from its head and the basket of water, balanced in its good hand, stayed steady, with not a drop of water escaping from it. The gong kept sounding intermittently, an empty intimidating boom. Then his attendant started a plaintive call, inviting the men of the compound to come out and meet '*Ajo Ofia*', keeper of the spirits, tamer of the devil, and the personification of mystery. As he called, he recounted all the victories of this lonesome spirit in battles with other masquerades from as far afield as Ngwo in Enugu State and how the earth trembled when the masquerade walked. Was there no giant in this compound to come do obeisance to this king of masquerades?

Suddenly, Nweke came out, swaying slightly. He had obviously busied himself with the beer, freely on offer as part of the day's celebrations. In his hand, he held a brown bottle of Guilder beer and he started singing, sweetly cajoling the masquerade to show mercy on this special day. He reminded the masquerade of how he, Nweke, had served him in days of old when his limbs were young. He told the masquerade that he Nweke had been taught the secrets of the dark and the calls of the spirits in the time when men were boys, and boys were not allowed out to play in the village square in the dark, lest the spirits possess them. The masquerade nodded and made a strange, guttural sound.

"Nweke, I salute you," said his attendant. "The spirits remember you and acknowledge your timeless service. The spirits thank you for your forthrightness and your sacrifice. *Ajo Ofia* will retire in deference to you, old friend. *Ajo Ofia* only asks that you present him with the gifts befitting a spirit like him."

Nweke bowed in respect, staggering slightly at the effort, then went back to the house and came out with a kola nut and a bottle of gin, then picked up a white fowl from the side of the house and handed all the items to the helper. The masquerade made its guttural sound again, waved its basket of water around and with a plume of smoke puffing from its head, made its way out of the compound with its helper announcing that *Ajo Ofia* was on its way and advising all to clear the way so that harm would not befall them.

As soon as the Masquerade left, the compound slowly filled again with guests and various traditional dancers. The parents and Uncle Udozor sat in the gazebo and drank palm wine and all the talk was on the antics of *Ajo Ofia* and why it was still allowed out on occasions like Christmas. One of the Nduka's cousins, Otosi, spoke about a time when some poor fellow ran into a ditch and broke both his legs because he believed the masquerade was coming. Between bouts of laughter, the men all reiterated that something needed to be done to curtail *Ajo Ofia's* appearances on civil occasions. Nweke could contribute little to the conversations as his constant drinking all afternoon had finally caught up with him. He sat peacefully in a corner snoring softly in a haze of beer and whiskey consumed quickly and happily, largely because someone else was paying for it.

Siyonna and Odera had also come downstairs and were sitting in another gazebo, together with Chieme, Ebele and Dele. Mama Obele was regaling them with tales from her youth, telling them the exploits of all the masquerades in the village and how masqueraders also used festival days to settle scores with girls who had jilted them, making sure the *Ojionu* masquerade chased down a hapless maiden and laid a few strokes of the cane across her back for good measure. She recounted how one day, on her way back from the stream she had encountered another girl running away from a masquerade. To save herself from a whipping and also save the water on her head, she had quickly picked up soot from the roadside and painted her face, tore her blouse a bit and ruffled her hair, then talking at the top of her voice, continued on her way. When the unsuspecting masquerade troupe confronted her, she stood her ground, wild-eyed and loud, babbling incoherently at the top of her voice. They took one look at her, shook their heads at the ill fortune that turned maidens mad and went off to harass other travellers. The young people were in stitches!

"What did you do next?" asked Adanma, Uncle Udozor's daughter.

"I was so scared and after they left, I put a hand to a tree and steadied myself. I couldn't believe I had escaped a flogging. But I also knew that I needed to get that water home, or my mother would make the *Ojionu's* caning look like child's play" replied Mama Obele, to a fresh round of laughter from her young audience.

As evening wore on, dinner was served outside and with a dessert of *ugba* and *okporoko*. Siyonna, full enough to burst, suddenly felt very tired, made her excuses and took herself off to bed. As she dropped off to sleep, she imagined a baby-faced masquerade dancing and singing her lullabies. Suddenly she realised she hadn't spoken to nor heard from Dante since she left Lagos a week ago. Must call him on Boxing Day, she thought as she finally drifted off to sleep.

12

Ma Coker's Dome Party

The New Year began and the months sped by. Suddenly, the summer term was coming to an end and the girls of Our Lady's were all looking forward to the long six-week holiday, which for some of them marked the end of an era. Some girls were going on to university in Nigeria and some were leaving the country to study in universities abroad. Amanda was returning to the United States to attend university there. Over the years they had been together, Siyonna had formed a close bond with Amanda and she had really surprised everybody. Growing up with little access to Nigerian culture, apart from what she learned from her father, Amanda had adapted so well to life in Nigeria and at Our Lady's, that all the teachers and most of the students had grown quite fond of her. As for Siyonna, Amanda's keen intelligence and easy manner marked her out as a go-to person and they had become firm friends. She would miss Amanda a lot and she knew it.

Siyonna wasn't quite sure where life would take her in September but really didn't want to think that far ahead. When she told her father that she would like to take a degree in creative writing at a US university, he looked at her and muttered a non-committal 'hmmm.' She knew it was a stretch. Studying abroad was expensive and she wasn't sure her father could afford to foot the bill, so she really didn't hold out much hope of getting there, especially since all her siblings had gone to Nigerian universities for their degrees. However, it hadn't stopped her from applying to New York State and a few other universities in the US in the hope that when the time came, she could secure a scholarship. She had also sat the Joint Admissions and Matriculations Board examinations in Nigeria to get into one of the federal universities and wouldn't know whether or not she had been successful until the end of the summer. All that would come later. Right now, what mattered to everyone was the long summer holiday ahead.

Siyonna had just finished her last Senior School Certificate examinations and sat on a bench in the courtyard waiting for her friends to join her. Dupe, Bunmi, Amina, Amaka and Amanda were finishing their final exams and would be out shortly.

"So, my grandma turns 80 on Saturday," said Dupe, when they were finally all huddled together on the bench. "My parents are planning a big *Owambe* for her. You must all come."

As the girls jumped up in excitement and hugged each other, Amanda looked bewildered.

"Ahem," she said. "Not meaning to spoil the mood or anything, but what's an *Owambe?*"

The others fell about laughing. Bunmi recovered first and put her arm across Amanda's shoulders, a bit like a parent talking to a slow child.

"Well, my dear sister of the Yankee persuasion, what is an Owambe if not the greatest party on earth? It is a Yoruba street party, loud and rambunctious, where everybody shows up in the finest garbs, dances to live music and eats and drinks to their heart's content! It is the very essence of life itself. You have not lived, dear girl, until you have attended an Owambe! But be careful with your dressing! You have got to wear a *gele, buba* and *wrapper*. You have got to look the part. Who knows? You might even meet your future husband there?" Bunmi finished with a wink and again all the girls fell about laughing.

As the girls linked arms and walked away, Siyonna put concerns about her future aside and promised herself that she would embrace the spirit of the six weeks, the spirit of the summer and give herself up to enjoying the moment. At the end of the summer, she would worry about the future again.

When she arrived home that evening, she found her father packing for a business trip to Germany. Ike had ordered some machinery for the firm and needed Mr Nduka to go and inspect the goods before they were shipped. As Siyonna sat at the foot of her dad's bed watching her mum fuss over him and help him pack, she marvelled not for the first time at her parents' relationship. Even though there was quite a big age difference between them, the love they had for each other was impossible to deny. Both of them treated each other with great tenderness and Siyonna always prayed that when it was time to marry, she would find someone who would love and care for her like her father cared for her mum. As her mum once said to her, she should neither expect, nor accept, anything less.

"So, dad, how long are you gone for?" she asked.

"Oh, not long. Just a few days to a week, tops. As soon as the equipment is inspected and agreed, I will be on the next flight back," he replied.

"Siyonna and Amina have an Owambe to go to on Saturday. We are working on an outfit for both of them," said her mum.

"Owambe, eh? Brilliant!" said Mr Nduka. "Take loads of pictures. You know how I never get enough of seeing my little girl in *Iro* and *buba!*" he laughed and gave her the usual playful pinch on the cheeks.

Siyonna smiled. In the eyes of her dad she may well never grow up, she thought but that was fine by her. They had a deep and enduring bond. As the youngest child, she had spent the most time at home and got to know both parents quite well. Her sisters always told her she got away with murder that both parents were spent and when it came to her, they quite happily gave in to all her demands. Siyonna always vehemently denied this of course. She felt she got the requisite number of 'nos' from her parents and pulled her weight when it came to helping around the house. Some of her classmates were already driving and she hadn't even believed the subject important enough to broach with her parents. No, Siyonna thought, she was not indulged, oh no. Then again, no one was listening.

She turned to look at her dad finishing off his packing.

"Nne," he said. "I have a meeting with the Governor of the state that owes our company money this evening. He's in Lagos and I thought I'd try again to see if I can reason with him, so I won't be home for dinner tonight."

Siyonna started to say Ok, then remembered her dream and Ma Mabel asking her to go with her dad for his meeting.

"I also wanted to tell you," he said. "You won't be visiting Ebele this summer. With the business struggling, we have to conserve as much cash as possible. I will make it up to you when things improve, ok Siyonna?"

Siyonna nodded, and then something prompted her.

"Dad, can I come with you for your meeting with the Governor?"

Zach stopped packing and both he and Obiageli looked at their youngest daughter in surprise.

"Why?" he asked. "It certainly won't be a fun visit and besides it will be all about business and may take a while. I'm really not sure it would be the sort of thing you'd enjoy."

"I know dad, I just want to keep you company especially since you're travelling tomorrow. Please can I come with you?"

"You might as well take her," said her mum. "What have you got to lose? Besides, it may help your case when the Governor sees you have a family?"

Zach shrugged.

"Ok," he said. "Get ready, we leave in half an hour."

Siyonna went to her room and changed into a simple *Ankara dress and* a pair of pumps, with her necklace visible around her neck, she went downstairs to wait.

Zach came down, dressed in a smart white caftan and they walked to the car together. He was driving tonight and Siyonna sat in the passenger seat. As the Toyota Land Cruiser roared to life and they pulled away from the compound to join the traffic, Zach glanced at his daughter.

"Lovely necklace," he said. "Very nice. I have seen it on you on many occasions but never quite thought to ask where it came from. Mum?"

Siyonna hadn't seen that coming.

"Thanks, dad, Ebele gave it to me," she said easily, hating herself for the deception but not knowing what else to say without inviting more questions. Zach looked at her and nodded slightly and the rest of the drive passed in silence. Siyonna knew her dad had a lot on his mind, so thought it best to let him be.

They drove through the toll gate and passed 1004 flats in Victoria Island, making their way onto Adeola Odeku Street, turning off the main road to one of the closes. Right ahead of them appeared a heavy iron gate with policemen in front and behind it. One of them walked up to Zach and said good evening. When Zach told him he had an appointment to see the governor, the gate swung back and they were directed to a spot off the main building. Zach parked, locked the car and both he and Siyonna followed a burly security man who led them into a wood-panelled room with lush red carpets. He told them to wait there until they were summoned. Zach thanked him, turned to Siyonna and smiled apologetically.

"Sorry Onna-mma'm, this could be a long night. Buckle up my darling."

He grabbed an old newspaper from the stool as he acknowledged the other people in the room. There must have been at the least six or seven waiting to see the governor.

Gabriel Ama, the police officer who had brought them in, worked as the Governor's aide-de-camp and made it a rule not to get involved in pushing through visitors. What his boss did and how he did it was of no concern to him. All he focused on was security. However, there was something about the gentleman in white with the teenage daughter that tugged at his heart. A man like that, accompanied by his daughter in this day and age, must be a good father. Children these days hardly ever wanted anything to do with their parents so this guy must be special. So, he found himself going into the Governor's living room where the great man was just finishing a phone call. Gabriel waited patiently for the governor to finish then calmly informed him that Mr Nduka was here to see him. The Governor frowned. He'd heard that name before but couldn't remember where. Oh well, he thought, last meeting tonight. After this, he was going to bed. He had an early start tomorrow. He nodded and Gabriel went back to the sitting area and invited Zach and Siyonna in.

They walked through a myriad of rooms until they came to the Governor's private reception room. He waved them in and Zach stepped forward and introduced himself and his daughter, always referring to the Governor as "your excellency". Siyonna had never met a Governor before, apart from seeing them on television, so she curtsied and shook his hand, following her dad's lead and saying "Your Excellency."

The Governor was younger than her dad but portlier. He was tall, with a big smile. He looked at Siyonna's necklace, fixated on it for a while and turned to Zach and smiled.

"How can I help, Mr Nduka?"

Zach explained that his firm had constructed roads, factories and housing units for the state and showed him the contracts. The state had failed to pay, putting both the company and other projects at risk of failure. The work had been completed over three years ago, so there was very little excuse for the delay in paying for it. The Governor looked surprised. There had been a budget for the work and he had been assured that all payments had been made. Mr Nduka shook his head.

"No, your Excellency, we have not been paid."

The Governor's face lost its smile as he grabbed a phone.

"Have Chief Appa call me immediately."

Almost immediately the phone started ringing. Without taking his eyes off Siyonna's necklace, the Governor issued a series of instructions to someone on the phone, who must have been Chief Appa. He peppered his orders with words like 'outrageous' and 'immediately'. When he was done, he turned to Zach and spread his arms expansively.

"I can only apologise for the pain we have caused you and really don't know what came over my staff. The Finance Commissioner will have your cheque in your office tomorrow morning. If there are any problems, here is my card, Mr Nduka, call me?" he said, handing Zach a card with his mobile number scribbled behind. "That's my personal number. I tend to answer that one because only people I have personally given it to will know it."

Zach smiled, thanked him and the Governor walked them to the door, handing them over to Gabriel. As they left the Governor turned to Siyonna.

"That is a remarkable necklace you have. It is quite unusual and beautiful. Look after it, young lady."

Siyonna curtsied and thanked him, then followed her father out.

On the drive home, Zach couldn't believe what had happened at the meeting.

"This is quite incredible," he said. "I have tried to meet the Governor six times in the past three years, sometimes waiting for hours on end only to be told 'sorry, come another day.' This is simply incredible. Onna-mma, you are my good luck charm! Perhaps I should take you to all my meetings, eh?" he said, still shaking his head.

Siyonna smiled, leant back in her seat and rubbed the beads on her necklace. Thank you, Ma Mabel, she thought.

The next morning, Odera dropped her at school as usual. It was the last day of school and all the boarding students were also leaving. As with most holidays, Amina was coming home with her. She would spend a few days with her and then travel on to Abuja to her family. After the assembly, Siyonna went to find her friend Lola to say goodbye. As she left the hall, Lola spotted her and called out to her with a smile on her face. The two girls hugged and promised to speak the following week. Lola was not sure what her summer plans were going to be. Her parents wanted her to come with them on a visit to Canada so she was likely to spend the summer abroad but promised to let her friend know what she was doing.

Siyonna continued outside where all her friends had gathered and they headed back to the dormitory to help Amina and Bunmi, the only two girls in the group who boarded. Of the two, Amina probably needed more help with her packing. So, while Amanda helped Bunmi, all the others went to pack Amina's things. Amina's usual protestations of 'guys I am quite capable of packing my stuff and I have already packed most of my things' were ignored as the girls got to work pulling her things into suitcases and scouring the room to make sure she hadn't left anything important behind. With everyone working together, Amina was packed in record time and they all met with Amaka and Amanda and headed to the car park.

With Saturday came the frenetic effort to dress for the Owambe. Since Amina was staying, Mrs Nduka had also adjusted a top for her. The wrapper (*Iro*) was more flexible and could be tied to size. As for the *buba* (blouse), Amina wasn't very big so Obiageli only had to adjust it down a few sizes to fit her slim frame. The girls then rushed out to go to the Palms Shopping Mall to pick up presents for the celebrant. There, Amaka, Bunmi and Amanda joined them, and they trouped from one store to the other trying to find things they could afford.

"Why don't we all pool our resources and get her one good gift rather than four not-so-impressive ones?" suggested Amanda and they all agreed it was a splendid idea.

"I have a good birthday card we can all sign, to go with the gift?" said Siyonna.

They continued the search for a worthy present with renewed vigour now the kitty had increased. After what seemed an eternity, they found a beautiful leather purse, which fit the budget. In dark red, it looked the epitome of class. They had it gift wrapped and headed triumphantly to the ice cream parlour, *Fluff and Cones*, at the edge of the shopping arcade.

"Oh, the guilt of it! But guilt be damned, nothing beats a chocolate ice cream," said Amanda joyfully, as she tucked in.

"Soon we'll have to start worrying about what we eat," said Amina, as the girls laughed. "Do you guys ever worry that this phase of our life is speeding away from us? Come to think of it, this may be the last time we will all be here together."

They all paused, lost in their own thoughts.

"Come on girls, it's just a phase," said Amaka. "My dad says you must enjoy the journey. Every phase presents different challenges and opportunities. We must embrace the opportunities and enjoy where we are in life as we prepare to carry on and transition to the next phase. Live in the moment. We are here, we have a party tonight. Let's enjoy. We will always be close, no matter where life takes us."

As they all agreed, Amanda started crying and they rubbed her back gently, assuring her that it would all work out well. Soon, they were talking and laughing about their costumes for the evening and enjoying their ice creams. The Ice Cream Parlour felt nice and cool as the Lagos sun shimmered on the glass and more people ventured inside, mostly parents and children. A lady with a set of triplets, aged about four came in and found the place so full, she couldn't find a table. The kids grew really agitated at being so close to the ice cream and not getting any. Siyonna suggested they give up their stools to the lady since they were done. They all agreed and Amaka and Amanda jumped up as Siyonna invited the grateful lady and her little ones to come and take their table.

The girls were headed for the door when Siyonna told them to hang on and sign the card, which she had in her bag. They all signed the card and headed out into the warm sunshine of the Lagos afternoon.

It was hot today and everything seemed to have a haze of heat, what Amanda famously described as 'the hot halo', around them. The girls made their way to the car park where the various drivers had left the cars and dived into whatever shade they could find, to keep cool. Amanda's car was the first and as the driver emerged from under a flimsy palm tree, the girls all said hello to him, hugged Amanda and agreed for the umpteenth time to meet at 3 p.m. when the Owambe started. Siyonna knew her parents wouldn't want her out too late, so they all agreed to meet at 3 and leave no later than 8 for the journey home. After Amanda left, Siyonna and Amina hailed a cab for the journey home.

Just as a cab pulled up, Siyonna saw the lady from The Ice Cream Parlour come running out.

"Femi! Femi!" she screamed at the top of her voice.

Siyonna exchanged glances with Amina and they both left the cab and ran towards the lady. The furious cab driver drove off. *All these small girls, he thought, always happy to waste someone's time.*

Siyonna got to the flustered lady and knew immediately that her child was missing. As she saw Siyonna, she grabbed her hand.

"It's Femi, my little boy," she cried, desperately. "He's only four. I had just turned to make sure his sisters did not soil their dresses and when I looked back, he was gone!"

"Don't worry ma," said Siyonna. "We will help you find him."

Siyonna looked towards the gate and felt her necklace get warm, so she spun around purposefully and walked towards the exit. Amina ran to catch up with her.

"Where are you going? How do you know he's there?"

"I just know," replied Siyonna with firm conviction.

She walked out of the Shopping Centre and saw a woman carrying a sleeping child, half-walking, half-running some 300 meters ahead of her. She broke into a run with Amina in tow and as she caught up with the lady, she grabbed her arm.

"Put the child down," she said simply. "He's not yours."

The lady started to protest and in typical Lagos style, a crowd immediately started to gather around them. A burly man stepped out of the shadows and stood in front of the lady, glaring at Siyonna.

"Wetin you dey talk? Na we get pikin!" he said, then turned to the woman. "Abeg carry de boy go house 'joor!"

The crowd looked first at Siyonna, then at the burly man who was now shouting threateningly and wagging a finger at Siyonna and Amina. Suddenly, he froze mid-sentence, finger still up in the air and the lady simply started walking back to the shopping centre, the child still held firmly in her hands. The crowd decided it made more sense to follow the walking woman, rather than stay staring at a frozen man. Meanwhile, Siyonna pulled Amina back a bit as they followed everyone from a safe distance. The woman crossed the gate and the distraught mother ran across the car park to claim her child, tears of joy and relief pouring down her face. Without waiting to see what happened next, Siyonna dragged Amina across the road to a waiting cab and they left. As they drove past, the hitherto frozen man was in full flight, with an angry mob in hot pursuit.

"What was that, Siyonna?" said Amina, when they returned home. "It almost felt as if you made the lady change her mind about kidnapping the child. Did you?"

Siyonna looked amazed and denied it completely. She had seen someone carrying a child out of the shopping centre earlier and thought nothing of it until the lady came out crying that her child was missing. As for the kidnapper changing her mind and returning the child, Siyonna surmised that she had just been overwhelmed by a sense of guilt. No, Siyonna protested, she had no more special powers than anyone else. Amina thought about it for a while and shrugged, smiling. It made sense. If her friend had any special powers, she would surely have known about it by now.

It was party time! Amina and Siyonna got dressed. Siyonna chose a gold buba and red Iro made from shimmery lace. Her mother had made a red buba for Amina and also an off-yellow Iro. Both girls also had *aso-oke* scarves on their heads and with make-up were transformed immediately into glamorous young women. Obiageli Nduka was quite proud of what she had done with them and took copious pictures to showcase her work, interspersing every effort with loud 'he-ey-eh's in the excitable Nigerian fashion. Odera had been volunteered as chaperon for the evening and he came in wearing an embroidered white brocade piece, with a traditional, Yoruba *fila* in red brocade on his head. His aunt hugged him, complimenting him on just how handsome he looked. He smiled shyly and herded the girls out to his Honda saloon car.

As the car pulled out of the drive, Cook ran alongside it banging on the window, forcing Odera to stop.

"Amina," he gasped. "Your wrapper has been caught outside the car door."

He opened the car door and helped Amina gather the loose yards of material, trailing behind after she had inadvertently shut the door on it. They all thanked Cook and continued outside the compound onto the thoroughfare that would lead them from Lekki to Victoria Island.

Although Dupe's grandmother lived in Surulere, on the Lagos Mainland, her parents had hired an events hall on the Island for the party. Quite a few such places hand sprung up in Lagos, designed specifically for hosting events such as wedding receptions, parties and conferences. The Dome was one of the newer halls and sat in its own grounds in Victoria Island. It was called the Dome because it was effectively a huge tent draped over a steel frame and anchored on a concrete base. Inspired by luxury tents found in Saudi Arabia, it was lavishly furnished with no expense spared.

The drive to the Dome was uneventful as Odera and the girls chatted about everything from fashion to the latest in Afrobeat music. Odera loved Flavour and could be heard humming to one of his tunes in the bathroom every morning as he got ready for work. The girls thought there were more contemporary Afrobeat acts and loved Wizkid and Davido. The Honda's air conditioning kept the car cool as the outside baked in the late afternoon sun.

Traffic was rather kind to them this afternoon. On any other Saturday, the build-up on the toll road could be unforgivable. As they got into Victoria Island, the traffic got slower and *okadas*, motorbikes used for ferrying passengers all over Lagos, weaved in and out much to the annoyance of many car drivers, and on more than one occasion a car driver could be heard in fierce argument with an *okada* operator. These motorbike taxis had been banned on the island because it was believed they were much too disruptive to the normal flow of traffic. However, over time they had slowly but surely crept right back in, this time interspersed with converted motorbike tricycles built along the same lines as the tuk-tuks of Thailand. These rickshaws were called *Keke-Marwa* in Lagos after the Governor who was in power when they were first launched and were more suited for use as taxis because they could hold more passengers in a single journey than the conventional motorbikes. However, just like the *okadas*, they too were quite disruptive and unpopular with car drivers.

When they pulled up in front of The Dome, they all gasped at how impressive it looked. From the outside, it resembled a smaller version of the London Millennium dome. They parked in an allocated car space and were welcomed by an usher who handed them a program and pointed them to the entrance. As the three walked into the dome, they saw a temporary bar, serving cocktails and sodas. They all grabbed glasses of orange juice and stood together. Shortly after, Amanda arrived with Amaka and Bunmi. The girls hugged and chatted as Odera stood back and admired the genius of The Dome. From the inside, it looked almost like a cathedral with its high ceiling. It felt cool with air conditioning units strategically positioned all around the foyer.

As he stared, admiring the sheer engineering ingenuity of the luxury conference venue built out of a tent, he felt a tap on his shoulder and turned to see Angela Ude smiling at him. Angela was at the University of Nigeria with him, majoring in Pharmacy. They had mutual friends but had never quite gone beyond the cursory civilized 'hi' of strangers.

"Why hello," Odera smiled. "What brings you here?"

"I could say the same to you," she teased. "The Cokers are family friends and Ma Coker is my mum's godmother. So you see, I have to be here! There's no way I could pass up this invitation!"

Odera had never quite noticed Angela before. Well, he had but was too much of a gentleman and way too shy to go beyond those famous cursory 'hellos'. Angela was tall and quite pretty, with a very easy smile. She also smelled of fresh flowers and he smiled at his own naivety. Of course, she smelled of fresh flowers, she was wearing perfume, probably in bucket loads like his cousins whenever they went out.

"Shall we get a drink?" asked Angela, angling her head suggestively. Odera nodded immediately and followed her.

From the corner of her eye, Siyonna noticed the striking girl chatting with her cousin, and watched as they went off to get drinks. She smiled to herself. Good to see Odera talk to a girl who wasn't her or her sisters. He was so incurably shy around girls, that boy, she thought. She couldn't remember ever seeing Odera with a girl. Her dad always said he was a focused student and did incredibly well in school because he did not waste time with all the love nonsense, teenagers got entangled in, which always made Siyonna and her sister Ebele laugh.

Siyonna was still watching her cousin when Amanda tapped her lightly on the arm and pointed to Lola, who had just walked in. Siyonna was pleasantly surprised and called out to her friend. Lola came over with a huge smile on her face and hugged all the girls. She was wearing a long, simple maxi, made of Chiffon and lace and she looked absolutely magnificent.

"I know, I know, I didn't tell you I was coming," said Lola. "Apparently my mum and Dupe's mum are tight, so here we are. My mum insisted I come with them," she said, indicating the other side of the room where her parents were busy chatting away with some of the other adults.

"I must go and say hello to them," said Siyonna.

"I'll come with you," said Lola, linking arms with her.

Lola's parents were deep in conversation with another couple. Both girls stood courteously and waited. When there was a break in the conversation, Siyonna said "Good afternoon Sir. Good afternoon Ma." As Lola started to introduce her, her mother cut in quickly and said they knew who Siyonna was. They asked after Siyonna's parents and said to be sure to give them their best greetings. Siyonna curtsied and as both girls walked back to their group, the MC announced it was time to go in and be seated so the event could start.

Siyonna looked around for Odera who was now firmly attached to Angela and walking into the hall with her. Siyonna shrugged and turned to Amina and Amanda.

"That pretty girl over there appears to have stolen my cousin," she said.

The girls laughed.

"Never mind, you still have us," said Amanda. "I must say I am a bit jealous though. I always hoped that whenever Odera decided to start noticing girls, he'd notice only me and then close up again."

All the girls laughed and promptly told Amanda again that she was far too young to date a boy in university.

The hall was even better decorated than the foyer, the walls draped in fine gold and red organza. The girls found a table and were joined by other teenagers. In typical Owambe style, there was a live band belting out *Juju* and *Afrobeat* tunes to the great delight of the seated guests. Soon the MC interrupted the music to introduce himself and requested those still not seated to hurry up and do so because the celebrant would be making an entrance soon. A few minutes later, the MC came back on stage and asked everybody to rise for the entrance of Ma Modupe Adekunbi Coker, the celebrant who was turning 80 today.

As everyone rose to their feet, the band started playing one of Sunny Ade's songs extolling the virtues of the new octogenarian. Ma Coker came into view to great and rapturous applause from the guests. She was dressed in stunning purple lace *Iro and buba* set, accessorized with beautiful coral beads. As she danced through the doors, all her children, grandchildren, sons and daughters in law followed her in a train, dancing and the guests went wild, cheering and clapping as the procession made its way through the middle of the hall to the podium that had been decorated for the celebrant. It was slow going as the procession danced slowly, soaking up the applause, as it guided the celebrant to the dais where the celebrant would sit.

As she came to the middle of the hall, some of the guests went over to where she was dancing and joined her, spraying her with money as was customary in *Owambe*. As the notes began to form a small mound around her, Dupe and her cousin went over and started gathering the notes into piles and putting them in plastic bags. As each bag filled up, it was handed to an adult relative for safekeeping. When the dancing had gone on for about ten minutes, the MC asked the guests to kindly sit down.

Introductions over, a beautiful buffet of fried rice, jollof rice, *ewedu*, various salads and different types of meat was laid out and guests were invited to eat. Siyonna and her friends all went for the jollof rice, always a party favourite, and also took some salad and beef cubes. The food was delicious and between mouthfuls, the girls talked about the beauty of the

Nigerian salad that came with diced hard-boiled eggs and generous quantities of salad cream.

"Heinz" Amanda piped up. "It has got to be Heinz or it really isn't salad cream at all!" and all the other girls laughed.

When most people had finished eating, the band started belting out popular tunes and people hit the dance floor. Most of the songs were classic Yoruba Juju songs and the band did Sunny Ade and Ebenezer Obey justice as they played tune after tune to the joy of the guests. Every time Ma Coker came out to dance, people surrounded her and sprayed her with even more money! Siyonna thought it was amazing. It almost felt that the pockets around the room were self-regenerating! Where was all the money coming from, she wondered. Out of the corner of her eye, she noticed a man in a billowing navy *agbada* with red borders and matching fila going from table to table. She wondered what he was doing as he seemed to hover around the tables and then move on.

Every so often Dupe would do a sweep of the room and drag her friends back to the dance floor. As Siyonna and her friends danced to Juju music, the mood suddenly changed as from the back of the hall, D'banj appeared to strands of 'Oliver' and the crowd went wild. As he finished his set, Ice Prince showed up as well to wow the crowd. When the two major artistes were done, the band came back on stage to belt out even more favourites.

Siyonna had danced for over an hour non-stop and was having such a great time. However, when Amina told her that there were mini-baskets of fried yam and plantain being passed around as dessert, she made a beeline for one of the waiters who smilingly handed her a mini-basket with the goodies. As she tucked in, Siyonna turned to Amina.

"Surely heaven couldn't get any better than this, could it?" she said and they both laughed.

Soon a sweaty Amanda joined them.

"I guess we'd better give the celebrant our present, shouldn't we?"

Siyonna yelped in relief and thanked Amanda for remembering. The girls went to find Amaka, who was busy chatting with a group of girls from Holy Trinity College in Lagos and happened to be in the same class as Dupe's cousin Yinka. Siyonna said a quick hi to the girls and grabbed Amaka.

"Come on, we need to find Dupe and give her grandma the card and present we bought. It's getting late and we probably should be heading out soon."

Amaka agreed and the girls found Dupe helping a child who had spilt her drink on her dress. The little girl must have been about 3 or 4 and was quite happily gulping down a bottle of malt as Dupe worked feverishly to get the stain off her lovely brocade dress. Dupe hugged her.

"Ronke say hi to my friends?"

Little Ronke took the big bottle out of her mouth long enough to mumble a hello, and back again it went. They all laughed.

"Give me a minute," said Dupe. "I need to hand little madam here back to her mum and I'll be with you."

When she got back, the girls told Dupe they had a gift for her grandma and asked if they could leave it with her.

"Guys that is really sweet of you!" said Dupe. "You will give it to her yourselves. Come on let's go before she leaves. She's getting tired now."

As they headed for the stage, something again caught Siyonna's eye as she saw the gentleman in the navy *Agbada* sweep through their table and started to beat a quick retreat towards the door.

"Amina," she said. "Where's your purse?"

Amina's jaw dropped as all the girls looked at her.

"I guess I left it at our table," she said, sheepishly.

At that moment, a lady wearing a large, gold Organza headscarf and gold lace buba and Iro started screaming.

"*Ole!* Thief!" she cried.

With her hands on her head, the distraught woman was screaming that her purse and mobile phone were gone. Siyonna looked at Dupe.

"I think that guy in the navy *Agbada* heading for the entrance just stole Amina's purse."

Dupe acted very quickly, breaking into a run, followed by her friends. As she ran past him, a suited security guard looked questioningly at her and she simply pointed to the figure now sprinting towards the door.

"That guy stole my friend's purse," she shouted.

The security guard ran after the retreating figure who realised he'd been rumbled and ran even faster.

"Stop that guy! *OLE!*" yelled the security guard.

Lola, who had indulged quite liberally in the fruit punch, was just coming out of the toilet at the foyer when she heard the shouts and saw a figure sprinting towards her, clutching his billowing *Agbada*. She stepped aside and as the thief came parallel to her, stuck her leg out to trip the man, but he had somehow anticipated that, feinted slightly to the left and kept running. Siyonna stood very still, watching the surreal scene unfold before her. She rubbed the beads of her necklace and as the thief got to the door a heavy bar stool inexplicably fell and rolled directly into his path. The man saw it too late and crashed to the ground, just as the guard got to him. As he fell, his *Agbada* tore and out spilt purses, wallets, phones and other accessories he'd stolen in what would have been a very profitable evening for him.

As the man lay on the ground, yelling about his broken ankle, the security guard grabbed him. Siyonna came over and picked up Amina's bag, which had flown out of his grip when he fell. Lola looked at her friends, all gasping for air, then looked at Siyonna with the bag.

"Let me guess," she said. "Amina's?"

The girls all burst out laughing, despite the aftereffects of running full-pelt in high heels.

"No point asking how you guessed," said Siyonna as a grateful Amina muttered her thanks and checked her bag for her phone and cash.

"All there?" asked Dupe.

"Yes," said Amina, timidly.

The lady in the gold headscarf and other guests arrived and identified their belongings from bags and wallets strewn all over the place, as the other security guards gathered up the rest of the loot and waited for the police.

"What will happen to him?" Siyonna asked the guard, hustling the thief away.

"We'll hand him over to the police. It's now a matter for them." He replied.

They thanked him for his help and watched as the thief, limping badly and protesting his innocence, was dragged away from the lobby and into the security office to await the arrival of the police.

"Shall we go see grandma now?" asked Dupe, still trying to catch her breath.

The girls nodded, waved Lola goodbye and followed Dupe back into the hall. They made their way through the crowds to the podium where Ma Coker was seated, still receiving guests. Fortunately, there was just one couple ahead of the girls and as they finished, Dupe went up to her grandmother and told her that her friends had all clubbed together and bought her a gift. The old lady smiled and hugged each girl in turn, asked their names and added that as she got older, she couldn't promise to remember the names, but she would remember each of them and their kindness. She thanked them again and blessed them in Yoruba, promising they would each have children who would care and look after them in their own old age, to a chorus of 'Amen' from onlookers who were themselves waiting to see her.

As they left, Siyonna saw Odera waiting at the door.

"Ready?" he asked.

Siyonna smiled. Yes, she certainly was ready to go now. What an evening. What a way to start the summer holidays. This one would be hard to top. "Thank you Dupe!"

13

London

Siyonna rolled off her bed and jumped up. It was Sunday and she had to go to church with her parents. If you asked Zach and Obiageli Nduka if they were modern parents, they would both yell, yes. They had, after all, supported their children's dreams, and were liberal enough to let the kids do what they liked, within the rules of decency and of course being mindful of the rules of the house and family. But where they were both unbending was when it came to the question of Mass on Sundays. All children and guests were expected to go to church, whatever their denomination. Even the Bakaris accepted that when Amina stayed with the Ndukas, she had to attend Mass with them.

Zach Nduka and Nazir Bakare, Amina's dad, had met at University as scholarship students from Nigeria. They had developed a strong friendship and found they had very similar experiences even though they were from different parts of Nigeria. As Zach was an engineering major, he left Glasgow a few years earlier and returned to Nigeria. Nazir did the same when he qualified. He returned home and got his first job at the Lagos General Hospital.

One day he showed up at his friend's flat unannounced. Zach opened the door, saw his friend standing there with his suitcase, hugged him, fed him and showed him to his guest room. Only when his friend was comfortable did they settle in for a long chat about life, plans and what had brought him to Zach's door. And so it was that Nazir lived with his friend for the next two years, only moving out when it became obvious that Obiageli, who was an occasional visitor to the two bedroom apartment in Surulere, was about to make the transition from girlfriend to the resident Mrs Nduka. As soon as Zach Nduka announced he was headed to the village to ask for Obiageli's hand in marriage, Nazir took the flat directly next door.

Over the years, they stayed close to each other, even after Nazir married. They finally lost touch when Nazir got a job first in Kano, then moved to England and the United States for his specialist training. They only reconnected when Amina and Siyonna found each other at Our Lady's and it was like time had stood still for them. Amina was always at the Ndukas largely because she had so much in common with Siyonna. She had two older brothers, both at University in the United States.

Amina had gone back to Abuja the day after Dupe's Granny's *Owambe*. It had been a week now but the girls spoke almost every day. Amina's brothers were back home for the summer break and the family would spend the summer together at home in Abuja. Siyonna hoped she could head for England at some point but since no one had said anything more about it, she slept, read, helped around the house and waited. Whenever Odera was around, which wasn't that often anymore since he discovered Angela, they would hang out and watch movies until Odera had to go to bed. Odera was still working at her father's firm and would do so throughout the summer and go back to university in September. Angela's family lived in Ikoyi and it was quite convenient for Odera to drop by and see her on his way back from work most days.

Siyonna had not thought about Dante in a while. When he went back to the United States, they spoke a few times and it just stopped. Siyonna imagined this was partly because of distance and the cost of calls, and then sensibly thought that perhaps they were in different places in their lives. His interest in her, flattering as it was, never quite extinguished that little sliver of doubt that accompanied her every day, willing her to wake up from her dreams of 'happy ever afters.' So, when the calls simply stopped coming, she neither felt hurt nor disappointed. It was what it was.

However, at Sunday lunch yesterday, her mum announced she was meeting Mrs Saul-Obi on Monday to go through designs for a new line of clothes for her stores. Siyonna stopped and looked at her mum, knowing exactly what was coming next.

"So how is that Dante boy sef?" her mum started. "Are you two still seeing each other?"

Siyonna almost giggled. How many times had she seen her mum put her sisters under the spotlight like this? It was her turn now, she guessed.

"Mum we were never seeing each other. Dante's in university doing university stuff and I am here trying to get good enough grades to get on with my life. In future, who knows? Right now, I just want to be 16. Could I have some more chicken, please mum?" she asked before her mum had the chance to prod some more.

Zach smiled and buried his face in a particularly juicy piece of meat on his plate. Touché, he thought, the girl is an Nduka through and through.

She was getting bored staying at home and knew it. She decided to ask her mum for a job. She could work in the fabric shop in the market. It was hard work, but she loved the banter and the stream of interesting ladies who patronised her mum. She loved helping them choose fabrics and also loved the healthy tips she got! Yes, she decided, she'd ask her mum for a job, since London really wasn't on the cards anymore. The travails of being 16!

She got out of bed and looked out the window. It was Monday morning, and everybody had gone to work. Same old, same old. She headed to the family room and plopped on the sofa, turning on the television and picking up CNN. She listened to the news for a while and as usual, there was some war somewhere, natural disaster somewhere else. She was just about to switch off when she saw an advert for scholarships to New York University for degrees in English and creative writing. The scholarship was for students from developing countries and the application was to be accompanied by a 3000-word essay on any subject. Siyonna grabbed a notepad and took furious notes of the details on screen. Now, all of a sudden, her summer began to look busy.

As soon as the advert finished, she switched off the television and was just about to go back to her room when she heard her father's voice as he came up the stairs. Odd, she thought, dad is never home this early on a weekday. As she got to the top of the stairs, she ran into him.

"Onna-mma quick, start packing," he said. "You fly out to England on Saturday. You have to go Saturday because Ebele's off and can pick you up from Heathrow when you land. Anything else you'll have to make your own way and I really wouldn't want to risk that."

Siyonna opened her mouth to speak but nothing came out. She flew into his arms. Zach Nduka rubbed her head as he used to when she was a little girl.

"Now tell me you don't have the best dad in the world," he teased, as Siyonna hugged him and held on tight.

She knew then that the government cheque had cleared. "Thank you, Ma Mabel!" whispered Siyonna.

The next few days were frenetic, to say the least. Siyonna packed for her trip, finished the essay for the scholarship application to New York University and submitted it to USAID in Lagos. She spoke with her sister and did her best to stave off her mum who was hell-bent on making sure Siyonna took every Nigerian foodstuff known to man on her trip. Fighting Obiageli off was not an easy task and eventually, Siyonna relented and agreed to take a little of everything her mother was sending to Ebele.

Unbeknownst to her, Zach had already applied for her visa and the British High Commission had issued one, without requesting an interview. All she recalled of the exercise was being asked to sign visa forms long before she even knew she was travelling. And today, she was flying out to the UK, to spend three weeks with her sister Ebele! Siyonna had never been to London. There had been a trip to Canada with her parents to see Adaobi just outside Toronto but that had been a long time ago. She had been really young then and had only a passing memory of the trip.

She got to the Murtala Muhammed International Airport Lagos and Mr Sunday dropped her off at the entrance to the departure hall, helping her lift her single suitcase out of the car's boot. He looked at her in a sombre fashion and reminded her to remember all the good advice her parents had given her and also told her not to talk to strangers.

"People dem bad my pikin. If person give you bag to hold for dis Airport, no 'gree oh, you hear?" he said, his thumb and index finger gripping his right ear lobe and pulling it as he spoke.

"Yes Mr Sunday, I go remember everything wey you tell me. Thank you sir," then gave him a quick hug and headed into the departure hall.

She joined the Virgin Atlantic queue and it was soon her turn.

"Hello there, could I have your passport and ticket please?" asked the lady at the check-in counter.

Siyonna stuck her hand in her bag and froze. She had left the ticket and passport on the car seat. As her eyes welled up with tears, she explained her predicament to the lady, who turned out to be quite sympathetic. She had seen this before.

"Go call your driver and see if he can come back. Leave your suitcase with that gentleman," she said, beckoning a Virgin Atlantic Airline assistant, and asking him to keep the suitcase for Siyonna for a few minutes whilst she got her travel documents.

Siyonna mumbled her thanks and ran for the exit, phone at her ear. Mr Sunday answered at first ring.

"My pikin, I get your ticket dem I dey return now now."

Siyonna heaved a huge sigh of relief, looked heavenward and mumbled a thank you to God, and headed to where Mr Sunday had dropped her. He took a while as traffic was now beginning to build up into the airport. As the car came into view, Siyonna ran to it and Mr Sunday handed her the documents through the passenger window.

"*Abeg my pikin, shine your eye o, you hear?*" he said, then waved her goodbye and pulled away.

Siyonna ran back to the check-in counter, found the porter who she'd left her suitcase with. He wheeled it out to her and she joined the queue again. Finally, armed with boarding pass and her completed exit forms, Siyonna went through immigration and customs and arrived in the departures lounge, waiting for her flight to be called. Sitting down, she pulled out the copy of Buchi Emecheta's novel, *Second class citizen* and was just about to get lost in the pages when she heard a familiar voice.

"Siyonna! What are you doing here?"

She turned and saw Sally Eze standing over her, oversized bag on her arm and a sulky boy standing next to her. Siyonna looked up and smiled, doing her best to hide her shock.

"Sally," she said. "What a surprise. I'm on my way to the UK to visit my sister for the summer. How are you? I take it you're also headed to London?"

"Yes oh! My younger brother and I are going to join my mum over there for the summer. I am sooo excited! We're staying at our place in Hendon and I might stay on for A Levels and University, I don't know."

With that, Sally plopped herself right next to Siyonna, forcing the rather buxom lady sitting to the left of them to move and leaving her brother standing in front of them and glaring at both of them. Sally launched into a speech about how conflicted she was. As Siyonna knew, (actually Siyonna didn't until then) she held British citizenship because, you know, her parents had lived in Britain and had her whilst they were still in Britain. So, she had a choice to stay on and seek a place at University after A Levels. But oh, she really couldn't be sure! Oh, decisions, de-ci-si-ons! So what did Siyonna think? What were Siyonna's plans? Was she going to stay in Britain or come back? Siyonna shrugged and said she was coming home after her break. She was hoping that the Joint Admission & Matriculations Board would have released university entrance examinations results by the time she came back. If she wasn't successful, then she might have to try her luck with one of the new private universities. Sally crinkled her nose in obvious derision and was just about to launch into a discourse on the inadequacies of private tertiary institutions in Nigeria when mercifully, their flight was called and they headed for the gate.

Siyonna presumed Sally had a seat in a different section of the large Virgin Atlantic flight to Heathrow because she did not see her on the flight. She could have sworn she heard her arguing with her brother as they boarded but thought it best not to turn to look.

The flight was smooth. Siyonna had a window seat in economy and gladly lapped up her surroundings. Not for the first time in her life, she marvelled at the ingenuity of lifting a plane full of people over 30,000 feet high and flying it across continents and oceans! She marvelled at the science of jet propulsion and the sheer brilliance of the inquisitive human spirit. She was still staring out of her window, lost in her thoughts as the huge Boeing soared through clouds and there was nothing to see but clouds when suddenly there was that familiar voice again.

"I was looking for you. Charlie and I are in front if you ever need company. There is a free seat there too, if you want?" said Sally, standing in the aisle.

Siyonna looked up and smiled, thanking her and saying she'd stay at her seat for a while. Sally smiled and went on to the lavatory at the other end of the plane. Siyonna sighed softly and picked up her book. She must have drifted off because the next thing she remembered was being woken up to eat. She picked at the rice and beef she had chosen and enjoyed the dessert more. Lunch over, she thought it might be a good idea to get up and stretch her legs, so she squeezed past the lady sitting next to her and headed to the lady's. Her row sat 3 but fortunately, they had a spare seat between them, much to Siyonna's relief.

For the rest of the flight, Siyonna watched movies and slept when she was tired. The flight took 6 hours and they finally landed at Heathrow late in the afternoon. As she made her way to immigration, she saw Sally and her brother ahead. At the barrier, they headed for the UK citizens' queue which moved much faster than the non-EU citizens' queue Siyonna had to go through. When it was her turn, the Immigration officer wanted to know why Siyonna was in the UK, how long she was going to stay, was she going to work? Did she plan on staying back with her sister? The questions were so quick and practically followed the script her dad had told her to expect. As the Immigration officer turned the passport and fired off these questions, her face was completely inscrutable and Siyonna half expected her to look up and tell her that her "leave to enter the UK is hereby revoked." But the lady suddenly broke out into a broad smile.

"Welcome to the UK, Miss Nduka, enjoy your stay," she said, handing her passport back to her.

Siyonna muttered a thank you and with great relief, followed the signs for luggage retrieval. She found her suitcase on the carousel and dragged it off, following the signs for the exit when Sally turned up again.

"I was waiting for you. I sort of thought it might take you longer to clear immigration because you were travelling on a foreign passport. Anyway Siyonna, here is my mum's number where you can reach me if you want to do something or just want to hang out? I know I wasn't always nice to you during our time at our Lady's and I am sorry. I will try to be a better person from now on. If you need me, just call, please? Promise you'll think about it?"

Siyonna nodded and instinctively hugged her and said goodbye, then headed for the exit just as Sally gathered her things and with her brother beside her, pushed her trolley towards the exit.

As Siyonna went through the green 'Nothing to Declare' exit, customs officials stood by, idly watching the passengers as they passed. Siyonna's heart skipped a beat as she remembered the carefully packed food parcels her mum had insisted on putting in her suitcase. Fortunately, the customs officials were not there for her. She walked right out, heaving a huge sigh of relief and as she came through duty-free out onto the concourse, she saw her sister, hopping up and down and calling out to her. She half dragged, half carried her suitcase over to her sister and they hugged for what felt like an eternity. Ebele pushed her back and studied her from top to bottom.

"Good Lord Siyonna'nma, you have grown into a beautiful woman! I am surprised your father let you travel on your own!"

Siyonna laughed, smacking her sister playfully.

"Your father let you come and live here all by yourself, didn't he? I am not a baby anymore. I'll be in Uni this year, you know?" she said, as Ebele made a face and mimicked her before they both collapsed into each other's arms in laughter.

"Come on, Uni-girl, we have a long journey home," said Ebele.

She linked hands with her sister, they grabbed Siyonna's suitcase and headed out. Ebele led them to a ticketing office and bought a ticket for Siyonna, then she led her through the turnstiles onto the tube platform where they got on the Piccadilly Line. Siyonna had never been on a tube train before. When she thought about it, she realized she had never been on any train at all. Rail travel was not very big in Nigeria so most journeys tended to be by road or air. Siyonna marvelled at the fact that this subterranean mode of transport could whip you across the city avoiding all the traffic jams common with big city travel. As Ebele reeled out facts on tube travel, Siyonna listened attentively as she went through the tube map identifying London landmarks, she'd mostly seen on a Monopoly board. The first underground rail line had been built by Marc Brunel in 1843, and by 1902 most of the underground had been electrified. The tube line at over 150 years old was the oldest in the world.

Ebele lived in Cockfosters, a suburb in North London and it was on the Piccadilly Line so they did not have to change trains. It did however, take a long time to get there. Cockfosters was the northernmost end of the line and by the time they got there, about an hour and a half later, most of the other passengers had left. Siyonna did not mind this in the least as she lapped up the experience and took in the sights as the train went from subterranean to above ground travel, and back under again at different stops. At Cockfosters Station Ebele got her an Oyster card and put enough money on it for a week's travel, explaining to Siyonna that they could top it up when her travel plans became clearer. Siyonna thanked her sister.

Ebele's flat was on Ebony Crescent and the girls caught the number 296 bus from Cockfosters Station to Chase Side which led to Ebony Crescent.

"This is probably your quickest route into town. You always get on this bus from the station to get to mine," explained Ebele, as the bus arrived at their stop.

The girls then walked the two minutes to Ebele's block. Ebele was renting a one-bedroom flat in a modern block. It was beautiful and Siyonna told her sister that she loved the whole block.

"It's perfect for me," she smiled. "I am always working and needed somewhere not too far from the station. I'm mostly in Barnet General Hospital thankfully and that isn't too far from here."

They took the lift to the second floor and Siyonna followed Ebele to flat 12. They walked into a tastefully furnished living room that opened onto a balcony overlooking a common garden. It was cool and welcoming, with an open plan kitchen. As Siyonna gushed over the property, Ebele smiled and showed her sister round the flat.

"We'll share the room. A bit like old days when you practically slept on my back because you were scared of the ghost of Zupa!" she laughed.

Zupa was the imaginary ghoul who had terrified Siyonna until she was about six. No-one ever quite worked out where Zupa came from but he became a constant in Siyonna's dreams. So, before the screaming would start, Ebele would take her into her own bed and hold her until she slept. And so, the two slept together, wrapped around each other, until Siyonna forgot about Zupa when she turned six. Either that, or as their father dryly remarked, Zupa went on to terrify another hapless 3-year-old!

As the sisters finished an early dinner, they sat in the living room and talked. They caught up on life and Ebele wanted to know what had been going on since she was last there. Siyonna filled her in as much as possible and appeared to save the best for last when she suddenly told her sister that Christian, Mama Obele's son, had come home from Italy. Ebele whooped with joy and held Siyonna's hands firmly in both of hers.

"Tell me all about it?" she said, wild-eyed. "Is he normal? Is he married? What is the story with him?"

"Not a lot to tell from what I hear," smiled Siyonna. "He is fine and had not written because it took him a while to settle. He is married to an Italian, has two sons and owns a haulage business over there. I did not see him and he was coming over to the house, tomorrow I think, on his way back to Italy. From what mum said, he is doing just fine and his visit has given Mama Obele a new lease of life."

"I am really pleased for Mama Obele," said Ebele. "I am thrilled the story has a happy ending. It really could have been worse."

They called home and both girls spoke to their parents. Siyonna told them she'd had a good flight and Ebele had been there to pick her up. She had made a list of things she wanted to do whilst she was in the UK, and she also wanted to travel to Surrey to see Mr Bellamy's parents, fulfilling the promise she had made them.

The next morning, Ebele woke her up. The girls got dressed and headed out for a quick mile run around the neighbourhood. Siyonna could not believe she was struggling to keep up with Ebele. This was the first time in their lives she had ever found herself behind her sister in a jog! Must be England, she thought wistfully. They showered and headed out to church. After church, Ebele took Siyonna into town. They went to Oxford Street where they spent the afternoon going to more shops than Siyonna had ever seen. They did Primark where Siyonna picked up a few casual things for the summer, then went on to Jigsaw and Zara, and just walked the length of Oxford Street, also popping into Selfridges. At most places, Ebele would pick up something for her sister and at the end of it, Siyonna was laden with a few shopping bags. The girls popped into Wagamama, the Japanese restaurant on Bond Street, for dinner, then headed home.

That evening, Ebele's boyfriend Jon came to visit. Ebele was always coy about him, not saying a lot to Siyonna's prodding, aside from "you'll see when you meet him." Jon was a Trauma Surgeon. Like Ebele, he was keen to work abroad and was applying to join the World Health Organisation, hoping to work for them in war-torn areas for two years. Jon was slightly taller than Ebele and quite handsome in an understated way. He had the firm build of someone who spent time in the gym and had an easy smile. Whenever he smiled, he looked even younger than his 28 years, and he smiled a lot.

Jon Derring was a surprise for Siyonna. He was white and in all their years growing up, Ebele wouldn't even date light-skinned boys. She always stated she would never date or marry a boy who was not dark and wore glasses. Siyonna would smile and ask what difference the glasses made, and Ebele would say it showed the boy was serious. Well, Jon was neither dark, black nor wore glasses.

As Siyonna smiled inside, she kept trying to catch Ebele's eye and Ebele did her best to avoid her gaze. This was so funny, Siyonna thought.

"So, Siyonna, Ebele tells me you want to go to Egham?" he said. "We can take you on Saturday if you like? We can make a day out of it and grab lunch afterwards. What do you think?"

"Thanks, yes that would be lovely," she smiled.

"Good," he said. "That's settled then. We'll go to Egham on Saturday."

After Jon left, Siyonna quizzed her sister: how did they meet? Was this love? Had she told the parents? Initially, Ebele tried to fob her off with the big sister 'you are just a child, go away' attitude, but Siyonna was persistent and kept coming back so, an hour later, Ebele capitulated. Yes, it was serious with Jon, she had never, ever met anyone like him before, and yes this was love. Yes, she had told the parents she was dating but not whom. She would tell them at the end of summer after Siyonna went back. Or perhaps Siyonna should tell them? Oh no, Siyonna insisted, their father would wonder why this sort of news was coming from Siyonna.

"You should tell them yourself," said Siyonna, firmly.

Ebele grudgingly agreed. It was the right thing to do. Then the girls talked till late that evening until Ebele declared she was off to bed. She had an early start the next day. Siyonna was out like a light, lying next to her sister. She woke up to Ebele sitting at the side of the bed and gently shaking her awake.

"Sleepyhead, I'm off to work," she said. "I have left my spare mobile phone for you to use," and she pointed to the bedside table. "You can't reach me because I'll be stuck in clinics all day. I will call when I get a minute but you should go out and see London if you like. Text if you need anything. I'll see you later."

Ebele kissed her sister lightly on the top of her head and was gone.

Siyonna lay in the bed for a while. She turned on the bedside radio and listened to music. It was a pop station playing some of the current hits. Bopping to music, she got up, made the bed and wondered what to do with the rest of the day. She jumped into the shower and let the warm water and strong jets wake her up fully. When she stepped out, she felt alive and ready for the day ahead. As she dressed, she tried to plan her day. Dressed in a pair of jeans, trainers and light top, she went out to the balcony and looked out at the courtyard below. It looked so peaceful and bright in the London summer light. She should explore London, she thought. Yes, she should head out and look at London. But to do it alone? Perhaps it would be more fun if she actually went with somebody else?

The only other person she knew who was in London was Sally and gosh, she really did not see how she could spend the day with Sally. No, Siyonna thought, I'll venture out on my own.

She grabbed a toast and marmalade and sat on the barstool in the open-plan, kitchen-living area, planning her day. She thought she'd do some of the sights, maybe the London Eye and some of the other attractions around the city. She wasn't quite sure how it worked but she had some money and felt she should head out and explore.

Getting into London was quite fun as she hopped from tube train to tube train until she got to Waterloo. She had to be vigilant so she didn't miss her stop and she studied her tube map as if her life depended on it. When she finally alighted from the Bakerloo Line at Waterloo, she followed the signs for the exit and when she got to the ticket barrier, she walked up to a young lady in the blue London Underground uniform and explained she was trying to get to the London Eye. The lady was very helpful, telling her how to get there.

"You can't miss it," she said, with a smile. "It's less than 10 minutes from here. Do you already have tickets?

When Siyonna said no, the lady, who Siyonna now knew as Sharon from the badge on her blouse, told her where to go for tickets and then added that she could get combo tickets that would let her do the London Aquarium and London eye today if she wanted. When Siyonna said yes please, she'd like that, Sharon gave her directions. Siyonna thanked her and made her way to the Aquarium, where she bought her tickets and was given a map to follow and walked into the dark and blue London Aquarium. Because it was right in the middle of summer the aquarium was busy with tourists. Siyonna made her way around the Aquarium and watched their live shows. She held her breath a few times as she watched some of the divers in a shark tank with sharks around them! Siyonna could not understand how anyone could be brave enough to want to go into a tank with sharks. Simply amazing, she thought. The sharks seemed quite uninterested in them.

There were also other shows with giant stingrays and divers with giant turtles and Siyonna also stayed for the penguin feeding. Siyonna loved the way the penguins waddled and even though she had seen them on nature shows, this was the first time she had ever been up close to them.

She left the Aquarium after one and a half hours and frankly, would have liked to stay for another live show but wanted to catch the London Eye. So, she walked over to the Southbank and joined the queue. It took about half an hour to get to the front and get on a capsule. As the capsule began its slow, deliberate climb, she saw an outlay of the city in front of her. In the 30 minutes it took to complete the cycle, she saw the Houses of Parliament, Buckingham Palace, the Shard and other London sights. She saw Tower Bridge and also watched in amazement as its bridge opened to let a big ship go through. She took as many photographs as she could on her smartphone.

As she left her capsule with the other passengers, she heard a phone ringing. It took her a while to realize it was the phone her sister had given her. She quickly grabbed it and pressed the green answer button as she walked, looking for a quiet spot to take the call. She walked into Jubilee Gardens and found a park bench.

"Hello?" she said.

"How are you getting on?" asked Ebele.

Siyonna smiled and gave her sister a brief update on her day. Ebele said she was aiming to be home a little after 5 and Siyonna promised to be home when Ebele came back. She put the phone back in her pocket and for the first time, took a look around her. She already felt too warm as she sat on the exposed park bench under the English summer sun. But all around her, she saw people lying on the beautifully manicured lawn. It was quite a sight for her. Back home in Nigeria, people dived for the shade whenever the sun was out. You walked purposefully in the sun but you didn't stop and ask it to bathe you! But even as incongruous as this appeared to her, she still loved the buzz and energy she got from this space just beneath the London Eye. It was busy as the holiday crowd milled around.

After a few minutes, Siyonna got up and made her way back to the Southbank Centre, where she stopped at a café for a muffin and coke. As she bit into the muffin, she noticed the amazing Southbank water fountains and watched people standing right in the middle of them as the water rose for about a minute, then walked out without getting wet. As she looked longingly at the fountain, the middle-aged lady sitting next to her at the café noticed her.

"It's called the appearing rooms," she said. "Would you like me to take your picture in the fountain, love? Go on, give me the phone and I'll take a few. Don't forget to take your bag," she said as they both walked out and Siyonna stood in the middle of the fountain and struck different poses as the lady snapped away with her phone camera.

At the end of the minute, Siyonna came out from the water wall that had disappeared just before the next sequence started and thanked the kind lady who smiled, handed her the phone and left. Siyonna walked into the Southbank Centre and looked around the ground floor. There were tourists and also a few events going on and she wondered whether she should stay for any of them. Then she looked at her watch and thought, better not. It was already 3.30 and she wanted to be back at Ebele's by the time she came back from work. So, she ran across the pedestrian bridge down into Waterloo tube station and started her journey home.

That evening, Siyonna recounted her adventures to her sister and posted her pictures on social media.

"You have always wanted to write, right?" said Ebele. "Why not start with a travel blog capturing your time in

England? Your adventures, what you thought, where you went?"

Siyonna thought about it. She did have enough material to share. Sitting at her laptop, she worked with Ebele to set up a blog on Google's free blog space. She called her blog *Siyonna's space*, and she started talking through ideas for her first blog with her sister.

"Might be best to do your draft in Word first and review before you post on your blog?" warned Ebele cautiously.

Siyonna agreed and pulled up a Word document and started writing.

Siyonna spent most of the next day, Tuesday, in her sister's flat, only popping out to the high street to look around. There wasn't really a lot on the high street. Cockfosters was pretty suburban and Siyonna began to regret her decision to take a rest day. Had she woken up early, she could have headed up to London. However, after Ebele went to bed, she had stayed up in the living room writing and finally finished her blog post about 1 a.m. By the time she finally woke up, she knew that heading out to the West End would be a waste of her fare. She might as well stay home today and head out tomorrow, she decided.

After exploring the short parade of shops on Cockfosters High Street, she decided to go down to Southgate, about a mile away. As she made the walk down to Southgate, Siyonna realized that she really could use some company. Ebele was busy with work and would struggle to spend a lot of time with her. She had promised to take Friday off so they could spend a long weekend together but between now and then, Siyonna really thought she could use a wingman. So, as she made her way back from Southgate, she called the only other person she knew in London, Sally. Actually, it was

Sally's mum because that was the only number she had for Sally.

"Hello?"

"Good afternoon ma," said Siyonna. "Please may I speak with Sally?"

"Hold on, I'll give her the phone," said Sally's mum.

"OMG Siyonna!" said Sally. "What a pleasant surprise! Where are you? Let's meet up! What are you doing now?"

Siyonna tried to answer the barrage of questions as best as she could and when she told Sally where she was, it turned out they were not too far from each other. Sally explained her parents had a place in Hendon and having taken Siyonna's address, promised to come and get her within the hour. Siyonna skipped home and spent the next hour, or what felt like an eternity, waiting for Sally. True to her word, Sally rang the buzzer to Ebele's flat exactly an hour after they spoke. When Siyonna asked if she wanted to come up, Sally said no, she had gotten a lift from her older sister who was in a hurry. So, Siyonna locked up, took the lift downstairs to a waiting Sally who hugged her, linked hands with her and walked her to a smart little Ford with her sister behind the wheel.

"This is my big sister Gabby. Gabby this is my friend Siyonna," beamed Sally.

Gabby smiled and said a quick hi, put the car in shift and drove off. As she cut through the busy London traffic with the ease of someone who had spent a lifetime driving in London, Siyonna mused at the absurdity of driving on the wrong side of the road. The United Kingdom was in the minority of countries that drove on the left. It took 20 minutes and a myriad of back roads to get them back to

Sally's parents in Hendon. Sally jumped out of the car and held the door open for Siyonna, thanked Gabby who smiled and screeched out of the compound back on the road and vanished in a screech of spinning tyres.

"Jeeze that girl drives like a nutter," said Sally, linking arms and walking Siyonna into the house.

Sally's parent's house backed onto Sunny Hill Park. Passing through the double doors, the girls walked into a big Victorian hallway that led into two living rooms. Sally's brother was plopped in front of a huge television screen, playing a video game and hardly acknowledged them, even when Sally yelled at him.

"Charlie that is so rude! Say hello to Siyonna."

He turned a petulant head, mumbled a perfunctory hello and went straight back to his game. Siyonna smiled and went with Sally to say hi to her parents who were watching the news in the next room. Mrs Eze was surprisingly soft-spoken and extremely attentive to her husband, who didn't say much. He looked up from his newspaper, smiled, welcomed Siyonna and went back to his paper. Siyonna and Sally quickly retired to Sally's room where they listened to music and Sally filled her in on the London buzz. Apparently, there was quite a contingent of Our Lady's girls over for the summer and Sally had spoken to a few. She offered to show Siyonna some of the fun things to do in London.

"Don't worry," she said. "You will have a lovely time, I promise."

Elsewhere in Tottenham, an area in the North London Borough of Haringey, Tyrell Parker was sitting on the porch in front of his mother's block of flats in St. Ann's Road waiting to be picked up by Jamie. Tyrell needed to raise money fast. As he chewed on a fingernail and watched his cigarette burn towards the butt, he wondered again how he could have shown such poor judgment. Derek 'Fishneck' Gaines had pulled up on Saturday morning as he walked down Green Lanes and called him over to his jeep. He'd gone over and Derek handed him a large dirty brown envelope filled to the brim with fifty- pound notes and asked him to deliver it to Mad Tony, 'personally'.

Now had Mad Tony been around when Tyrell went over to his usual haunt at the Rose and Crown Pub, perhaps the story would have been different. However, Mad Tony wasn't there, and no one knew when he would be back. So, Tyrell left, with Mad Tony's cash burning a hole in his pocket.

He returned to the flat he shared with his mum and younger sister Shauna and went to his room. Fortunately, both his mum and Shauna were out working so he had the place to himself. Sitting on his bed, he pulled all the money out of the envelope and tried to count the notes. He got lost after £20,000. He really did not have a head for figures. Truth be told, Tyrell did not have a head for much at all. So, having concluded that there was a 'lot of money' in the envelope, he surmised Mad T wouldn't miss a note or two, so helped himself to 10 of the £50 notes. Then he popped out and soon found his friends Jamie and Donnie. They set off to get something to eat from the Green Lanes Kebab shop and as Tyrell explained his good fortune, Donnie suggested they double the money. Jamie knew a place and off they went.

They ended up in an underground gambling place in Hackney, less than five miles south of Tottenham, in a bar just off Stoke Newington, where Delphus ran a scrap game place. As the boys walked in, the men sitting around the bar stared at the three friends. Tyrell was tall and lanky, quite good looking, soft-spoken and likeable. His father had been from Trinidad, not that he knew his father. But he was so handsome people always told him he must have gotten his looks from his dad. Tyrell had to admit his mother wasn't that much of a looker. But she was still his ma, and he loved her dearly. Donnie was short and thickset, very dark and even at 19, already had a receding hairline. Jamie was pimply and ginger-haired. He was also gangly, like Tyrell. And like Tyrell, he really wasn't very smart.

What Tyrell lacked in intelligence, he made up for in charm and with his good looks, his mother told him he could charm the bark off a tree. So, as he swaggered in behind Donnie who was the brains of the operation, he focused his charm on Delphus. Donnie showed Delphus the money, starting with £250 and Delphus let him into the room. Half an hour later, the boys had lost £400.

Hands in pockets, jeans sagging beneath their boxer shorts, the three friends walked out of the bar towards Jamie's car - and Mad Tony.

Mad Tony Nathan was a relic of the East End gangsters of old. He was shady and exceptionally cruel, building a reputation first as an enforcer, then heading up his own crew. After a stint in jail for armed robbery, Tony refined his act and now concentrated on narcotics and people-smuggling. He also financed gigs and house parties, which became easy avenues for selling his products. The moniker 'mad' was added to his name as a reflection of his unpredictability and the ease with which he visited extreme forms of violence on those who crossed him, even in the slightest.

As the boys walked to Jamie's car, Mad Tony stepped out of the shadows with two of his hoodlums. Jamie froze first, just as the hoodlums grabbed Tyrell and Donnie. Mad Tony was intimidating. Black and heavily muscled, he had once been a heavyweight boxer and was only kicked out of the sport when, Tyson-like, he bit a chunk off an opponent's ear lobe.

"Come over here and stand with ya mates," he said to Jamie.

Jamie did as he was told and Mad Tony turned his attention to Tyrell.

"Where's the package you were asked to give me?"

Tyrell said it was at home and started explaining his efforts to find Tony. Tony raised a hand to stop him.

"In an hour," he said. "Bring the package to me. One hour, or you'll be eating out of a straw."

£500 short, Tyrell handed the envelope to Tony. Tony had the money counted whilst Tyrell sweated. When Tony discovered £500 missing, Tyrell received a punch that almost tore his insides. Tony calmly informed him that nobody stole from him. He had 48 hours to make good the missing money with £100 interest, or find him two girls, instead. At the end of the 48 hours, Tyrell's sister would be taken and he would lose an eye. Tyrell swallowed in pure, unadulterated terror.

As he recounted the conversation to his friends, Jamie surmised it would be easier to find girls than replace the £500. There was a place he knew in North West London where they just might find what they were looking for. Jamie pulled up in his 15-year-old black Vauxhall Corsa with Donnie in the back and the boys set off for Sunny Hill Park.

Sally took Siyonna to Sunny Hill Park and as they walked, Siyonna marvelled at the British love of the outdoors. It was early evening on a weekday and the park still had a buzz to it, with people walking their dogs, children playing, or people merely sitting around and chatting. Siyonna was beginning to get a feel for just how important open spaces were to the British. On a warm summer's day like today, the park was simply teeming with people. She spent the rest of the evening with Sally and her friends and as they ate ice cream and talked, she found she actually had a lot in common with the girls. She struck up a conversation with Kiki, a slim, 17-year old who was very curious about Nigeria and pumped her for answers on all things Nigerian. When the questions descended to, 'you really live in houses?' Siyonna bit her tongue to hide her irritation, whipped out her phone and took Kiki on a virtual tour of Lagos, including Banana Island. Siyonna found her anger dissipating with the increasing realization that Kiki was genuinely curious and had only been feeding off the misinformation she had picked up all her life about how backward Africa was.

That is when the girls met Tyrell. He sauntered into the park looking like a younger version of Snoop Dogg, the rap star, with his silky black hair in a man-bun on top of his head. One of the girls, Funmi, had gone to buy a bottle of water, met Tyrell, got talking to him, and brought him back with her. Siyonna thought he was incredibly handsome, like a model, but not like Dante's athletic looks, a different kind of handsome. As he swaggered assuredly towards them, with his two friends following him, the girls all turned to look.

"Hey I'm Tyrell, and these are my boys Donnie and Jamie. Can we hang with you girls?"

As the evening wore on, Tyrell regaled the girls with stories of parties and escapades. It was obvious Funmi and Nikki were smitten by him, hanging on his every word. Soon it was time to go. Kiki suggested they meet up tomorrow to do a tour of London. Tyrell popped up and suggested they all go to a rave instead. He knew a place in Camden Town run by his friend that was running a rave tonight and he could get everyone in for free.

"Please come, please?" He cajoled, holding his hands together in fake supplication, "please?" This time pursing his lips and bending one knee, and all the girls laughed.

As they said yes to him, all eyes turned to Siyonna who hadn't said anything.

"Please come," implored both Sally and Kiki.

"Is it alright?" she asked Tyrell. "Will we be safe?"

Tyrell laughed at such a ridiculous question.

"Of course, it's safe man! I wouldn't ask you if it wasn't. Please come?"

Siyonna did not quite trust Tyrell. It was his eyes, very bright, very shifty. But if her friends were going, she agreed, she'd go. As they left, Tyrell said goodbye and confirmed they all had the address.

"It's settled then," said Sally, taking Siyonna's hands. "I will ask Gabby to give us a lift into London.

Siyonna waved the girls goodbye and walked with Sally to the bus stop.

As Jamie drove the guys away, Tyrell called Mad Tony to report that he had girls, lots of girls. Tony muttered a looking-good-we'll-see-how-we-get-on-tonight and hung up.

"Wicked!" yelled Tyrell. "We're in boys! Who knows we may even get a job with Mad T if we play our cards right.

The others nodded. Then they drove listening to the Drill beat pumping out of Jamie's stereo. The stereo would have cost more than the car, had Jamie paid for it. Tyrell hummed happily, then suddenly sat up.

"Hey lads, notice the rocks on that gal Lu-utah's neck?" he said. "That necklace has gotta be worth a lot! I say we take it off her tonight, bro, wha'ya say?"

Donnie nodded and suggested they get to it as early as possible as no one knew exactly what Mad T had in store for the girls. The opportunity may well slip away before the night was over.

"You're so right Don," said Tyrell. "So right."

Siyonna had called her sister and told her she was going to a party. Ebele asked her to text Sally's number so she had an alternative number to call should she need to. Then she asked her sister to be safe and call if she needed any help.

True to her word, Sally got Gabby to drop them off in Camden Town and the three girls squeezed into the back of the little Ford. Gabby and her friend Ken were going on to Regent Street to meet friends, so the girls would need to make their own way back after their party. Gabby shot down through Finchley Road, turning off into Lyndhurst Road, swinging right and past Southampton Road and turning into Kingsford Road. Going past the station and heading towards Finsbury Park, she turned off and followed a string of warehouses until she pulled up to a quiet warehouse with cars outside and bouncers at the door.

As the girls clambered out, Gabby turned to Sally.

"Yo Sal," she said. "Watch yourself, you hear?"

Then she spun her car around and disappeared with tyres screeching, towards West London.

The girls called Tyrell who appeared in the same dirty jeans and blue converses he'd had on earlier. He invited the girls into the warehouse where they were hit with the sound of booming music and a dance floor full of swaying young people. Tyrell led them to an area where five or six other girls from the park were sitting. As Siyonna walked in, she noticed that a few of the girls looked glazed and one of them was already curled up on the chair, fast asleep. Strange, Siyonna thought. Then again, she'd never been to a rave before.

"Where are your friends?" Siyonna asked Tyrell.

"Oh yeah, they're here somewhere," he replied with a sneer, all the time staring at Siyonna's necklace.

He must have also felt Siyonna staring back at him because he suddenly changed tack.

"Sorry, would you girls like something to drink? Some food?"

Siyonna and Sally said they'd rather dance first but Kiki was hungry and wanted a drink so Tyrell said he'd get stuff in ready for when the girls came back.

"Looks like the idiot Tyrell came through this time," said Mad Tony, lurking in the shadows. "Damn these girls are fine and young. Hey Danski, take stills and see if any of the regulars are interested, will ya?"

Danski was a muscular, bald-headed Albanian who worked as Tony's assistant.

Siyonna had to admit she was having fun. The music wasn't the Afrobeat she was used to but good music had a beat all of its own. As they danced for about 30 minutes, Kiki joined them then left after 10 minutes saying she felt tired and quite lethargic. That's strange, thought Siyonna but she just shrugged and kept dancing. As they danced, Siyonna grabbed some of the random bottled water being passed around and gave Sally one. They were both drenched. After dancing solidly for an hour or so, both girls agreed they needed a break and went back to the VIP area. As they got in, Siyonna noticed that the area was almost empty. Most of the girls from the park had gone and the girl who'd been sleeping when they came in was also no longer there. Kiki was fast asleep, a half-finished glass of Coca-Cola by her side. Siyonna sat down, tired, and nudged her.

"Hey Kiki, wake up sleepyhead, you're meant to be dancing!"

Kiki just grunted and kept sleeping. Siyonna was finding this behaviour stranger and stranger. Something did not feel right here.

Anton Barnard and his partner Eileen Derby were just starting their shift. They would patrol Euston, King's Cross and Camden Town as part of an early response police presence tonight, their shift ending at about 8.00 a.m. tomorrow. Both Anton and Eileen seemed quite young but at the age of only twenty-seven Eileen was a veteran with five years' experience at the job. As they cruised through Euston Road, Eileen suddenly turned off and started heading towards the warehouses.

"All Ok?" asked Anton.

"Dunno," she said. "I have a funny feeling about this place this evening. Let's just check it out, shall we?"

Anton agreed. He'd learnt not to disregard Eileen's instincts.

As Siyonna and Sally sat resting after all that dancing, they were both on their phones and sipping from their individual bottles of water when Tyrell showed up with a tray full of drinks.

"'Ere, get this lot into you. Will refresh you!" he said.

"Oh cheers," said Sally, as both she and Siyonna grabbed drinks from the tray.

"Do you know what's up with Kiki?" Siyonna asked casually.

"No man, dunno," said Tyrell, that laconic smile playing on his lips. "She says she's tired and just wants to sleep, know what I mean?"

Siyonna did not know what he meant but was desperate for the coke Tyrell offered. As she got the drink to her mouth, her necklace suddenly felt very warm around her neck and to everyone's amazement, the glass shattered in her hand. Sally stopped and stared at Siyonna as the coke spilt all over her and the glass lay in pieces at her feet. One of the men immediately jumped up and handed her tissues as Tyrell offered her another drink. The necklace around her neck felt heavy and even warmer. She turned to Sally.

"Don't drink that," she said urgently. "It's drugged."

Too late, she thought as Sally seemed to collapse back into her chair, staring at Siyonna with a look of desperation.

"Grab them and let's get out of here!" yelled a man at the door.

The two men moved quickly towards Siyonna, who instinctively went for her necklace, rubbing it for comfort and got up from her chair, standing very still as the men approached. The necklace felt reassuringly warm. Suddenly the men turned on each other. One of them raised a glass and smashed it violently across the skull of the other, who struggled to his feet, dazed, as his attacker then hit him with a punch that lifted him off his feet and sent him flat on his back, out cold before he hit the floor. The guy at the door who had been shouting orders turned out to be Danski and he couldn't believe his eyes. When the attack started, he had looked on in horror as Mickey laid out his colleague.

"Mickey man, what the hell's the matter with you?" he yelled.

Then swinging into action, he went for Mickey who, anticipating the attack, swerved and kicked Danski in the chest. Danski grunted, backed off then rugby tackled Mickey, knocking him to the ground. Two other hoodlums came in and inexplicably joined the fray, pounding on Mickey and Danski. As Danski shoved them off, he picked up one of the men and hauled him down the stairs towards the dance floor. People screamed as the second hoodlum kicked Danski from the back. Danski flew down the stairs headfirst, landing awkwardly right next to the guy he had thrown down and lay there, very still, very unconscious.

People started screaming and made for the exit, shoving, shouting and falling all over each other. Mad Tony heard the commotion from his office and zoomed the camera on the VIP area. He saw one of the girls trying to revive the other two, then Tyrell walked up to the girl, spun her around and made a grab for the necklace around her neck. The girl stood very still as Tyrell tried to pull the necklace. Then she calmly touched Tyrell's arm, very gently, almost as if she was caressing it. Tyrell screamed, pulled back his arm and clutched it like someone had set it on fire. Then he turned and ran out of the room, joining the throng of people escaping from the rave, still crying in pain.

Mad Tony was livid. What was that, magic? We'll see about that, he thought.

"You two, with me," he barked to the two other hoodlums in the room. "VIP room, now!"

He stomped across the narrow passage into the room, glaring at Siyonna.

"You two," he said. "Approach from either side of her, we need to get that damned necklace off her."

As the two tried to corner Siyonna, she suddenly spun around and spread her arms. The two hoodlums were picked up as if by invisible hands and slammed hard against the wall, lying very still on the floor. Mad Tony froze. Siyonna quickly walked up to him just as he raised a fist to punch her, ducked under the fist and touched his face. Tony stopped, put his hands to his face and saw nothing. Tony was blind. The two men who'd been slammed against the wall got up, shook their heads to clear the grogginess, looked at Tony who was now screaming, and ran.

Outside, Anton and Eileen had heard the screams and stampede from the rave, turned on their siren and headed for the warehouse. Siyonna poured the remnants of her water bottle on Kiki and Sally and grabbing both girls by their arms, yanked them upright with all her strength.

"Quick, we need to leave now!" she shouted, as the girls came to.

Pulling and dragging them, she managed to find an exit at the back of the warehouse and eventually started walking her friends towards the Euston Road, just as police vans, sirens blaring, sped past her towards the rave. She asked a couple standing by the bus stop for the nearest McDonald's and was pointed in the direction of Euston Station. Thanking the couple, Siyonna dragged her friends the 200 or so yards to the McDonald's and ordered up some strong coffee for them.

"Oh, my head!" moaned Kiki, between sips of hot coffee. "What happened?"

"You were both drugged by Tyrell. I managed to escape him and his gang. The police are there now," said Siyonna.

"Good Lord," was all Sally could say and she sat there staring into space.

Long after they got home and had all slept well, Siyonna was curled up in Ebele's living room watching the news. A report came up about the police smashing a prostitution ring which specialized in abducting and grooming young and teenage girls for sex with paedophiles. The leader of the gang, Anthony Nathan, known on the streets as 'Mad Tony' had gone on and on about a girl with a necklace who'd made him blind. When the reporters asked the arresting police officers, Eileen and Anton, whether there was any footage of the arrest and underage girls drugged at the scene, they said they had footage of the hoodlums turning on each other and fighting, and they found some girls who had been drugged and locked up in one of the rooms, but there was nothing showing any girls with necklaces and certainly nothing showing Mr Nathan going blind.

The next day, Siyonna went over to see Sally who looked very subdued. She greeted her in a baggy sweater and jogging pants, hugged her and they went to her room.

"Thank you, Siyonna," she said. "God knows what would have happened to Kiki and me if you hadn't been there. Not sure how you got us out but I am so grateful. If my parents knew I'd been in a place like that, I'd be on the next flight back to Lagos!"

Siyonna smiled and agreed they'd all had a lucky escape.

"By the way Siyonna, did you see the news? Did you see any girl with a necklace? That guy Mad Tony kept going on about some girl and a necklace?"

"Nope," said Siyonna, shrugging. "Not sure what the man was on about. Perhaps he saw a ghost?" she said and made Sally laugh.

Then Siyonna hugged her friend, promised to see her again before she went back to Lagos and left. She had a lunch date with Ebele at a restaurant in Whetstone and really couldn't be late.

On Saturday, she made the much-anticipated trip to Egham with Jon and Ebele to visit Mr Bellamy's family. Even though she'd only known Mr Bellamy a very short time, he had made such a huge impact on her life.

It was a modest semi-detached house. The living room opened up into a dining room and kitchen. The family had a love for education and learning that was palpable. The walls of the living room were lined with bookcases and small photo frames with pictures of generations of graduates and educators, proudly displayed on polished furniture. His father Andrew was a Professor of Geography and his mum Alice, a lecturer in Comparative History. Alice told Siyonna that Adrian had always wanted to work in academia and make a difference in the developing world. If they had any regret, it was that he did not live long enough to fulfil his dream of setting up a school for disadvantaged children in Africa.

She spent about an hour talking with them, then Sam arrived, Adrian Bellamy's only sister, who was training to be a marine biologist.

"That's quite a remarkable necklace you have there," said Sam, smiling. "It is absolutely beautiful."

Siyonna thanked her and they sat for a while longer, exchanging news about their lives and of course, discussing dear Mr Bellamy. It was obvious to Siyonna that they all missed him very much.

When they got up to leave, Adrian's mum gave Siyonna a brand-new book of poems, 'Poetry by Heart' by Andrew Motion. It was, as she explained, a collection of ageless English poems to remind Siyonna of her time in England.

"Keep us in your thoughts child and pray for us. We still haven't come to terms with Adrian's death," she said, sadly.

Siyonna hugged her and thanked her. As they said their goodbyes, they all had tears in their eyes. Sam, Adrian's sister, hugged her for what felt like an eternity.

"I am so happy I got to meet you, Siyonna," she said. "Please don't be a stranger and if you're ever in England again, let us know?"

"I promise," said Siyonna, between tears that were now flowing freely.

Ebele put an arm around her and led her out to the car. As they made their way back, there was a certain quiet in Jon's car.

"All right, girl?" Ebele asked.

Siyonna smiled and nodded. Jon suggested they stopped for lunch and chose a lovely, warm pub-restaurant just on the outskirts of Egham. He recommended the lamb shank for Siyonna but when it came with mash and veg, Siyonna thought she would rather have fries. Jon laughed and ordered a side of chips for her. Perfect, Siyonna thought, as she tucked into her chips and mayonnaise with the lamb shank. The vegetables on her plate did not get a look in.

After lunch, Jon drove them to Hampton Court, where they spent the rest of the day touring Henry VIII's beautiful palace on the banks of the River Thames near Richmond. Originally built for Cardinal Wolsey, the palace had been seized by Henry VIII when Wolsey fell out of favour. The grounds were well kept and absolutely beautiful, a glorious picture of green lawns and summer flowers. As she made her way through the magnificent halls, she was blown away by the sense of history and preservation and thought about how this had been the same on every historical tour she had taken in London. She learnt that the palace had been built in 1514 and when Henry VIII died, had been used extensively by his daughter, Queen Mary I. Over the years, succeeding monarchs made changes to the palace and it remained in active use until the 18th century. With all that history, Siyonna felt she was travelling through time as she walked from room to room, especially through the Great Hall, where Henry VIII entertained visiting dignitaries and nobles.

They headed for home. Siyonna had enjoyed a full day and frankly was ready for bed. Jon dropped them off and left.

"I'm so glad you're with Jon," murmured Siyonna, as they climbed into bed. "He loves you."

"You came to that wise conclusion after spending one full day with us?" said Ebele, laughing.

"Nope," replied Siyonna. "A girl knows these things. It's the way he looks at you when you're not looking and the gentle brushes of skin between you when you guys think I'm not looking."

"Well, I hope the girl is right," said Ebele. "Because this girl is crazy about Jon. It wouldn't do for him to break her heart, now would it?"

As if, thought Siyonna before she finally fell asleep.

The time came for her to say goodbye to Ebele, Jon and her friends in England. She was sad to leave but also felt she needed to go and sort out her future. Her results had come out whilst she was in England and she had done incredibly well, all A's. To celebrate, Jon and Ebele had taken her to a fancy Asian restaurant in the West End.

She had also been incredibly surprised by how quickly her relationship with Sally had changed. Sally had become a friend, a mate, as the Brits would say! Her stay had been so very enjoyable, in part because of Sally. Their adventures, walks and historical tours would always bring a smile to Siyonna. Saying goodbye to Sally and Kiki had been hard. They enjoyed a picnic in the park and talked about their summer of discovery. Both Kiki and Sally were going to start their A Levels in September and they made Siyonna promise to stay in touch. They toasted their precious new friendship with a bottle of fizzy non-alcoholic wine, poured into plastic champagne flutes, as they sat chatting on the grass in Sunny Hill Park. The girls laughed and giggled, recounting stories of their incredible summer and cried as they hugged one last time. Kiki declared she was firmly off cute boys after the Tyrell affair.

"Yeah, right," said Sally.

"Give it time!" laughed Siyonna.

When Siyonna got on her bus back to Cockfosters, Sally and Kiki waved her goodbye all the way, until the bus was out of sight.

Ebele and Jon took Siyonna and her ever-expanding luggage to Heathrow Airport. Siyonna had bought gifts for everyone, including her nephew and Odera, her cousin. Coupled with the things she bought for herself, it meant her suitcase now weighed an absolute ton and she prayed fervently that she was not over the 23 Kg weight allowance. Fortunately, it wasn't and she checked in successfully. Between the little wheelie bag, Ebele had given her and her suitcase, she'd been able to spread all the extra weight.

After she checked in, Ebele and Jon walked her to the security gates. Siyonna hugged Ebele long and hard and told her she'd miss her, thanking her for giving her an incredible holiday. Then she turned to Jon, hugged him and made him promise to look after her sister. Fighting back the tears, she walked to the security gate, swiped her boarding pass and turned for one final look back. There stood her sister and Jon, with arms around each other, smiling and waving madly. She smiled through her tears, gave them one last wave and walked towards airport security, to start her journey back home to Lagos.

As Siyonna's flight took off, Tyrell was sitting on his bed at home with Donnie and Jamie. On the bed lay £200,000, minus the £500 he had helped himself to. After Tony was arrested, Donnie had suggested they break into his car and search for the money before the police impounded it. They found the package in the glove compartment. Tyrell loved cars and it was a shame to smash the lovely 7-series BMW's window but it was no use to anyone now. It would only sit in a police pound forever, and where Mad Tony was going, he wouldn't be out for a long time.

Tyrell had handed the money to Donnie, who had been lying low, waiting to see if anyone came asking. No-one did. Today they divided the loot amongst the three of them. They got £66,500 each. Donnie knew exactly what he was going to do with his share. Start a business. His cousin was a builder in Spain and had been at him to go and learn a building trade. He fancied plumbing.

"That's it, lads," he said to Jamie and Tyrell. "I'm leaving London. You take care, yeah? And don't hang around. Sooner or later, Mad Tony will leave jail and figure out who took his money."

As he walked out of the North London flat, he could still hear his two hapless companions whooping with joy at their windfall.

"Poor beggars," he thought. "That money won't change a thing for them."

Meanwhile, from her window seat on the plane, Siyonna looked out at the clouds and gently touched her necklace. As she remembered those bad men back in London, she could have sworn it glowed with a warning heat. But now, as she travelled further and further towards Lagos, to her home and her loved ones, she felt it breathe a sigh of relief and settle itself peacefully around her neck. Siyonna also thought about her sister Ebele, Jon, and all the friends she made in London and concluded it had been a wonderful holiday. She would miss London, despite the 'Tyrell' experience. She had had a fun summer and would love to visit again someday. Next time though, she really would be very choosy about which parties she would attend.

———————

Available worldwide online and from all good bookstores

---

www.mtp.agency

www.facebook.com/mtp.agency

@mtp_agency

www.dollobies.com
contactus@dollobies.com

Michael Terence
Publishing